THE BLOOD STONE

CURSE OF THE DRAKKU: BOOK ONE

Jason J. Nugent

Jason J. Nugent
jasonjnugent.com

Book Layout © 2016 BookDesignTemplates.com

The Blood Stone: Curse of the Drakku Book One/ Jason J. Nugent. — 1st ed.
ISBN-13: 9781099953637

For Joe Gray. Wizards, finally!

ONE

Lailoken's enchanted leather-clad arms strained against the ropes, his muscles regretting the improvised snare the longer he held.

"Hurry! The dragon's trying to break loose!" he called to Darlonn and Jor. The other two dragonslayers rushed the Onyx dragon, knowing time was not on their side. Lailoken was strong, but he wouldn't hold the dragon down for long. Sweat poured down Lailoken's chiseled face despite the cold bitter winds.

Magus Breen and his novice Myrthyd, both in heavy black robes, stood far enough away to stay clear of the violently thrashing dragon. They stayed close enough only to ensure their enchantments on the slayers remained active. Two crossbowmen, their part in the hunt fulfilled, drew their short swords in case their assistance was needed. If Lailoken had his way, that wouldn't happen. It was a source of pride for him.

"Hold, hold!" Darlonn called. He approached the dragon from the right, moving swiftly with his broadsword drawn. His dark skin was a stark contrast to the snow around him. The dragon rose, Darlonn staring at its chest as the beast loomed over him.

"Come on, Lai, you've held bigger dragons than this!" Jor called, grinning from ear to ear. Lailoken glowered at the woman.

"Finish him or prepare yourself to be my next victim!" Lailoken yelled back. His arms were on fire as he pulled tighter on the rope. The dragon was trying to break its mouth free but they only needed a few more minutes until the two slayers could end this battle.

Jor nodded, the mirth over. She was a great slayer and one of Lailoken's closest friends. Along with Darlonn, the three of them had been on several hunts in the name of the Black Magus from the Order of Eschar.

Jor crept closer to the dragon, her black handled blade held firm within her hands. Her long red hair flowed in the wintry breeze.

When the Onyx dragon was spotted in the skies west of Kulketh, the Black Keeper issued the call for the dragonslayers to the hunt. The crossbowmen Wendrake and Hilgren were brought along with Magus Breen and his novice Myrthyd to slay the dragon and perform the ritual.

Lailoken didn't care much for that part. Foreign words spoken over the pieces of onyx were supposed to infuse them with the spirit of the dragon and turn ordinary stones to magical weapons. All he saw were black stones bathed in dragon blood: of his enemy from birth and the creatures who stole his wife.

His thoughts didn't matter, though. As a slayer trained from youth to perform one function, he did so with a clarity of mind that rivaled many of the great masters within the Black Tower.

"Hold firm, Lai, we've got this!" Jor called. Lailoken pulled tight, and with a quickness he'd come to appreciate, Darlonn and Jor attacked the dragon from both sides, their long swords piercing its flesh. Though the dragon's mouth was closed with the rope, a loud roar of pain escaped. Darlonn withdrew his sword, avoiding a stray claw, and rushed in and pierced the dragon's side, He missed the bones and found the large beating heart inside.

"That's it, Darlonn! Again!" Lailoken called. The ropes grew taut in his hands as the dragon tried to free itself. Jor followed suit, slashing at the dragon's forelimbs to fight them off, slicing at its side, drawing large deep gashes in the thick hide.

Wendrake and Hilgren stood next to the Magus and his apprentice, their swords sheathed, watching the slayers perform their duties.

"Watch the tail!" Magus Breen yelled. Darlonn looked up at him as the strong black tail of the dragon knocked him to the ground.

"Hold, hold!" Wendrake yelled. He rushed toward the downed slayer.

"Get back!" Lailoken yelled. The crossbowman must not have heard. He ran at the slayer, waving his short sword wildly. The dragon broke from Lailoken's grasp and swung its tail at Wendrake. Magus Breen wove a spell on the crossbowman, hoping to protect him from the dragon's poisonous saliva.

Wendrake made it to Darlonn, kneeling at the man's side. "I've got you! Come, move with me!"

Darlonn groaned, rolling to a sitting position.

"Get clear! We have to finish this!" Jor cried out.

The dragon thrashed and broke from Lailoken's grip. It lurched toward Darlonn and Wendrake, the crossbowman placing himself between the dragon and the slayer. The dragon spewed its poison on him, but the Magus' spell held firm, protecting him from certain death. Wendrake screamed as the poison rained on his skin, but realizing it didn't burn, he was filled with a false sense of security and ran at the dragon.

Darlonn stood on shaky legs, freeing his broadsword, and readying himself for a fight.

"No! Wendrake, come back! The spell doesn't protect you from—"

The dragon swiped at the crossbowman, catching him in the face. Wendrake screamed as thin lines of blood appeared on his skin. He fell to the ground, dropping his sword. Before the rest of the slayers could stop it, the dragon leapt on Wendrake and clawed at the man, ripping into his leather armor. It roared loudly and gored him, ripping an arm off. Wendrake howled in agony as the dragon continued tearing into the man and shredding his flesh. His screams grew louder and louder.

Darlonn rejoined the fight, preparing to attack the distracted dragon.

"Now, Jor!" Lailoken yelled. Jor nodded and crouched under the dragon's forelimb. Lailoken did the same. Both slayers lunged at the beast, thrusting their swords into its side. Darlonn sliced into its back, cutting through its wing, and burying his sword in its bony back.

The dragon cried out but would not let its prize go, shredding what remained of Wendrake.

Lailoken and Jor pulled their swords free and plunged them again into the sides of the dragon. It howled one last, awful time and fell to the ground, a large gasp of breath leaving its putrid nostrils before its tongue rolled out of its mouth.

The slayers pulled their swords free and left the carcass on the ground.

"Do what you must," Lailoken called to Breen and Myrthyd. He watched as the wild-eyed Magus went into action.

The Magus slapped his novice on the head. "Come on, boy! Hurry before the blood sours." Myrthyd glared at Breen, a dark, deadly look that spoke volumes of the boy to Lailoken. Myrthyd was sixteen, the same as his own daughter Alushia. He was old enough to know his time as a Magus was close, but the way Breen treated him, it was a wonder the boy didn't kill him when no one was looking.

Magus Breen and Myrthyd scurried to the dead dragon, their long black robes flapping in the cold wind. Myrthyd opened his leather pouch and fell to his knees as Breen shouted at him.

"Come on, boy, hurry up! We need to be quick about our work. If this dragon's blood turns before we complete the ritual, I'll cuff you all the way back to the Tower. Do you understand me? We shoulda left you to die instead of bringing you in as a baby."

"Don't you think you ought to lay off the boy?" Lailoken interjected.

Breen spun on him. "If I want your opinion, slayer, I'll ask for it. This is Order business. You did your part; let us do ours."

Lailoken shook his head. He tried. The boy knew what he was in for.

"Hurry, boy!" Breen said, smacking Myrthyd across the face.

"I'm doing my best," he growled back. Lailoken placed his hand on the dagger in his belt. The tension was thick between the two.

Myrthyd spilled the onyx stones on the ground, which earned another smack from the Magus. He quickly picked them up and handed them to Breen. "Remind me to have you punished when we get back to the tower, you worthless novice."

Myrthyd lowered his head, then stared at the bloody remains of Wendrake near the dragon. He heaved, covering his mouth to hold back his sick.

Breen held the stones in his hands, lifting them high, and closed his eyes. He went into a trance, unintelligible words spilling from his lips. Then he approached the wound in the dragon's side, spilling blood from it.

"Infuse these stones with your essence. Live on in death. Give your power to those who guard the world from evil," Breen said. He then took the stones and plunged them into the wound, coating the stones and his hands with the dragon's blood. A faint glow surrounded the stones, illuminating the deep crimson blood. He held them inside the wound until the glow dissipated and pulled his hands out.

"Boy, the bag. Now!"

Myrthyd opened the bag and Breen poured the blood-soaked stones inside. "Guard them with your life. They're more precious than you right now. Lose them, and I have Tower permission to kill you."

"Yes, sir," Myrthyd replied slowly. Breen must not have noticed it, but Lailoken caught the sinister tone of Myrthyd's reply. The boy screamed of danger.

Darlonn and Jor stood next to Lailoken, the remaining crossbowman behind them.

"The boy is gonna be in for a long trip back," Jor said. She smiled. "Glad it's not me!"

"We live in Kulketh. It could never be you. Maybe if we were in Oakenvault..." Darlonn said. Jor punched his arm.

"Stupid Tower," she grumbled.

Lailoken wrapped his arms around his two friends. "Another fine hunt, my friends. The tale will be a great one to share when we return." The three waited for Magus Breen and Myrthyd to finish so they could leave. More than once, Lailoken's hand flashed to his dagger when he thought the two came close to blows.

CHAPTER

TWO

Myrthyd walked the streets of Kulketh with a basket of half rotten apples on his way to the archives to study. He'd spent his last half-dracs on them from a vendor just outside the Black Tower. As often as he could, he spent the meager money he earned to feed as many as possible, but it was never enough.

"Here you go. It's all I've got today," he said, handing one of the better apples to a little girl curled up and leaning against the side of a tanner's shop.

"Thank you, sir." She snatched the apple and shoved it into her mouth, the juices running down her chin. Myrthyd shook his head and kept going. There were many more like her.

Magus Breen scolded him for wasting his money on people that might never make it. Several weeks after returning from the hunt, he lectured Myrthyd on the merits of such actions.

"How much have you spent on those people?"

"Not enough."

Breen backhanded him.

"Respect, Myrthyd. You'd best learn it if you're ever to earn it."

"Yes, sir," he growled.

"I don't understand why you waste money to feed the hungry."

"Who else is going to take care of them, sir? It's only gotten worse since I was a boy. More and more families are struggling. As Magus, shouldn't we take care of them?"

"I'll tell you who we need to take care of. The Drakku, that's who! Their presence in Tregaron has brought this on us. The Magus have been weak and failed to enforce their ban. Maybe one day we'll be strong enough to do so."

"The Drakku? Dragons and halflings? How are they to blame for what's happening with our crops?"

"Our crops, our people, our society. Their blood has poisoned us."

"But...we need their blood for our stones. I don't understand."

"No? You wouldn't, would you? Gain some experience and then talk to me about why you don't think their blood has poisoned us."

Breen excused him from his chambers.

Turning the corner, he handed the rest of his apples to a family of five, all caked in mud and dung. "Here you go, a gift from the Order."

"Thank you," the man said. He carefully took the apples and shared them with his family. In turn they thanked him and said they'd pray to Menos for him.

With the apples gone, Myrthyd moved quickly toward the archive, hoping to return to his special project.

Magus Breen had been adamant that the Drakku were the root cause of the growing food scarcity. At first, Myrthyd dismissed him as an out-of-touch relic, but the more they spoke, the more he came around to the same line of thinking. Since then, he turned to the archives in search of information about the Drakku, hoping to find a way to fix things.

One day, he came across a reference to a tome created by a powerful Kull Naga named Drexon. The reference noted the spell book was forbidden for its "unscrupulous use of power affecting Drakku and people." Though it didn't sound promising for his current needs, it intrigued him enough to search for it.

It took three days of continuous searching and a few well spent dracs to find the tome in a special section of the archives. He made sure he was alone before he opened the book.

Immediately he knew it was something extraordinary.

"By Menos, look at this!"

The pages were adorned with colorful images and elaborately scrawled letters, unlike anything he'd ever seen. But more than that, it was the content of the spells. They were sinister in nature and he could see why someone would want these hidden from general use. But he also understood how, under the correct guidance, they'd be extremely useful to the Order.

He snuck the tome out of the archives and hid it in his room in the Tower.

Day and night, when not at Breen's service, he read from the Tome. He gained spells no Magus had known for close to a thousand years, and he advanced in his regular studies at a lightning pace.

As he scrolled through the tome and read over the Nightwraith spell once again, his door burst open.

"Myrthyd! Why weren't you at my quarters this morning?"

It was Breen, his face a deep shade of red.

"I'm so sorry, Magus Breen! I lost track of time! I was busy—"

"As my novice, you're never too busy to learn from me! Give me that!" He snatched the tome from the table and his eyes widened as he read the contents.

"Where'd you get this? No Magus should possess this! You stole it, didn't you?"

"No, sir! Please! It was only to learn from!"

Breen closed the book and slammed Myrthyd's head with it. "Never read from this! Never put these spells into practice, do you hear me? They lead to danger and death. They were placed here by a madman!"

He continued to beat Myrthyd with the tome, knocking the boy to the floor. He cowered from him, trying to deflect the attack.

"You dirty orphan! How dare you go behind my back to read this!"

"But, Magus Breen, I was only trying to help! The Drakku—"

"I don't care!"

Breen's stone glowed and Myrthyd felt an unseen force lift him from the floor, holding him steady. Breen stepped forward, their noses almost touching.

"We must never resort to these measures. No matter how difficult the situation may seem, we must never follow these spells!" He shook the book at Myrthyd.

"Yes, Magus Breen. I understand, sir."

Breen released him, letting him fall to the floor.

Rage grew within Myrthyd. He only wanted to help; he wasn't trying to do anything wrong. The people were starving. The Order did nothing to ease the situation. The Drakku were allowed to influence Tregaron in a terrible way, and yet no one stood up to them.

"Breen," he snarled. The Magus spun, shock crossing his face.

"What did you say, boy?"

"Breen, I won't tolerate this. You are part of the problem. You, and others like you."

"How dare you speak to me like that, boy!"

He took two steps toward Myrthyd and was locked in the air, Myrthyd's stone glowing as he cast the spell.

"Let me go this instant! I will have you hanged for this!"

"You will do no such thing. We have a duty to our people that you seem to have forgotten. I'm done with your disrespect."

Weaving a spell he learned from Drexon's tome, he slowly extinguished Breen's life. He watched as the Magus lost the battle, completely unable to reach his own magic as Myrthyd continued to let him die.

When the Tower grew quiet after dinner, he snuck the Magus back to his quarters and carefully slipped him inside the room.

He only wanted to help.

THREE

Returning from the hunt, Lailoken walked from Kulketh to his home north of the city. There were a few more beggars than before and he ignored their pleas for help. He had a home and a daughter to return to.

The road was dustier than normal, the lack of rain causing the hard-packed dirt to crumble. Fields to his right were blackened by rot, a common occurrence growing worse over the years.

I do hope the Order finds a solution soon, he thought.

The road was quiet and he turned his thoughts to his family.

His wife Etain was a beautiful woman full of life and joy. At least that's what he remembered. She'd been missing for close to sixteen years now, and he prayed to Menos every day for her return. Her image was burned into his mind and he would never rest until he found her.

Their daughter Alushia was all he had left in the world. She was a strong girl well equipped to handle the homestead while he was gone on a hunt. He never worried about her, trusting she'd take care of things as well as possible.

The blight on the land started not long after her birth. The first two harvesting seasons were traumatic for Tregaron, but the Order assured the people all was well and they'd bring in the Verdant Magus from

Woodpine to help grow food.

It worked for a time. Then, their efforts lessened as dragon hunts grew more frequent, with some Magus grumbling that the Drakku were to blame for it all. Honestly, he didn't care what the cause was. He was a dragonslayer, trained to kill the great beasts.

The Order needed their blood, and he needed the dracs to survive. It all worked. For him at least.

Many other families were not so fortunate. He witnessed more than enough young children die of starvation.

Working his way past the rotten fields, he passed through a wooded area.

Something scurried to his right and he froze. "Who's there?"

The sound stopped. He waited, listening for the intruder. When it made no further sounds, he moved slowly, watching the trees for whatever made the sound.

You fool, it's just an animal. What are you afraid of?

He heard it again and stopped, withdrawing his large dragon-eyed sword.

"You best show yourself! I'm not in the mood for games."

A small boy crept out from behind a tree.

"What are you doing here?"

"Please don't hurt me, sir. I only wanted something to eat. The Drakku—"

Sticks snapped behind Lailoken and he turned as two men rushed at him. "What the—"

They slammed into him and knocked him to the ground.

"Give us all your dracs and we'll let you live," one of the men snarled into his ear. They pushed his face to the dirt so he couldn't see who they were.

"I swear to you, I have no money on me. You'd do well to leave this place if you know what's good for you."

"Good for us? We need money. We need food. That's what's good for us!"

"Go to the Tower. They can help."

"Pah! The Tower cares only for itself!"

The second man was thinner and seemed hesitant.

"Druce, we should leave him be. Did you see his sword?"

"Aye, it'll fetch a nice sum at the market. Grab it, too. Take anything we can get our hands on."

"I warned you."

Lailoken forced himself off the ground. He was much larger than either of the two men and had no problem freeing himself from their grip.

"Get him, Tarry!" the one called Druce cried out. He was shorter with brown hair and with a slightly larger build than his partner.

Lailoken grabbed Druce and shoved him to the ground with ease. "Don't make me hurt you! Go to the Tower and ask for help. Tell them Lailoken sent you."

"Lailoken?" It was the boy. He'd snuck up on the fight and stood behind Lailoken.

"Yeah, that's my name. Tell them I sent you, and they'll take care of you. I promise."

"Lailoken?" The boy said his name as if it were a spell or contained magic.

"You're the slayer?" Tarry asked.

"Aye. Unless you want to share the fate of many a

dragon, I suggest you do as I say. Go to the Tower. They're there to help."

Druce backed away slowly, never turning his gaze from Lailoken.

"We...we will do as you say. Please. We only needed food," Tarry said.

"I'm sorry, but I have none to give."

The two men looked to each other and then at the boy. Without another word, they raced along the dirt road headed for Kulketh.

Lailoken dusted himself off and watched until they were out of sight.

"Something has to change. This is getting out of control."

He turned and continued on his way home, wary of vagrants.

***

Nearly two months after the hunt, Magus Breen turned up dead in the Black Tower. He was found in the company of a halfling girl who was later executed. Lailoken never shared his concern, but he was certain the novice Myrthyd had something to do with the death. As he was told, it was *Tower business.*

The fallout from the death set in motion a chain of events that lasted for two years before the unthinkable happened. The novice Myrthyd ascended to the rank of Magus on his eighteenth birthday. The more surprising appointment to Kull Naga, the leader of all Magus within the Order of Escaher in Tregaron, was more shocking. A growing sense of disorder amongst the Order took hold in the gossip of inns and taverns. Myrthyd shut down those fears when he ordered a gathering of all Magus in Kulketh, where they unanimously supported his appointment. It was an amazing achievement of harmony amongst the Magus that was unheard of for over a thousand years.

FOUR

Myrthyd, the eighteen-year-old Kull Naga, walked swiftly along the dark corridors of the Black Tower. His long black robe with the deep red embroidered crossed lightning bolts on his back hung on his gaunt frame. His hair was shorn in the tradition of the Kull. A black stone hung from a leather cord around his neck. His gray eyes darted back and forth, scanning the tapestries lining the corridors depicting victorious slayers over the centuries. He marveled at the detail; the embroidered dragon blood spilled in the images appearing real. Dragons were slaughtered in every scene he passed over, the watchful eyes of the Magus off in the far corner of every image.

He smiled. *Such lovely images*, he thought.

Despite the late Spring weather outside, the black stone walls offered a cool temperature inside. Torches that burned with eternal flame hung between the tapestries. An ancient Magus spell emitted heat when necessary, and during the warm months offered only light, yet the wood never burned down. As far as Myrthyd knew, these torches had been burning since the tower was built and would continue to do so long after his death.

Often, he spent his days in study or reflection with constant interruptions. As the Kull Naga, it was his duty to protect the land and his people. Problems and questions were never ending. He knew that would be so when he was elevated to his station and embraced the challenge. It was highly unusual for someone of his age to achieve Kull status, but the election was fair and unbiassed—as far as anyone else knew.

While a novice, Myrthyd had discovered an ancient forbidden tome written in blood by the Kull Naga Drexon, a Magus so reviled in the south that he was never to be spoken of. For the Magus in Tregaron, he was an anomaly. Powerful and devious, he tricked the dragons during the Great Council after the Wars of Reformation. Their people had been at odds with dragons ever since. He was also somewhat of a dark Magus, delving often into forbidden spells. Myrthyd had found many useful spells reading his book.

He was on his way to study further from the tome in his personal chambers on the second floor of the tower, hoping to learn anything that might remove the blight that had plagued Tregaron since he was a novice. Crops failed. Rain was infrequent. His people were starving. As a novice, Magus Breen chided him for wanting to fix things.

"It's because of the dragons!" he'd claim and cuff the boy. As he grew into his own, Myrthyd accepted Breen's reasoning, though the Magus wasn't around to know. Something had to be done about the dragons. They were the cause of all ills that befell their land. Too many people were dying or hungry, and something had to be done.

Myrthyd walked silently along the halls to his room. Though the Kull Naga traditionally occupied the top floor of the thirty-story tower, he preferred his lower level room.

"Kull Naga Myrthyd," a novice said, bowing as Myrthyd walked by. He gave a slight nod and continued. The novices and apprentices frustrated him. The incessant bowing and vying for recognition grew weary. He was once one of them, but now despised their sycophant ways. It was a necessary part of being the Kull, though it didn't mean he enjoyed it.

Myrthyd approached the large wooden door to his chamber. A tower guard stood in front of it with his arms crossed, scanning the corridors for any sign of danger, not that there would be, but Myrthyd never trusted the rest of the Magus. When he ascended to Kull, a large contingent decried his rise and swore to oppose him. They tried at first, but he soon forced them into submission, using ancient forbidden spells. Thus, his intent this day to study.

"Good day, Trenton. Any sign of trouble?" Myrthyd asked.

"No sir; all is good." The guard opened the door for Myrthyd to pass and closed it behind him, no doubt returning to his previous posture outside the door. Myrthyd passed through a smaller door into the bed chamber in the back. He closed the door to keep Trenton from hearing the spells or becoming suspicious of his studies.

Situated in the far corner of the room was a large cabinet where he stored books, potions, and powders, behind which was a secret compartment. It was to this hidden spot Myrthyd went. He moved the books aside and lifted the barely visible handle, revealing Drexon's tome. Reverently he carried it to the chair next to his bed. The candles were lit earlier by a novice whose job it was to maintain them for Myrthyd's needs, and the light flickered as he opened the forbidden text.

Inside, intricate images were drawn along the margins of the text and at the beginning of the spells. It was one of the most highly decorated books he'd ever seen, though most images were dark and gruesome, often depicting dragons attacking humans. Some images were of horrific acts of brutality inflicted by the Drakku—dragon-kind—such as disembowelment and decapitation. At first when he discovered this tome, the images had frightened him. Now, they enticed him. So far, his studies suggested new methods of attack against dragons while many of the minor spells dealt with subjugating people to his will, something he'd done a little of.

He returned to a spell that vexed him previously in hopes of unraveling its meaning in order to learn the secret. An image of a half-dead dragon introduced the spell. The colorful drawing depicted a black dragon with torn wings and smoke where its eyes should've been. It was devouring the dream of a woman sleeping in a bed. Without the large black dragon, the picture would've been serene and calm, but the dragon above her, eating the colorful dream turned the image into something dark. The page's simple title was *Nightwraith*. Myrthyd read the spell several times, unable to decipher the steps needed or the items required out of the text. It was to this spell he turned his attention.

From dark crystal once hidden, now found
Comes power unchecked, unbound.

Fill the onyx with a dragon's soul
And own the dream, the dreamer whole.

Myrthyd poured over the words, their meaning lost to him. *What crystal? What power? How do you fill a color with the soul of a dragon? How does one own a dream and the dreamer?* He stared at the image, trying to piece it together. The words continued.

Find the crystal on a dragon's back
Within a cavern, dark and black.
Slay the keeper and take the gem
Power eternal, over dragon, over men.

The words mocked him; their meaning hidden within the rhymes. Where would one find a gem on a dragon's back? He'd been with slayers as they killed dragons and feverishly searched along the scaly spines to no avail. He timidly inquired about such a thing and was rudely laughed at by the older slayer. That man, Karnath, no longer walked among the living for his insult.

The dragon soul you will bind,
A Nightwraith to destroy the mind.
The living will live among the dead,
When you control the visions within their heads.

The infuriating words meant nothing to him, yet something drew him back to them again and again. He gleaned a promise of power, yet how, he did not know. It seemed to him that a crystal held the ability to trap a dragon's soul, but what was a Nightwraith? How does the living live among the dead? Isn't that what people do anyway? The meaning of the verses vexed him. He had to decipher what they meant. If it was anything like the other spells he'd learned from studying Drexon's text, it held power, and so far, every spell he tried granted him control over someone or something.

> *Vile offspring of a dragon's lie*
> *Controlled by the onyx eye.*
> *Within the fatal dragon fate,*
> *Power of yours, a Nightwraith.*

Myrthyd closed the tome and leaned his head back, closing his eyes. He'd not studied the words in a few days, hoping his mind would see the connections, see the truth hidden within the verses. Still they alluded him. They avoided discernment, and that angered him even more. He was one of the wisest Magus in all Tregaron, and yet somehow these simple lines confused him. The Nightwraith, a term he'd never heard before, enticed him. If he could somehow work amongst the dreams of his people, how much power would that give him? No one had ever done such a thing, as far as he knew. He'd be the first and last Magus to ever have such knowledge. It was imperative he decipher the code and bind his people to his side. Their lives depended on it. If only he could break through, he might be able to remove dragons from Tregaron and restore the land to its former state, and save his people

FIVE

The spring sun's early morning rays washed the camp in life. Called to the hunt by young Myrthyd, the tower was in need of more bloody stones. It seemed there was a dire need for the magical gems and an Onyx dragon was spotted in the mountains to the west. Onyx dragons once swarmed the skies, but over the centuries, the need for their blood caused excessive hunting by the Magus. Now they were scarce and when spotted, the local Magus Keeper would gather the hunt together.

Lailoken was joined by his long-time companions Darlonn and Jor and the two crossbowmen, Tozgan and Ori. The Magus Driano and his novice Belthos completed the group, and they set out to the west.

Lailoken found it difficult to leave his daughter again. She was capable of running their small farm, and with her snowcat Brida at her side, he didn't worry about her safety. Still, leaving her alone always forced a touch of guilt to surface. She was all he had left in the world.

The party arrived at the mountains after searching for days for the Onyx dragon. The skies were clear without a dragon in sight, making Lailoken wonder if their informant was mistaken. Unless the great Onyx revealed itself, they'd be home sooner than expected. It wasn't like them to be completely outwitted by a dragon.

"Men, 'tis time to move. Our glory did not find us this day, but we shall once again rule these mountains and find our prey," Lailoken said, walking around the camp, waking the sleeping men and Jor. One by one they rose, bleary-eyed and rubbing sleep from their eyes.

"You're gonna scare the poor men," Jor said with a smile. She stood and clapped Lailoken on the back. "You drive them hard. Ori has yet to kill a dragon, and the Magus...he's not one for company," she said, nodding toward the sleeping plump man. His novice Belthos had risen and quickly prepared his belongings to leave, careful with the bag of sacred stones waiting to be bathed in blood.

"How many have you failed to kill?" Jor asked Lailoken, nudging him in the ribs.

Lailoken peered at her. "That's between me and Menos. I'm not talking. Ask him." He winked and walked away.

Out on the dewy plain with men united in a single cause, the scent of morning mingling with a dying fire wafting in the light breeze gave Lailoken pause. He loved his home and he enjoyed working the fields with his daughter Alushia, but out here under the heavens with a common enemy to fight was where he felt most comfortable. Leading the charge against dragons made his heart race and life seemed more real. "Forgive me, Alushia," he mumbled. He never wanted to leave her, but hunting dragons was an instinct too powerful to ignore. It was part of him.

The slayers broke camp and followed Lailoken's

lead across the plain and down the paths that wound through the mountains. It would take at least a day to reach the bottom, as their progress was slowed by narrow paths and the Magus, who insisted on resting every hour.

Around mid-day, the unmistakable sound of a dragon's roar echoed through the mountain pass. Lailoken stopped.

"Halt!" he called to the men. "We may yet have a trophy to bring home!" He scanned the skies for the dragon when it roared again. This time, the sound rose behind them. Lailoken spun. "There!" he shouted, pointing upwards.

A large Onyx dragon soared across the sky, its open wings casting a shadow on them as it flew overhead. It roared again, belching a cloud of acid across the sky.

"The dragon!" Belthos yelled. Being his first trip, he'd yet to see a dragon in person. He was younger than Alushia, and maybe one day would grow into the role of Magus, if his master would allow it. Driano, like most Magus he'd known, was a harsh taskmaster and never gave the boy any breaks.

"You speak when spoken to! Got it?" he said to Belthos, cuffing him on the head. The boy winced but said nothing.

"Be careful of the acid. Once on you, it will sear through your skin, leaving only bones," Lailoken said. Already Jor and Darlonn had moved to either side of Lailoken, each taking a crossbowman with them. Jor took Ori and Darlonn had Tozgan.

"Driano, if you please," he asked of the Magus. The stone around Driano's neck glowed faintly as the Magus enchanted them with protection against the dragon's acid.

Ori was a tall brown-haired man with a scraggly beard. Lailoken knew him from the tavern in Kulketh but was unaware of his slaying prowess. Jor recruited him to their group after the last hunt. Tozgan looked the part and wore a bright green cap with blue feathers. He'd been on many hunts, traveling across Tregaron and attaching himself to the latest hunt. It was rumored he understood most dragons better than anyone, but Lailoken had yet to see him in action.

"Jor, be ready. It looks like it might come your way," Lailoken called. The tall woman waved her hand at him dismissively. *Of course she knew*, he thought. She rivaled him in the hunt, something she constantly pointed out. Jor positioned Ori on a rise, pointing upwards. He'd soon have the opportunity to bring down a dragon.

Tozgan had already cranked the crossbow, the iron bolt ready to fire. Darlonn flanked him and held his sword at the ready.

The dragon roared overhead, the sound making Lailoken's adrenaline flow. He lived for these moments. No matter the size or variety, he relished the chance to take down the great flying beasts.

Over the centuries, Tregaron had grown a reputation as a dragon wasteland, and it wasn't an unfounded accusation. The needs of the Magus overruled the desire to protect the creatures. Their ability to shift into human form was an awful consequence of their attempt to live in the land, though halflings were mercilessly executed to stop their blood from mixing. In the south, Lailoken heard tales of griffons, the half lion, half dragon breeds that roamed freely along Rowyth's southern shores.

The dragon swirled in the sky, flying high and tumbling down toward the mountain to skim past the men and unleash its acidic attack. It belched an immense cloud as it flew by. The men held to their positions, the acid narrowly missing Driano.

Jor and Darlonn were poised with their crossbowmen, ready to penetrate the thick dragon scales.

"Be ready for the next pass. Do not flinch nor waiver. Stay resolute. Do you understand?"

Jor rolled her eyes. Lailoken smirked. He knew how he sounded, but the hunt was on and the thrill overcame him.

"We shall have our trophy this day!" Lailoken shouted.

Tozgan called, "Huzzah! Let's take him from the skies and drench our stones in his blood!"

The Onyx screeched across the sky, trailing behind a cloud of acid.

Darlonn shouted. "Fire now, you bleeding idiot!" Tozgan let loose an iron bolt that went wide of the dragon. "What kind of shot was that? Give it here!"

Lailoken smiled, knowing Darlonn's face was flaming red.

"Now! Fire now!" Jor called. Ori found the mark, the iron bolt piercing the dragon's leg. It roared loudly, acid arcing across the blue sky.

"Again! Again!" Lailoken called.

Another bolt flew from Darlonn's direction, this time clipping the dragon's ribs.

The dragon bellowed a piercing howl and thrashed its head back and forth, emitting a wild spray of acid from its open maw. It fell to the ground in a howling heap.

"Hurry! We have it now!" Lailoken called out. The rush of adrenaline pushed him toward his prey, the scourge of Rowyth.

The slayers yelled as they ran at the felled beast. Swords were raised with victorious shouts. Then as they closed in on the Onyx, it turned toward them and narrowed its large black eyes. It let out a fierce roar and covered the ground with acid.

Darlonn was too eager. He raced for the dragon but didn't pay heed and ran through the acid, his leather boots smoking as the dangerous liquid seeped into them. He yelled but to his credit, continued forward toward their prize.

"Darlonn!" Jor shouted.

"You will die, dragon!" she shouted.

"Go around! The beast is yet to die, and we still have life within our lungs!" Lailoken shouted.

Ori called to Tozgan, "Get your short sword! Come around the acid!"

Driano cast the enchantment on the group again, though his spell was weak with so many. "Be careful! You may not be protected!" he cried.

With their swords raised to strike, the crossbow-men raced to outflank the pool of acid. Driano and Belthos stood back, afraid to get close to the dragon until it was dead. Other than cover the slayers in a spell of protection, they were useless in the hunt.

Jor screamed. Lailoken crouched clutching his sword, anger fueling him. It was time.

On the other side of the acidic pool, Darlonn

worked his way out of his boots, their heels completely gone and smoking. He took up his sword and rushed barefoot at the dragon wailing on the ground.

In the middle of the acid, a small opening appeared as though it were retreating into the ground. "There," Lailoken growled, pointing his sword. Jor ran for the opening, Lailoken at her heel.

The dragon roared and belched acid at Ori and Tozgan. They were too close and almost got caught in the deadly bile.

Jor lunged at the dragon, catching it in the chest with her sword. The dragon howled and grasped Jor with its front legs. She screamed in pain.

"Let go of me!" she yelled, beating on the powerful claws. It opened its mouth, ready to devour her in one bite.

"No!" Lailoken shouted, unable to save his friend. The Onyx was winning, tearing apart the slayers.

Before it ended Jor's life, Tozgan fired a bolt from his crossbow, the iron bolt stabbing its soft mouth through the back of its neck. Jor freed herself while the dragon struggled to remove the bolt in its throat.

Lailoken seethed as he faced the dragon. "You will never escape me," he growled. The dragon frantically pulled at the bolt as Jor's sword swung with each movement. The blade and bolt both ran deep and the dragon struggled to remove them, its claws having difficulty grasping the handle.

"You've lost this day. You will die by my blade!" Lailoken hissed.

The dragon breathed acid, creating a wretched pool around the two of them. Lailoken held steady, fear long ago turning to resolve as he awaited his move.

The Onyx narrowed its eyes and moved its head closer to Lailoken.

Slayer, it said, to Lailoken's astonishment. The voice was in his head, an old trick many used before they died. *Do you not recognize me?* Its voice was slick and evil.

"Your words mean nothing to me! Your death is all I require!" he shouted back.

Slayer, you know so little. Its speech was slow and drawn out, each word emphasized. *What you presume to be a danger is far from the truth. Seek inside yourself. Do you see it? Can you feel it gnawing at your soul?*

"I feel nothing but anger. Your kind deserves the sword."

The dragon reared its head and looked down on Lailoken. He'd faced dragons before and never felt as sure of his abilities as he had at that moment. No matter what this Onyx did or said, he would find a way to kill it.

I sense something about you, Slayer, something weak. It snapped its jaws at him, feigning an attack. Lailoken drew his sword close in a defensive stance.

Jor rolled to the side, looking around for something to attack it with. Darlonn had shifted to the far right near Tozgan, shouting words Lailoken didn't understand.

"You will know the meaning of weak when I slit your throat and let you bleed out. I will bathe in your blood and rip out your innards, I will feed them to my dogs. You will die by my hand."

The Onyx reared his head back. Lailoken heard maniacal laughter in his mind. It was a deep, booming laugh that echoed loudly.

Slayer, it began in its long, drawn-out way. *You talk a lot for such a weak man. You don't even have the blood of the dragon within you, yet you speak with our power. You aren't blessed with a parent from my line.*

"Abominations, those vile halflings are! None live here amongst us! Those horrible creatures stay away from our lands, as you should have." Lailoken ran at the dragon, raising his sword high. The dragon inhaled and blew out small clouds of acid on either side of Lailoken, singeing his arm hairs.

Take another step, and I will end you, the dragon roared in his mind.

Lailoken hesitated. The dragon finally pulled the sword from its chest and tossed it on the ground. Dark blood oozed from the wound. It worked the bolt free, spitting it at Jor, and striking her leg.

I sense you, Slayer. I sense your past. I sense your fears. Why are you afraid of the halflings? They are but a better version of you. Fused my with race, they're superior to you in every way. What causes your fear?

"They are a disgusting mix of things that should never be! When your kind chose to change...to transform into our likeness to steal our women and seduce our men, you changed everything. It's unnatural. It's against all that Menos stands for. It sickens me to think of such evil." He peered around the dragon, hoping to see Darlonn. "And that is why you must die!"

The dragon extended his immense wings, one of them torn slightly from the crossbow bolt. Lailoken was bathed in shade.

Today is not the day I allow a human to take my life; especially not one so ignorant of his past. It breathed acid at Lailoken, blocking him from advancing, then roared and dove to the sky, flapping its large leathery wings. In a downdraft of air, it rose high into the sky. It circled a few times, peering down at Lailoken.

"Come fight me! Don't fly away like a coward!" Lailoken screamed at it.

It flew to the south, disappearing beyond the mountains.

The slayers stood in stunned silence, finally broken by Driano.

"You call yourselves slayers? How could you let the dragon escape? In all my years, I've never seen such terrible hunting. I've never—"

"You've never what?" Lailoken asked. His body ached, and his head hurt. He'd lost a dragon before, but it had been a long, long time.

"We need that blood! Without it, we don't have the power of the stones!"

"I'll show you what those stones can do!" Jor said. She stood next to Lailoken, brushed her hair back from her face, and held the pommel of her sword.

Belthos gasped. Lailoken thought the boy was going to speak, but he covered his mouth with his hand to prevent an unwanted smack to the head.

"Touch me, and I'll see you all hanged."

"That means you'd leave alive, and that won't happen," Jor said.

"If you mean to threaten me with your amazing killing skills, I've yet to be impressed. If what I just witnessed is any indication, I think I'll be fine."

Jor growled, unsheathing her sword. "I'll split you in two!"

As much as Lailoken wanted to see the fat rat Driano carved in half, he had to stop the tension.

"Jor, not now," he said, placing a hand on her shoulder. Darlonn approached, holding his hands up to stop Jor.

"He's not worth it. When we get back to Kulketh, we'll see about getting another Magus to accompany us. This one doesn't deserve your time," Darlonn said.

Jor's eyes narrowed. She shook her head and walked away, mumbling under her breath.

"Gather our things. It's time we left," Lailoken commanded. The crossbowmen scoured the camp for lost or stray iron bolts and packed up. Belthos finished with the Magus's items and hoisted the immense bag on his back. Darlonn convinced Jor to collect her things and the two of them talked alone for quite a while. She calmed down, though Lailoken understood her rage, and under most circumstances, he would've been fine with her anger. However, they had to be careful with the Order. They could be terrors to work with.

SIX

Soon after the dragon's escape, the camp was cleared and the party worked their way back down the mountain over treacherous passes and narrow ledges. Weariness made them move slowly and Driano's insistence on stopping for a break didn't help. As twilight approached, they'd only made it halfway down.

They were too far from the village in the valley below to make it safely by nightfall. Under an outward-facing ledge, Lailoken spotted flat ground that was perfect for hiding overnight. "Over there," he pointed. "We'll rest and continue in the morning."

"I hoped you'd see reason," Driano grumbled.

"You best hope he doesn't see my sword in your belly," Jor said as she walked past him, following Lailoken.

Lailoken's mind and body were weary, the fight and search having consumed much of his strength. Exhausted, he sat under the ledge and leaned against the far wall. Jor sat next to him, smiling, and lay down on the hard ground. Darlonn reclined on the other side of Jor, and Ori and Tozgan huddled close to each other nearby. Driano directed Belthos to build him a soft place to rest and the young novice tore through his bag looking for blankets and other items to give the Magus rest. Lailoken shook his head and leaned back, the cold stone comforting him. Exhausted, he soon fell asleep.

Sometime in the night, a dream came to him.

A brightly shining dragon raced across the sky, shimmering and gold. A horrid, black dragon with torn and shredded wings and eyes of smoke trailed behind it. The hideous thing reminded him of death. It devoured trees and fields as it pursued the golden dragon. Nothing was left in its wake but a black void, as though it destroyed creation, turning it all to nothing. Lailoken screamed, though not a sound came from him.

Suddenly, the golden dragon spun on the evil one, and poised to attack. The smoky-eyed black thing sped across the darkening sky and the two tangled in the air, gold and black intertwined in the throes of death. The golden dragon screamed a horrible cry of pain as the smoky-eyed dragon tore into its neck. Black cracked lines radiated outwards from the bite, streaking the brilliant gold. The golden scales became an ashy gray and the dragon was transformed into a similar black creature with smoky eyes. The pair turned their attention to the surrounding hillside and voraciously attacked everything in their path, leaving little untouched.

Lailoken woke in a cold sweat, startled and alarmed. *What are these dreams?* he thought. *What does this mean?* He looked out over the valley below, at the peaks rising through the clouds and the moonlight bouncing off them. It was a beautiful sight, but one he knew concealed danger. He remained awake for the rest of the night, his mind returning to the nightmare and the smoky-eyed dragon.

At dawn's bright light, he and the other slayers set off down the mountain toward the village and hopefully home.

Halfway down, Darlonn heard the unmistakable sound of a dragon roaring in the sky. He crouched, scanning the morning sky for the beast. Then he saw it. "The Onyx!" he called. The dragon had returned. "Cowardly thing! Now it's time to taste death!"

The Onyx soared in the sky, looping in on itself; twisting, and forcing acid from its mouth.

"Death comes for you!" Lailoken yelled. Though it was far away, the dragon turned toward them and dove at them. It streaked across the sky preceded by the acidic vapors it belched. Lailoken unsheathed his sword from his back and held it before him. "One of us will die this day," he said, narrowing his eyes, preparing to fight. Ori and Tozgan struggled to prepare their crossbows. Jor and Darlonn took position next to Lailoken, all three brandishing their swords. Driano and Belthos scurried away under a nearby tree.

"Driano, do your thing!" Lailoken called. The Magus summoned his power and cast enchantment over the slayers to protect them from the dragon's acid.

The dragon pulled up within reach of them and shot high in the air. It rolled and dove to their right, disappearing.

"Coward!" Jor called, returning her sword and charging toward where the dragon vanished. Lailoken and Darlonn followed, crossing the difficult, rocky terrain and narrow ledges, scanning for the beast. Lailoken looked over his shoulder at the rest of the group. The crossbowmen stumbled and the Magus was nowhere to be found. In the distance, they saw an enormous black hole.

"A cave," he said. "We've got you now."

They approached the opening carefully, their swords drawn in preparation of a fight. Ori and Tozgan were at their heels, crossbows cranked and bolts in place. The wind picked up, sending a chill running through Lailoken despite his thick fur coverings. "Menos, be with us now. Grant us vengeance on this dragon."

As they crept closer to the cave's mouth, it was eerily quiet. Lailoken thought it unnatural for something so large as the Onyx to be so still and silent. The hairs on the back of his neck stood on end. The sword felt heavy in his hands. Something wasn't right.

"I enter now to slay or be slain. It is no longer a matter of who, but when." He looked to Jor and Darlonn. "Stay here with them. Make sure it doesn't come out. If you see it flee, kill it."

"You aren't going in alone!" Darlonn said stepping forward. His large frame was imposing, but Lailoken knew his heart was pure, as was his loyalty. He held up a hand to stop him.

"We'll come with you. No dragon escapes us twice," Jor interjected.

"Stay here and guard this entrance. If it tries to escape, do what you must to bring it down. Station them to either side and wait. Maybe by then, Driano and his novice will arrive. They'll get their damn blood then."

Jor took a step forward, but Darlonn held her back. "It's a good plan. If we all go in there and die, it will be a tragedy. If only he does, we'll get the glory of the kill." He winked at Lailoken who grinned.

"You do anything stupid, the dragon won't be your biggest problem," Jor said, pointing her sword at him. She shook her head and stalked away.

"We'll be ready," Darlonn said. Lailoken nodded.

He stood at the cave's entrance and listened for the dragon. He heard nothing and had no choice. "So we begin," he said.

Moving slowly, he entered the void of the cave, wary of a surprise attack from the Onyx. All it had to do was spew deadly acid and he'd be helpless to stop it unless Driano's protection held. It was dangerous to track the thing, but it was his duty, his calling to do so.

The Magus of Tregaron preached on the necessity of dragon blood. Without it, their powers were weak. Blood-infused gems enhanced their powers exponentially. It had always been that way, at least as long as Lailoken knew. It was his calling as a slayer to do the work the Magus could not. This Onyx would not escape him.

Lailoken crept deeper into the darkness. Every sense was heightened. At any moment, he expected the dragon to lunge for him or unleash its awful acidic fury. No matter; death wasn't the end.

The cave took a sudden right turn and Lailoken hesitated, waiting for the attack that never came. One long look back to the bright entrance of the cave and he followed the path to the right, plunging himself into near total darkness. When he got so far that he could no longer see the light behind him at the bend, a sound startled him.

"Show yourself!" Lailoken called. A loud scrape like claws dragged across rocks answered him. "Come on, dragon, let's end this now."

A loud, deep voice called back in his mind. *I'm the one who will pay? I intended no harm to you humans, and yet you injure me and attempt to murder me. Does that seem right?*

"We only need your blood. It's our right. This is our land. You know the way of our people."

The dragon laughed heartily.

Do you really believe your words? Are we that bad? I believe your Black Magus have poisoned your minds and turned you against the truth created by Deavos.

Lailoken bristled at the mention of the false god Deavos, the father of dragons and heresy.

In the darkness, the sound of ripping flesh and crunching bones made Lailoken step back. "You disgusting, vile thing! How dare you speak ill of the Black Magus! They protect our people from the likes of you!"

Do you truly believe every word that little imp Myrthyd tells you? He's hiding more than you know. Ever wonder how someone so young earned the title of Kull Naga? The sound of a body being torn apart forced a grimace on Lailoken's face.

"It's not my place to question the Black Magus. Their ways are secret. I will not argue this point with you."

So you'd rid the world of my kind for our blood and the halflings because the teachings of the Order say so? Seems like a thin excuse to hunt us.

Lailoken was speechless.

Afraid to talk, human? You should be. I smell something...different about you. Something...

The dragon shuffled in the darkness, tossing something heavy on the cave floor. As a gust of wind whirled, a bright ball of white flame illuminated the cave. Lailoken shielded his eyes against the brightness. When his vision adjusted, he gasped.

Standing before him was a man in dark clothes, his eyes deep oily pools. To his left and behind him were the remains of an ox, the hind end missing. The man held his hand under the ball of flame as it floated as if on a cushion of air.

"By Menos!" Lailoken exclaimed.

The man smiled. "You might say that, though who knows for sure?" His short, black hair framed a face chiseled from stone with a hint of stubble on the chin. But it was those eyes, those black eyes that Lailoken couldn't take his gaze from.

"Have I stumped the slayer? How odd. You're familiar with our powers, are you not?"

Lailoken narrowed his eyes. "Demons you are! Spawn of Deavos, the false god of death!"

The man laughed. "You keep mentioning his name as though you don't know who Deavos is!"

"Father of lies and deceit. The creator of your horrible species."

The man stepped forward, blood dripping down his chin. He wiped it away with the sleeve of his black shirt. Lailoken raised his sword.

"Slayer, rest. I will not harm you. Your Magus have done that well enough." He paused, considering the ball of flame above his hand, then pushed it forward with an unseen force until it hovered near the top of the cavern between the two of them. Lailoken eyed the white ball suspiciously, wary of it crashing toward him.

"I recognize you. I've heard talk about you among my kind."

Lailoken puffed out his chest. "I imagine they fear me. I've slain many of your brethren."

The man nodded. "'Tis true. You have preyed on the weak, though the stronger amongst us don't have a flicker of fear. We'd destroy you in an instant if it weren't for one vocal female. She's made us promise not to kill you, though I must say, recently I was tempted to break that vow." He grinned, his black eyes boring through Lailoken.

"I've slain so many of your kind that it's a wonder you continue to travel to our lands."

"Slayer—"

"It's Lailoken. I want you to know the name of the man who will end you."

"Lailoken, then," the man said. "And you may call me Evros. There's a dark presence to your land. The colds of Tregaron are home to an evil so heinous and devious that we are compelled to seek it out and crush it. We cannot help but to come over the mountains. It is our duty."

"Your duty is to kill and destroy? Your methods make no sense."

"So your attempt to slaughter my kind *does* make sense?" He cocked his head to the side. Lailoken said nothing, his thoughts swirling.

"Lailoken, you have much to learn. I truly want to kill you; to exact vengeance on the man who murdered many of my younger and weaker brethren. My vows prevent me, and there is more about you that compels me to reign in my anger."

Evros shifted on his feet. Lailoken considered charging him and ending this debate. Nothing this dragon-man said held truth. True to the nature of his kind, he spewed lies intent on tricking his mind and twisting his thoughts.

"Lailoken, tell me about Alushia."

"You dare speak my daughter's name!" He raised the sword higher, stepping forward. "I'll split you in half if you've harmed her!"

"Easy, Lailoken. She is well, and I promise she will not be harmed in any way. It's part of my vow."

Lailoken tilted his head to the side. "What are you saying? I swear, if your lies go much further, nothing will stop me from killing you."

Evros turned his back. For a moment, Lailoken considered piercing him with his sword, but something in the man's manner and speech held him back.

"What do you remember about Alushia's mother, Etain?"

The mere mention of his long-lost wife felt like a dark force had gripped his heart and threatened to squeeze the life from him. He'd been searching for her since her disappearance soon after Alushia's birth. No note, no clue as to what happened, or where she went. "You dragons took her from me. I'm convinced of it."

"We did? Huh," Evros said, turning to face Lailoken. He set his hands on his hips and stared at him.

"You do know Etain is one of us."

Lailoken charged him, unable to stomach the lies he so causally spoke. Evros stepped calmly aside and gave Lailoken a nudge, forcing him to stumble and fall.

"How dare you speak such vile lies!" Lailoken

screamed at him. "Etain was no such creature! She was a beautiful, loving woman! Your kind stole her!"

"Etain lives. Far beyond the mountains, she lives and thrives. Who do you think my vow is to? She's an ancient dragon, more powerful and wise than any I've ever known. Like me, she can take human form. She speaks of you still. When you and your men first attacked me, I wasn't sure it was you. Not until moments ago was I sure you were the great slayer of legend. But here we are, face to face." Evros tensed. "Etain still loves you. She fears your anger over her deception."

Lailoken sat up with the sword across his knees. "You lie! Your tricks will not deceive me! This isn't true!"

"It is, and you know it. Myrthyd and his clan of false prophets have done much to destroy the truth."

Lailoken jumped to his feet, wielding his sword over his head, intent on destroying this giver of lies. "I will strike you down, no matter your form! Your words mean nothing to me!"

Evros stepped back. "Now, Slayer, I've been nothing but honest with you. I tell you nothing that isn't true. Think about what I've said. If Etain is a dragon, what does that make Alushia?"

"No! It's not true!" Lailoken lunged at him. Suddenly, a blinding ball of light erupted in front of him, stunning him. He closed his eyes and heard the stretch of skin and bones, and an immense whoosh of air nearly knocked him down.

Listen to my words, Slayer. The voice of the dragon, deep and slow in his mind again. *You know not what you do. She loves you still. Both of you.*

Then it roared, forcing Lailoken to cower. He had no idea where it was or if he was in danger from a surprise attack. He waited for death, for those long claws and pointed teeth to tear into his flesh, but nothing happened. The light fizzled, and in the last remnants of flame, he saw the empty cave.

SEVEN

When Lailoken stumbled out of the dark cave, night had covered the mountains and the moon cast its glow upon the land. Wispy clouds were illuminated by the orb in the sky, their thin tendrils reaching into the distance. Peaks rose above the clouds, breaking their form and reminding him of how precarious life had become.

Darlonn and Ori were sprawled out near the entrance as the rest slept near a small flame further away from the cave.

The dragon-man's words rattled around in his head. They couldn't be true. It was impossible. He had slain too many dragons to be duped by one now. It was a lie created to stall him from killing the creature. Lailoken closed his eyes and breathed in the cool night air. *Never again*, he thought. *I will never again let those beasts lie to me.* He opened his eyes and shook Darlonn awake.

"I'm back," he said quietly. The man smiled, and after waking Ori, they settled in next to the fire.

They said nothing for most of the night. Darlon opened his mouth to ask what happened, but Lailoken cut him off with a glare. Ori fell asleep again and Darlonn stayed up with Lailoken. When morning came and the camp stirred, Jor was the first to get him to open up.

"What happened in there? We heard something

and when Darlonn entered, we couldn't find you. We thought you were dead."

"Not dead, though if the dragon-man's lies are true, I wish I were."

"Come now, Slayer; that's a bit dramatic, don't you think?" Driano said.

Lailoken considered his words. Even a hint of dragon blood was enough to set the Magus after his daughter. He glowered at the Magus. "You weren't there."

Driano waved his hand dismissively. "Regardless, we must return to Kulketh since the hunt is over. I have pressing matters at hand."

Darlonn shook his head. After he helped Belthos pick up the camp, they began the journey back home.

Lailoken was quiet for most of the trek, brooding. Jor lead them down the mountain, the entire company silent.

The dragons stooped to new, despicable lows by claiming his wife was one of them. They knew how to needle him, to slide under his skin and force his anger. He'd never let them lie to him like that again. They must've been desperate to accuse his wife like so. Then to declare his daughter—his only child—a halfling? It was the absolute lowest thing they could've done. Whoever Evros was, Lailoken hoped to meet him again. "Nothing would give me greater satisfaction than slicing out your tongue and tearing you apart limb by limb," he said out loud. His anger had boiled to a point where nothing mattered other than finding and destroying that lying dragon.

"What was that?" Darlonn asked. Lailoken shook

his head, waving him off.

The mountain pass was difficult to navigate. The path narrowed near a ledge and Lailoken nearly slipped off the side. As he was considering Evros's words, he stepped on small rocks, and his leg was forced wide. He fell to the ground and dangled off the ledge.

"Lai!" Jor yelled. She pushed back through the small line and knelt to pull him up. Darlonn was next to her trying to assist.

Lailoken kicked against the sheer cliff and pushed himself up.

"Are you all right?" Darlonn asked. Driano huffed as though they were hindering his progress.

"I'm fine. My thoughts were elsewhere."

"Well, bring them back to now, would ya? It would be embarrassing to say we lost one of the greatest slayers in Tregaron to the whim of a couple pebbles," Jor said, forcing Lailoken to smile.

A few steps ahead, the path widened and Lailoken fell to the ground in a heap, panting, and wiping sweat off his brow.

"Menos, preserve me. Allow me to return home to see my daughter one last time so I may know for certain she is not what the evil thing claims she is." It was an impossible tale told from the mouth of a liar intent on preserving his own soul. There was no way Alushia was a halfling.

For his entire life, Lailoken had known nothing but hate for halflings. They were a plague upon Rowyth. The Order was clear: all halflings must die. Their blood polluted humanity and made them weak.

Lailoken rose from the ledge and dusted himself

off.

"Are you all right to continue?" Darlonn asked. The large man, had one of the kindest hearts he knew.

"He'd better be. We're wasting time here," Driano said.

"If you'd cut the man some slack, maybe we'd all get along better," Jor snarled.

"For a magnificent slayer, he sure does seem unsure of himself. We should've had that dragon's blood for our stones. Now we return defeated and humiliated. The Kull Naga won't like this at all."

"I don't care what that little man likes," Jor retorted. Driano arched his eyebrows.

"Be careful who you speak ill of, dear."

"Can we get moving now? I've seen worse situations than this with less tension," Tozgan said. He took his hat off and wrung it, then put it back. "This is not the first dragon a slayer has lost and it won't be the last. It happens. There are always more."

Driano peered at him but said nothing.

Jor once again began the trek down the mountain, moving faster despite Driano's protests. "Keep up. We need to get back!" she called when he asked for rest. He had no response. She heard Belthos giggle and then receive a cuff for it.

Several hours later as the sun rose higher in the sky, they entered Damol. The village was nestled at the foot of the mountains and surrounded by a thick forest.

"We can rest here for the night before returning to Kulketh," Jor said. There were no arguments from the group, not that Lailoken expected any. They were weary and discouraged. Driano's constant badgering of them and his novice wore on him. He relished the chance to spend a quiet evening in a room without the man's continual taunts. They walked the streets of Damol, passing the tavern and several shopkeepers eager for customers and headed straight for the Inn. Several villagers noticed the group with their long swords, leather armor, and crossbows and bowed slightly. Lailoken nodded in return. The villagers knew why they were there and where they came from. Damol had seen its share of slayers over the centuries, and the people knew when to engage in conversation and when to leave the slayers of Tregaron alone.

Lailoken opened the door to the Inn and approached the wooden counter. A small older woman sat knitting and looked up from her work.

"Aye, Slayer, have you come to grace us with your presence?" She paused as she took in the entire group.

"We need rooms for the night."

"I have a couple available. Might need to set someone up in the stall out back. The horses won't bite, but the bugs might."

"I'll take it," Jor said.

Lailoken tried to wave it off. "No, you take a room. I'll stay out there."

"Don't give me that! You need your rest. You and Darlonn take the room. I'll be fine," Jor said, running a hand over a dagger tucked into her belt. She was right. Anyone who dared mess with Jor was asking for trouble.

"Thanks. I owe you," Lailoken said.

"Yep. That's at least three now."

"If you two are done, I'd like to finish this transaction so we may rest for the journey tomorrow," Driano said.

The old woman nodded. "Follow me." She set down her work and rose from her chair, catching her balance on the counter. She waved them on and they went down a dark, narrow hallway. Keys from her waist rattled together with each slow, lumbering step. Finally she turned to the last door on the left, opened it, and held her arm out in invitation. "Your room, Slayers. Lunch is at noon and dinner is at six. Roast mutton tonight."

"Thank you," Lailoken said. He and Darlonn entered the room and closed the door. The wood inside was discolored from years of use. Lailoken stripped off his leather armor, draping it over a wooden stool in the corner, removed the rest of his fur outerclothes, and fell to the straw bed covered with a thin muslin sheet.

"I'll go check on the others," Darlonn said. "You rest. The hunt has been hard on you." Lailoken waved him on and soon drifted off to a fitful sleep.

A loud knocking on the door startled Lailoken awake. "Slayer, dinner is being served," he heard the old woman say.

"Thank you," he called back. He rolled to his back, rubbing sleep from his eyes and wondering where Darlonn was. His body ached, his mind was scattered, and his head pounded. He stretched and his stomach grumbled. Rising from the bed, he slipped on his boots and made his way down the hall to the dining room where the smell of roast mutton and freshly baked bread made his mouth water.

The rest of the group was seated at two tables, Driano and Belthos sat at one; and Jor, Darlonn, Ori, and Tozgan at the other. Jor waved him to their table.

"When was the last time you had a good meal?" the old innkeeper asked. There were other people seated in the dining room; a young couple, the man playing with the girl's long curly hair; an older man with a shaved head and thin white beard who looked like he could have been a former Magus; and a young man who looked to be a slayer.

"It's been some time. This looks and smells delicious," Ori said.

Lailoken sat at the wooden table and was promptly served a bowl of barley soup, a chunk of steaming bread, and a plate of mutton with root vegetables.

"I'll get you some ale," the innkeeper said. She shortly returned with wooden mugs full of ale and sat them down, splashing suds on the table.

"Thank you kindly," Lailoken said.

He ate in silence, savoring the meal and thinking about Evros's words.

When they finished dinner and countless mugs of ale, Lailoken excused himself and went to his room and fell back asleep. He never heard Darlonn enter, but when he woke in the morning to find the man passed out on the floor, he felt bad for not letting him have the bed.

They left as the sun rose and were soon on the path toward home.

It took considerably less time to return to Kulketh than when they left. Jor kept a quick pace, rarely stopping when Driano called for it.

Two days after leaving Damol, they arrived at the

gate to Kulketh.

A large black tower rose in the distance. The home of the Black Magus.

"I expect Kull Naga Myrthyd will want a full accounting of this expedition," Driano said. He tugged on his robes and tapped his shoulders to dust them off.

"You'll do just fine," Lailoken replied. They'd need to report in but it could wait. Finding Alushia was more important.

"But the Kull—"

"He'll either enjoy your tale or he won't. I don't care right now."

Driano hesitated, grunted, and slapped Belthos on the head. "Come, boy. It's time we rid ourselves of these brutes." The Magus and his novice scurried away for the Black Tower.

"Want us to take you home?" Darlonn asked.

Lailoken shook his head. "No. You go and rest. I'll be fine. Ori, Tozgan...it was my pleasure working with you. When the Kull Naga calls again for our services, would you be willing to join us?"

Tozgan replied for both of them. "It would be an honor," he said with a tip of his cap. Ori agreed. They shook hands and the crossbowmen walked away into the mass of people milling in the streets.

"'Til next time," Jor said. She shook his hand and Darlonn's, winked, and walked away, avoiding the beggars calling for coins.

"Are you sure you're fine to go by yourself? I don't mind," Darlonn said.

"If I were a scared little boy, I might consider your protection, but I'm sure I can manage," Lailoken said with a grin.

"Fair enough. We'll be in touch." Darlonn embraced him and left, going the opposite direction of Jor.

Lailoken stood within the walls of Kulketh and watched as his hunting party dissipated. Then he turned north for home.

He passed the busy town center where vendors called out, selling their vegetables and assorted handmade goods. A few people called out to him, recognizing the slayer, and thanking him for his service. Lailoken smiled and politely waved, though he didn't feel like being social.

Evros's words still bothered him, though he knew without a doubt they were false. He tried shaking them, but the cool, calm way he spoke to Lailoken made it seem like he was thoroughly convinced of his lies. *Were dragons that devious to truly believe their own falsehoods?* he thought. What other reason could it be? Clearly it was all a ruse to fool him and slow him down enough so he could escape.

Fresh fish!

Wheat for sale! Get your wheat over here!

Wanna new belt? I've got the best leather goods in Tregaron!

The vendors hawked their wares but he ignored them all. He had no need of their overpriced goods. All he needed was at home...except for Etain.

Other than to bother him with smoothly delivered lies, Evros forced Lailoken to think of his lost wife Etain.

He remembered when they first met. It was at the mid-summer Order of Eschar celebration when he was eighteen-years old, close to Alushia's age now. Etain had long flowing red hair like Jor and the most gorgeous green eyes he'd ever seen. They were like summer fields after a rain, glistening and vibrant. The sprinkle of freckles across her nose made him think of the stars above.

For a long time that night, Lailoken watched her from a distance. She danced and twirled to the music. At one point, she stood on a wooden stage and sang along with the musicians. Her voice was powerful and alluring. He never expected to fall for someone at the celebration; he was there to meet with older slayers and hear their tales of the hunt, but when he caught sight of Etain, he was ensnared.

Long into the night, he debated if he should approach her. Then, after several mugs of ale, he made his move. It wasn't pretty at first.

"Hey, I've never seen you around here," he said and hiccupped.

She giggled. "No, this is my first time in Kulketh. I'm from the village of Evenmount to the east."

"The—hic!" he hiccupped again, "the forest people?"

"That's what outsiders call us. We prefer to be called people. Like you."

"Well, that's the best thing I heard all night!" Lailoken stumbled and caught himself before he fell over his own feet.

"Maybe you should have a seat. I think you've had too much to drink."

"I don't need no seat! I need—" and those were his last words before falling down and knocking himself out. When he woke, Etain was gone, as were most of the revelers. Several scowling Black Magus stood around him.

"We cannot have our slayers inebriated at the first sign of drink," the tall skinny Magus said. He was bald and without facial hair and clad in the traditional black robe of the Order.

Another Magus, shorter but with a full black beard, chuckled. "Come on, let the boy be. He's just excited like the rest of us. Midsummer is here and not a dragon for ages. Life is good."

"Brother Burham, do not give this one an excuse to slack on his morals."

"Bah. Brother Elorin, leave him be. He'll face death soon enough. Let him enjoy what life he has left."

The two left him lying in the street, sore and hungry.

Days later, he tracked down Etain who hadn't left Kulketh yet. He gave her red roses daily, and she accepted each one and promised to one day reveal herself to him. Excited at the prospect of being with a woman, Lailoken dutifully continued bringing the roses every day for a month. Finally, Etain gave in.

"Lailoken, I will reveal myself to you, but first we must marry. I am not one to disrespect custom. We must first do that above all else."

Three days later, they were married by a low-level member of the Black Magus whose duty it was to attend to such matters.

That night, the couple consummated their marriage well into the night, Etain praising Lailoken for his prowess. Nine months later, Alushia was born while he was on a hunt.

Lailoken was very proud of his small family. He'd gone on two hunts during Etain's pregnancy and returned with a reward both times. By the time Alushia was born, they were on their way to a long, prosperous life on the small homestead he'd earned for his skill and bravery.

Then the unthinkable happened.

When Alushia was only four months old, Etain disappeared. Lailoken came in from the fields to find their daughter crying on the floor. "Etain! Etain, where are you? Why'd you leave Alushia alone?" he called out. The prolonged silence sent fear through his body. He scooped up his little girl and scoured the home and neighboring fields but found nothing. No clue gave away what happened to her. There were no footprints, no sign of a struggle; nothing. After several days of searching with the help of his brother and fellow slayers, they came to the conclusion that a dragon had stolen her away, though the only account of seeing one was made by a small boy at the edge of town who, when questioned further by the Black Magus, recanted his story and was whipped for his lies.

He never saw her again. How did Evros know her name then? How did he know about her disappearance?

By the time he reached the edge of his property, twilight was settling across the land. Far away, a small flame flickered through a window at his house. The smell of the animals blew in along the fields, a scent so comforting to him. His daughter would be inside, possibly with a pot of stew, and she'd be surprised by his presence. It had been too long since he'd been home.

He reached the door and hesitated. He heard noise inside that didn't sound like Alushia. *Had she taken a man?* With as much as he'd been gone, he understood, though it was his daughter. *His* daughter. No man would have her without his permission. Lailoken pushed open the door and raced inside.

"Father!" Alushia exclaimed. She jumped up from the floor where she'd been stroking the head of Brida, her snowcat, and gave him a tight hug. He smiled, more to himself for thinking she'd been sneaking around behind his back. "I'm so glad you're home!"

"So am I."

EIGHT

Lailoken's return to his homestead didn't assuage his concerns about the lies told to him by the dragon-man. When out in the rotting fields, he had a difficult time focusing on the task at hand with the oxen. His mind returned to the conversation he had with Evros over and over.

"Is that how a slayer leads a team?"

"What? I'm doing my best. Whatever you did to these oxen while I was gone, I now have to undo. You didn't talk to them like they were pets again, did you?"

Alushia laughed. "Like Brida? Maybe."

Lailoken rolled his eyes. He struggled with the ox, pulling tight on the reigns to urge it forward in a straight line. At this rate, planting the winter wheat would take a lot longer than expected, and when he expected less than half the field to return anything to eat...

Brida prowled along the edge of the field, her bright white fur in stark contrast to the dark ground.

"Maybe if you'd talk about your trip and share what's on your mind, you'd stand a better chance of getting BoBo to work right," Alushia said. She'd been behind him, planting the wheat and having an easy time catching him.

"Nothing from the hunt would interest you. It was brutal and we lost the dragon."

When they finally finished a row, they took a break, sitting against a tree at the edge of the field.

Lailoken's gaze followed Brida creeping after a small animal in the distance.

"Father, you were gone so long. I wondered if you'd been taken by the dragon. I had terrible dreams most nights. Black, tattered dragons soared in the sky, their eyes plumes of smoke. They devoured everything in their path, turning my dreams into nothingness. I had the oddest sensation staring at the void they created and feeling--truly feeling—a threatening abyss. I'd wake most nights and fear going back to sleep because the void felt dangerous."

Lailoken didn't know what to say. The visions Alushia shared sounded like they were invented by Evros, though he experienced something similar once.

"I wish you didn't have to deal with those nightmares, Alushia. I'm here now, and unless called to hunt soon, I should be home for quite a while. Let's finish these next rows before it gets dark. The way BoBo is moving," he squinted at her with a mock scowl, "it will take days to finish this field." He winked and stood, extending his hand to her to help her up.

Her eyes reminded him of Etain, though her hair was a much darker black. Her eyes were full of life and so bright. They were the same shape and color as her mother's, and when Alushia smiled, his heart broke as he thought of Etain's disappearance. One day, Alushia would find someone to share her life and leave him, and only then would he possibly find rest for his grieving soul.

For the rest of the day, Lailoken's thoughts dwelled

on Evros and his lies. The thought of Etain still alive gave him hope that maybe she might be found. He convinced himself they were lies, though he couldn't shake them from his memory. He had to report to Myrthyd anyway and considered speaking with the Kull about his encounter.

The next day, he went to the Magus Tower. Lailoken left early so to reach Kulketh by mid-morning. The interrogations often lasted several hours and he wanted to be home before dark.

The road to town was crowded as villagers and beggars from around Kulketh travelled to the market to enjoy a few days of the vices offered by the town. Most often they'd end their stay with time in the Magus Tower, seeking forgiveness for their sins committed while in Kulketh. For a half-drac, they'd be able to wipe their slate clean and return home cleansed of their sins. The Black Magus hoarded those coins to pay the slayers for their service and for the upkeep of their tower, not to mention the robust meals and generous consumption of ale. Most of the order wore round bellies like a talisman against hunger.

Lailoken avoided the main market area, not wanting to deal with the crowds and constant barking of the vendors. There was an ever-increasing presence along the streets of families that begged for food and money. It seemed like they increased daily.

He travelled along the outer edges of the market near the smaller established shops and inns where the noise was not as bothersome. Young boys cleaned the streets and were busy about their task as one of the Black Magus novices clad in a black robe with a white sash supervised their work.

"You missed that pile of dung!" the novice scolded one of the boys. He whacked him on the head with his hand, sending the boy reeling. The boy dusted himself off, asked forgiveness, and cleaned the dung from the road. His face twisted and he turned his head to the side as he scooped up the dung with his hands and dropped it into his wooden bucket.

"Better. Now get back to it. At this rate, you scoundrels will be out here till sunset, and I've got better things to do than watch you scoop dung from the road." The boys hurried back to their jobs, no doubt worried the novice would strike them, too.

Novices often remained in their stations for a year or two before being tested by a special council of the Order. If they passed, they were ordained a Magus. If they failed, they were relegated to manual labor and their powers silenced. Their hard labor of menial tasks was to harden them for a life of service.

Lailoken left the novice and his apprentices and walked by several blocks of buildings until he approached the immense Black Tower of the Magus. It rose high into the sky, its peak piercing the clouds. At each entrance stood two large Tower Guards clad in black-coated armor with long pikes held upright. Lailoken approached the pair nearest him and they crossed their pikes, blocking entrance to the tower.

"Halt. What business do you have with the Black Magus?" a guard asked. The other one narrowed his eyes, the scar on his face twisting into a gnarled river of red flesh.

"Bilgron, must you act so impersonal every time I

come to the Tower?"

Bilgron grinned warily.

"No one approaches the Magus without reason."

The scarred one spoke. "What's yours?"

Lailoken sighed. If these idiots were going to force him to be formal, he'd oblige. "I've been summoned by his highness the Kull Naga Myrthyd to report on my hunt. My name is Lailoken, slayer for Kull Naga Myrthyd."

Bilgron spoke. "Let him pass, Troyer. He's telling the truth."

Bilgron and Troyer moved their pikes aside, allowing Lailoken to pass, and turned back to the street, waiting for the next visitor to harass.

"If they were any dumber, the Order might need to use sheep to replace them," Lailoken muttered as he stepped inside the cavernous hall.

He followed the immense entrance to a central open area ascending into the building. Standing in the center on the mosaic image of Rowyth, he looked up. Sunlight streamed in through stained-glass windows as floor after floor rose higher in the air. He often wondered how such a large building with nothing in the center remained standing for so long. It was a marvel to look at. Black wood and white marble streaked with black and grey were offset by beautifully colored tapestries that hung on all the walls. They depicted the origins of their world and the settling of Tregaron. The mighty feats of past soldiers led by former Kulls told the story of how Tregaron had established itself after the reformation a thousand years ago. They fought back the weak southerners who chose the path of the dragon and Deavos instead of the one true god Menos, a demanding god who outlawed the union of dragon and man.

Standing in the central hall, he could hear whispers all around as Magus and their guests discussed current policies and Myrthyd's mandate to secure their borders against invasion from the south. The rise in halflings was a sign the southerners were stirring against the north, a common theme amongst the snippets of conversations.

Myrthyd was young; about the same age as Alushia but projected a wisdom and confidence that no one disputed. As a champion dragonslayer, Lailoken had met with him several times, even while he was still yet a novice, and always left impressed by the young lad's composure.

"Fascinating, isn't it?"

Lailoken turned, startled, and faced the Kull Naga. The Kull was almost as tall as Lailoken with a shaved head and black mustache and beard, though the beard wasn't full and betrayed a boy of eighteen. It would be years before he looked like a man. He wore the black stone pendant of the Magus, a tool to enhance his innate abilities.

"Kull, I didn't notice you there. My apologies."

Myrthyd waved him off. "Pah, enough with the formalities. It's great to see you, Lailoken! Come, regale me with your latest exploits. I've heard from Driano, but I want your take." Myrthyd led him down a dark stone hall with red tapestries of some of the bloodiest hunts ever depicted. Red and green dragons were slaughtered by slayers while a figure representing the Kull Naga stood in the distance. Near the end of the hall, they ascended a small staircase where Myr-thyd stopped at a guarded door. The guard opened the door, Myrthyd waving Lailoken into his study.

"Please, have a seat." Myrthyd flicked his fingers and the two candles on his desk came to life, instantly illuminating the room.

Lailoken sat across the large black wooden desk from Myrthyd. The room was sparsely decorated in contrast to the halls outside.

"Tell me, Slayer, how did the last hunt go? I hear one got away. Driano was most upset, though his nov-ice thought his anger a bit funny. Poor lad, he'll pay for that I'm sure."

Lailoken shifted in his seat. He came here for this, but still, explaining his failure to the Kull unsettled him.

"A large Onyx dared to show itself. We attacked, but somehow it escaped. We then tracked it to a cave and I went in for the kill. It used its evil ways, trans-forming itself into a man, and spoke with me."

"It shifted? Interesting. It's rare they shift here. At least not where we can see. It must have been anxious to speak with you."

Lailoken cracked his knuckles and spoke. "It did. The dragon-man spouted lies about..." he paused. Speaking her name brought so many memories. "He spoke about Etain. He claimed she was a dragon her-self."

"A dragon? Your wife? That's not possible! A slayer would know the difference!"

"I agree. He was confident in his lies. Almost had me doubting the truth."

Myrthyd crossed his arms and leaned back.

"It cannot be true, can it? There's no way Etain was one of them. Right?"

"Those beasts are cunning, but you'd have to know the difference," Myrthyd said in a smooth, deep voice. "A man such as yourself committed to their extinction must surely know a shifter from a real person."

Lailoken nodded. Several awkward moments passed before Lailoken spoke.

"Alushia has had dreams. Bad ones of a half-dead black dragon devouring everything in sight."

Myrthyd sat upright and stroked his scraggly beard. "Half-dead? And it destroyed everything?"

"Yeah, but not as if what she was watching was a dream, but more like it was devouring her dream. She claims she had the sense that if it finished, something bad might happen. She woke before it turned everything into a black void."

Myrthyd stroked his beard again and peered at Lailoken with his unsettling gray eyes, making him squirm in his seat. He didn't like the way Myrthyd stared at him as though about to accuse him of heresy.

"So your daughter had these visions. Do you think she made them up?"

"She's much smarter than that! She told me of her own volition. There must be something causing them."

"If she has these again, come to me immediately. I expect they're nothing more than coincidence, however I want to be sure. So," he said, "tell me all about the hunt. Every little detail. You know how I enjoy the demise of those filthy dragons."

Lailoken spent nearly three hours recounting their two dragon encounters. When he was done, Myrthyd closed his eyes as if in meditation. When he opened them, Lailoken felt like Myrthyd's gaze bore into his soul. It was more unsettling than he expected.

"You kill one beast and allow the shifter to spew lies and escape? I had higher hopes for you, Slayer. I was told upon my ascension that you were the best in Tregaron. None were more ruthless and cunning than you, yet you let the Onyx simply walk away. On top of that, you allow it to infect your mind with lies about your wife. I bet your next thought was if your daughter was a halfling."

Lailoken was taken aback by the shift in Myrthyd's tone. "Kull, it's not exactly that at all."

Myrthyd leaned forward, resting both hands on the desk. "Then tell me what it's exactly like," he said, drawing out each word; accusing him, daring him to argue.

Lailoken stumbled to find the words.

"Slayer, this is your last failure. We cannot allow those creatures to poison our people with their treachery."

"I will not fail you, I ask your guidance to help find this dragon-man. Help me to seek him so I may exact my vengeance on him for his deceit."

Myrthyd's lips cracked in a sinister smile. "That's the slayer I've come to adore. I'll help, but I need you to do something for me in turn. Do we have a deal?"

"Of course, I'm here to serve."

"We must hurry. Time is not on our side."

NINE

Myrthyd enjoyed watching Lailoken squirm. The great and mighty slayer was no match for him. He may have been stronger and more experienced in the ways of dragon hunting, but he was not smart. Like most around him, Myrthyd assumed he was a brute with little intelligence. Now that he spun his tale, Myrthyd was ready to make the slayer more uncomfortable.

"I've heard of this Onyx. He's been known to lie to humans in order to preserve his hide. I fear he may have poisoned your thoughts with his lies. I can help you rid Rowyth of it. But to do so, I need something from you."

Lailoken shifted in his chair. Myrthyd knew he had him.

"What do you require?" Lailoken asked.

"There is a gem. A blood gem. It's hidden inside the Dragonback Mountains and has been there for centuries."

***

Before Lailoken's return, Myrthyd had studied Drexon's tome carefully. The verses taunted him.

From dark crystal once hidden now found
Comes power unchecked, unbound.

Fill the blood with a dragon's soul
And own the dream, the dreamer whole.

Find the crystal among a dragon's back
Within a cavern, dark and black.
Slay the keeper and take the gem
Power eternal, over dragon, over men.

What did the words mean? How were these more powerful than a normal spell? He mulled it over day and night, racking his brain to discover their meaning. Then in a moment of sheer brilliance, it dawned on him.

Find the crystal among a dragon's back
Within a cavern, dark and black.

The mountains. The Dragonback Mountains. He'd been searching the backs of real dragons, but to the south bordering the land of the infidels was an entire range of mountains—the *Dragonback Mountains*. It must be there! Whatever they needed must be hidden within those accursed peaks.

He'd understood the part about a dark crystal and a blood gem. Whatever they were seeking was a dark, blood-like gem of some sort. Not the easiest item to find hidden somewhere inside a mountain range, but at least it was a start. Leaving the tome aside, he spent days within the Tower archives searching for clues to the spell and the implications therein.

Two days before Lailoken arrived, he spotted an anecdote from one of the earliest Kulls of the Magus; a man named Doothan. Doothan wasn't well known in the Order, he hadn't done much of anything important. Myrthyd vaguely remembered the name let alone anything he'd accomplished. In truth, none of the former Kulls would matter if he had his way. If he lifted the curse upon his land, they'd all be forgotten in favor of him.

In an ancient history of the Order, Doothan mentioned a blood stone that was "forbidden and hidden" within the mountains as to deny the power to any human soul. He claimed to have a slayer in his service who knew of a cave on the southern side of Opaline Mountain where such a thing might be hidden. The problem was, Myrthyd had never heard of Opaline Mountain. Where was it? Did it exist amongst the Dragonback Mountains or was it somewhere else? There were a few mountains within that range with names like Dragonfire Peak, Mount Routhan, to name a couple. But nothing called Opaline Mountain. However, if the spell were to be understood as real, then it had to be within the Dragonback Mountains. That was where his studies ended. He tossed the book against the wall, startling a novice who was silently attending those in the archives.

Myrthyd closed his eyes and held his fingers to his temples, massaging the tension growing inside. He was so close to the truth! The sooner he uncovered the meaning, the sooner his power would be complete and the Drakku wiped from Rowyth forever, and Tregaron returned to its former state.

He locked himself in his room until Lailoken's arrival, turning the spell over in his mind trying to discover some other hidden meaning within the text.

It eluded him, though he felt on the edge of a discovery. It was like he saw the silhouette of something he couldn't bring into focus. The lack of insight aggravated him.

***

With Lailoken seated across from him in obvious discomfort, Myrthyd issued his orders.

"I need you to canvas the Dragonback Mountains."

"For what?"

"Do not interrupt me, Slayer!"

Lailoken shifted in his seat, a sign pleasing to Myrthyd.

"You are tasked with searching the mountains for the gem called by some the Blood Stone."

Lailoken's face flashed surprise. "A gem? I'm a slayer, not a treasure hunter. Send someone else to find your wealth. I have land to tend to and a daughter to take care of. I've been gone long enough. Like everyone else, my fields are in terrible shape, and food is growing scarce."

"This is not an ordinary gem. It is not a treasure in the sense that it will bring great wealth. Let me ask you something...would you care to see the elimination of all halflings from Rowyth?" Myrthyd leaned back with his hands interlocked behind his head, waiting for Lailoken to reply.

"They're part of the reason our fields refuse to yield their bounty."

"Then find this gem. I believe it will unlock something so powerful that we can make it a reality. No more dragons. No more halflings. They'll all be wiped from existence. With them gone, we'll be able to march on the south, bring them to the truth, and end our misery. No longer will they worship a false god and spread their evil ideas. With halflings eliminated, nothing would stand in our way."

Lailoken's green eyes widened and he stroked his long beard. The lines on his chiseled face were deep.

"Tell me, Slayer, would that appeal to you?" His eyes were far away, lost in thought.

"Anything to help Tregaron recover. I've witnessed our land grow bleaker as halfling and dragon influence grows. I will not allow my daughter to one day have a family, only for them to starve."

"And tell me, Lailoken, how many dragons have you slain?"

Lailoken looked down at his leather gauntlet. It was adorned with dragon scales. He pretended to count them.

"Come, Slayer; you know the number without counting those. How many?"

"Twenty-two."

"Twenty-two. Now imagine doubling or tripling that number and eliminating the source of all halflings. In fact, imagine an entire suit of armor created from the scales of all the dead dragons. It would be enough to outfit an entire army! We can do that. With this Blood Stone, it can happen."

"But how?" Lailoken cocked his head as though not understanding.

"That will be up to me. With my powers, I can make it happen. But only if you find me that gem."

Lailoken crossed his arms on his chest. "I still don't

understand why you need a slayer to find a gem. Do you even know where to look?"

Myrthyd went into his bedchamber and returned with Drexon's forbidden tome, though he figured Lailoken would know nothing of what was allowed and what the Magus had declared to be dangerous. He opened it to the Nightwraith spell and read the spell aloud.

"From dark crystal once hidden now found
Comes power unchecked, unbound.
Fill the blood with a dragon's soul
And own the dream, the dreamer whole.

Find the crystal among a dragon's back
Within a cavern, dark and black.
Slay the keeper and take the gem
Power eternal, over dragon, over men.

The dragon soul you will bind,
A Nightwraith to destroy the mind.
The living will live among the dead,
When you control the visions within their head.

Vile offspring of a dragon's lie
Controlled by the onyx eye.
Within the fatal dragon fate,
Power of yours, a Nightwraith."

When he had finished, he slammed the book shut. "The crystal is in the dragon's back. The Dragonback Mountains. It has to be. It clearly states the gem is in a cave hidden in the mountains. *Slay the keeper.* I need a slayer to fight what might be the strongest dragon known to man. Who better than the greatest slayer ever known? It's you. I need you, Lailoken, to find the cave, find the gem, and slay the keeper. When you return that gem to me, my power over dragon-kind will be absolute."

He watched as Lailoken considered his request. Silently, he cast a spell he learned from the tome on the desk to compel Lailoken to agree to his suggestion. So far, the spell didn't force someone to do something they normally wouldn't do, but it did make them much more agreeable to the question at hand, especially if it was something they would consider anyway. This just cleared internal boundaries to make the decision easier and more to Myrthyd's wishes.

"I will do as you ask. I will need my team of slayers, and I will need to collect my things. Alushia will not be agreeable to this."

"Do not worry about your daughter. I will personally ensure she and your homestead are properly taken care of. You have nothing to worry about while you go on this most important hunt. I'd prefer a certain level of...discretion. Do you trust your slayers? I need your party to understand the need for silence on this matter. If this gets into the wrong hands or the southerners somehow find out, it would be devastating. It must remain private. Find this cave, find the gem, and slay the keeper. I care not if it's a dragon, a person, or something else. Bring that gem to me."

"I will do as you bid."

"Good," Myrthyd said, a grin spreading across his face. "Within a week you must go. Until then, prepare your daughter for your absence once again. Know that you are now part of the greatest hunt in the history of Tregaron. Do not fail me."

Lailoken stood and bowed.

"One last thing. The cave you seek is on Opaline Mountain."

"Where is that?"

"That's all I know. Now hurry; time will not wait for us."

Lailoken excused himself and left the chambers.

Myrthyd closed his eyes and let out a deep breath. The longer they waited to find the gem, the more chances it could fall into the wrong hands. No one was actively searching for it, at least not that he was aware of. Once in his control, the Drakku would be over. Their reign of terror would end.

During the meantime, he'd figure out what the rest of the spell meant. All he knew was that it started with the gem. How he'd use it was still a mystery, but not for long. He'd discover its meaning by any way necessary.

TEN

An hour later, Lailoken entered the door of the Wandering Sailor, his favorite place to have a drink and unwind. It was near Kulketh's northern wall and often frequented by the Black Magus. He hadn't been there in a while but when he entered, he could see nothing had changed. The walls were still grey wooden boards, worn and useless to stop the elements from entering. The bar was made of the same grey wood. Oil lamps ran along the walls, flickering and casting shadows in the corners. A small band played music at the far end of the room where several people were up and dancing.

"Well, look who decided to grace us with his presence!" Wichard, the tavern owner said. He was short and still held firm to his pot belly and long stringy hair. It looked like he'd lost a few teeth since the last time Lailoken saw him.

"Hey Wichard, it's good to see you again!" They shook hands and Wichard poured a large wooden mug of ale and slid it across the bar.

"First one's on me. The rest, you gotta pay for."

"Thank you. I appreciate it."

"You slayers have a rough job. It's the least I can do." Wichard brushed the hair from his face then pointed toward the dance floor.

"You two idiots start fighting, I'll club ya both!" he

yelled. Lailoken turned and watched as two young men around Alushia's age prepared to fight. Suddenly they hugged each other, almost toppling over.

"Good to see you again, Lailoken. I gotta take care of them. See you around." The short man left and scolded the two men as the band played a fast tune, bringing many around the dance floor to their feet, surrounding Wichard in the chaos. Lailoken laughed and drank his ale, asking for another from the woman behind the bar. She did most of the counter work while Wichard worked the crowd.

"Lailoken, is that you?" a gruff man called behind him. Lailoken turned around and instantly recognized the man, though it had been at least a year since he'd seen him.

"Tibaut? Is that you? It's hard to tell from the ugly on your face!"

Tibaut frowned. Then his lips turned up in a smile. "Lailoken! The best slayer in the land and one of the worst jokers around! Come, let's have a drink. More ale!" he called to the woman barkeep. He led Lailoken and two other men to a table far from the dance floor, though the music was still loud. They sat and Tibaut introduced the two other men.

"This here is Reinfrid. He's a southerner, but don't worry none about him. He ain't got the stomach for those halfling lovers! He's up here to learn about us dragonslayers. Says he wants to be one someday!" Reinfrid nodded. He was a thin man, maybe a few years older than Lailoken. His long grey beard was full and he wore a deep gray wool coat and pants.

"And this one over here, he's Alfan. Been courting

my sister for over a year and still ain't asked her to marry him. It might be he don't want to be related to me!" Tibaut let out a loud bellow of a laugh.

"He might be right!" Alfan chimed in. He was younger and had a mangled ear. His blond hair was dirty and he had the sturdy build of a farm hand.

"What brings you in here, Lailoken? It must be what, a year since you last came in?" Tibaut asked.

"I suppose it has. Been back from the hunt for a while now. Just me and Alushia at home, and I needed to get out. She's a great girl, but I miss being around drunks like yourselves." He laughed and the others joined him, raising their mugs high in a toast to their inebriation.

"The hunt, you say?" Reinfrid asked.

Lailoken nodded. Wichard dropped off another round of ale for the men and cleared their empty mugs.

"Went in search of an Onyx. Nearly caught him, too, but he eluded me."

"The great Lailoken missed his mark. That calls for a drink!" Tibaut called. He raised his glass, urging the rest to do the same and they gulped in unison.

"Damn dragon shifted on me, too; turned right into a man."

The group fell silent.

"*Shifted?*" Alfan asked.

"He means turned into a human. Many dragons have that ability, though why they do so is beyond me," Reinfrid said. Lailoken narrowed his eyes and stared at him. "What? I'm from the south. I've seen it a lot."

"When that Onyx shifted, he spoke a pack of lies to

me, too. Said my wife Etain was a dragon, making my Alushia a halfling."

The table went silent. Then Tibaut burst out laughing. "A halfling? Are you kidding me? The great dragonslayer lay with the enemy, and now raises a halfling? Ha ha! That's too good!" He slammed down the rest of his ale and called for more.

Lailoken seethed inside. He was no fool. He did not lay with a dragon, and Etain was no such thing. Alushia was as human as human can be, not a drop of dragon blood filled her veins. He clenched his fists as Tibaut and then Alfan laughed harder, pointing at him.

"Will you two get a hold of yourselves?" Reinfrid asked. He refused to laugh at Lailoken's words. Concern crossed his face. Even after several mugs of ale, Lailoken caught the look.

"Fine, fine," Tibaut said, wiping away the tears from laughing so hard. "It's just too good to imagine. The man who spent his life killing dragons is accused of laying with one and having a halfling. It can't be true, but it is funny to think about!"

The men drank long into the night, mug after mug of ale making its way to their table and down their throats. When at last Tibaut had enough, he stumbled out the door with Alfan at his side. Reinfrid remained behind, and the moment the other men were gone, he turned to Lailoken.

"Slayer, you say the Onyx spoke to you and claimed your wife was a dragon?"

"Aye, that he did. Lies, lies, and more lies. They'll do anything to get away from me."

"I'm not so sure it was a lie. I think these men

would kill your daughter if they believed a shred of truth about your tale."

Lailoken narrowed his eyes. It was difficult to focus after so much drinking. "What do ya mean, you aren't sure it was a lie?"

"Dragons shift all the time. They aren't harming anyone, and we've grown quite accustomed to their changes in the south. They aren't bad...not all of them. Like us humans, there are good ones and bad ones." He went quiet, looking around the tavern, then turned back to Lailoken. "Come with me to the south. The queen could use someone like you. Bring your daughter. She won't be safe here, not with the way the Order insists on slaughtering all dragons and the halflings. Your knowledge and expertise would be invaluable to Queen Pethinia."

Lailoken tilted his head, unsure if he'd heard Reinfrid right. "Are you telling me my girl *is* a halfling? You don't even know her! You speak southern blasphemy!"

Reinfrid motioned for him to calm down. "I'm not saying she is a halfling, but the possibility is real. I've heard of a Garnet named Etain. She lives near the western shores. Quite a powerful dragon, too."

Lailoken slammed his fists on the table. "I will *not* listen to your lies, southerner! You say another word about my wife, and I'll kill you right here!" A couple patrons turned their way but left them alone.

Reinfrid leaned closer and spoke in a quiet voice. "When you're ready to accept the truth, I'll be at the Dragon Bane Inn in Woodpine. I'll be leaving in a few days and could use some company on my journey. Please consider the offer." He rose and left the tavern, leaving Lailoken in a greater state of confusion than when he entered hours ago.

ELEVEN

The cool morning was a lie, as the sun would rise higher and turn the day scorching. Myrthyd walked in the garden on the south side of the tower among the apprentices out tending to the shrubs and flowers. One of their first tasks was to learn how to harness enough power to envelop a weed with poison and destroy just that weed and not the precious plants around it. The harsh clime of Tregaron made farming difficult, and in Kulketh, they dealt with it differently than in the other cities. The novices were allowed small black stones dipped in dragon blood to aid their magic, though those stones weren't the same strength as the larger, more powerful stones the Magus carried.

Turning the corner, Myrthyd heard the crowd before he saw it. They were raucous, calling for the deed to be done. Men and women—children even—were calling for the deaths of the boy and girl on the platform raised for all to see, both maybe a year younger than him, but far different.

They were thin and dirty. It crushed him to see them that way. It was why he adhered to his policy against halflings. If the Drakku thought they'd destroy Tregaron, they'd have to face him. He peered into the shouting faces around him.

"Settle down, settle down," a tower guard called out to the crowd. "As soon as the Kull Naga arrives, we will begin the sentence."

"Evil traitors!" a woman called out.

"Death to the halflings!" a man countered.

"Our people are dying because of them!" another man cried out.

The crowd erupted in chants again, the guard trying to quiet them down by waving his arms.

"There's the Kull!" a boy shouted, pointing at Myrthyd. In a sudden shift, the crowd reacted and roared louder at the sight of their leader, their protector. Myrthyd smiled. This was what he lived for.

He waved, not wanting them to see him as an equal but as their leader. The crowd hushed when he raised both hands high. He approached the platform and walked up the four creaky wooden steps. Guards beside the halflings took a step back as Myrthyd inspected them. He held the boy's chin in his hands, turning his face back and forth as though inspecting an ox. He did the same with the girl. She was an ugly thing; large wide nose, warts above her left eye, and dirty hair. Her brother didn't look much better, though his nose was considerably smaller. Myrthyd turned to the crowd.

"Today we fulfill our calling as protectors of Tregaron. As your rightful leader and humble servant, I declare these halflings guilty of treason and guilty of polluting our land with their wicked nature. Are there any among you who would counter these charges?"

He knew well there would be none. These two were halflings discovered hiding with their father and step-mother near a small village to the east. Their parents were hanged last week.

"Please don't kill us," the boy said.

Myrthyd turned to him. "What did you say?" he growled.

"Please let us be. We've done nothing wrong. We're one of you. We belong among you. We had no choice. Please Kull Naga, have mercy on us." The boy's sister sobbed, snorting. The scene disgusted Myrthyd. He scrunched his face and turned back to the crowd.

"These abominations beg for mercy. What say you?"

"Kill them!"

"Destroy the wicked!"

"Rid Tregaron of their kind!"

The crowd shouted, louder and angrier than before. Myrthyd faced the two again. "You know the penalty. You have no rights in our land. We cannot allow your blood to infect our people."

"Please! No!" the girl screamed. She tried running off the platform. A guard grabbed her and held her in place as she thrashed. The bindings around her wrists prevented her from attacking. The other guard held the boy tight. Myrthyd nodded and the guards fixed their bindings to the large charred pole in the center of the platform.

"No!" the girl screamed. "Let us go! We've done nothing wrong!"

"I beg for mercy! Have pity on us! We have no choice in who we are!" the boy screamed.

The guards stepped back after checking to make sure they were securely attached to the post.

Myrthyd held his arms high in the air, scanning the quiet crowd, then turning back to the two on the platform. The guards departed, leaving only Myrthyd with the children.

"Never infect our land again!" Myrthyd yelled, then produced two clouds of acidic vapor above their heads. They struggled against their bindings. Blood ran down the girl's arm as the metal cut into her flesh. Then, Myrthyd moved his hands down.

The vapors above their heads descended down around them, growing larger and darker. The crowd silenced in awe of Myrthyd's raw power and the execution playing out before them.

When Myrthyd ascended to Kull Naga, he quickly reintroduced the public executions of all halflings. Before him, they were done in private. He needed to make sure his people knew his power and understood their roles in ridding Tregaron of the infection plaguing their lands. He'd personally put to death every halfling discovered since he became Kull Naga, using a spell he learned from the secret tome.

The first time he produced the vapors, a council of Magus convened to discuss if his behavior was forbidden or not. The council debated for days until he could stand it no more. With a spell from the book, he compelled them to conclude his magic was not forbidden and they decreed the Kull Naga—because of his stature and role in Tregaron—should have the exclusive use of any magic known or unknown to further their cause. It was a blanket decree that he really didn't need, but made it happen anyway to squash the undercurrent of dissension brewing amongst the Order and the populace at large. He'd use whatever spell or whatever means necessary to wipe out halflings from the face of not only Tregaron, but all of Rowyth.

The boy and girl screamed horrific cries of pain as the acidic vapors consumed them. The smell of burnt hair and charred meat filled the air. Some in the crowd cheered their deaths, calling for the eradication of halflings from their land. Myrthyd was pleased at the reaction. The more public executions they had, the more the people feared him and accepted his demands to remove halflings from Rowyth. He had grand plans for his people. They would one day rule over all and bring a sense of normalcy to an otherwise unruly and heathen world. And he would be at their head. The grand Magus of Rowyth, a title he considered for himself once all his plans were set in motion.

Myrthyd watched as the acid engulfed the pair from head to foot. Their screams were deafening. The crowd grew bolder, shouting for their deaths. Shouting for the vapors.

First the girl and then the boy went silent, their heads falling downward. The vapors intensified, melting the flesh from their bones. The crowd silenced again, filled with awe and morbid curiosity as Myrthyd's acid finished the job.

A few minutes later and the muscles were sizzling and shrunken from the intensity. Myrthyd smiled wider as the spell neared its conclusion. With a loud pop, the vapors died out, leaving smoking, charred bones in place of the two living people who had struggled against their shackles only moments before.

Myrthyd turned to the crowd. "And thus, we cleanse our land of these two unnatural beings; two creatures born of sin, never to have been in existence at all. We must be vigilant in our search for truth and peace. No longer will we tolerate the evil of halflings in Tregaron. Their time is over. It is time for us to rise and reclaim what was given to us centuries ago. No more will we allow this. *No more!*"

The crowd erupted in frenzied applause and shouts of "No more! No more! No more!"

Myrthyd felt the sense of pride in his people. They understood now what it meant to be from Tregaron and how evil halflings were. If not, he'd make sure they knew it soon.

He left the smoldering skeletons and walked through the crowd, grateful people reaching out to touch the great Myrthyd. He waved and placed his hands on as many people as possible while trying to cross through the thick crowd. He had a book to read and a puzzle to solve to make these executions unnecessary. The results would only make him stronger, and in due time, save his people.

TWELVE

Two days after meeting Myrthyd and Reinfrid the southerner at the tavern, Lailoken joined Jor, Darlonn, the two crossbowmen Ori and Tozgan, and Magus Driano with his novice Belthos at the Black Tower.

"Lai! It's good to see you again!" Darlonn said, embracing his old friend. Jor did the same as the crossbowmen shook his hand. Driano barely acknowledged him with a slight nod, but Belthos was all smiles.

"Lailoken, it's a pleasure to join the hunt with you again," Belthos said, earning a quick rap on his head from Driano.

"Boy, another outburst like that, and I'll send you back to the fields where we found you." Belthos hung his head in silence.

"Are you gonna be like this the entire way?" Jor asked. "The boy is excited, and with you berating him like that, he might snap and come after you. I'm not so sure I'd stop him."

Lailoken and Darlonn laughed. Ori looked surprised and Tozgan grinned.

Lailoken felt comforted in this group. He was his best while on the hunt. Though he loved Alushia dearly, tending the fields and livestock did nothing for him. Out in the wilds tracking dragons was all that mattered. Having Jor and Darlonn at his side meant so much. An image of Etain bubbled up in his mind and he forced himself to push it down. *Not now*, he thought.

"Ready?" Lailoken asked. Each member of the group carried large leather packs on their back with their weapons except Driano, who used Belthos like a pack mule. The Dragonback Mountains were at the southernmost edge of Tregaron beyond the great wall that ran between Woodpine, the home of the Verdant Tower; and Fearglen, the home of the Crimson Tower. It was the edge of their world and a natural boundary with the southern lands. The trek would be difficult as they'd go on foot, the Magus adhering to an ancient ban on riding horses with the rest of the group sworn to abide by their customs.

"Get on with it, then," Driano scolded and started for the southern road. Those on the streets cheered them on, knowing not what they were after, only that a hunt had been started. Many recognized Lailoken, Jor, and Darlonn. The slayers had been on many hunts and gave the same parting accolades.

"Slay that dragon!"

"May Menos guide you!"

"Lailoken, will you marry me?"

Jor laughed at the question. She looked around to find the source of the voice. "I guess you might have an offer of a wife, Lai! Maybe when we get you back, you can find her and marry again." She was grinning from ear to ear.

"Unless it's Etain come back from her imprisonment, I want nothing to do with her."

"How long has she been gone?" Ori asked.

Darlonn turned to shush the crossbowman, but it

was too late.

"Long enough. She has to be alive. I know it," Lailoken said quietly.

"Slayers!" a voice from the crowd called out. A short balding man limped toward them.

"Tibaut!" Lailokan said, embracing the man. Last they met, they were drinking hard in the tavern. Tibaut no longer hunted dragons due to the injury suffered on his last hunt. The dragon thrashed when he plunged his sword into its heart, slamming the long tail of the Onyx dragon into his leg and twisting it in such a way that it was beyond repair by the time they returned to Kulketh and the Black Magus tried to properly heal him. He was given a stipend and spent most of his days in taverns telling tales that he made up. He was fun to be around and shared with Lailoken a mutual affinity for the hunt. And ale.

"Jor and Darlon, may Menos comfort you," he said. He leaned close to Lailoken. "Be safe, my friend. I have a bad feeling about this hunt."

Lailoken pulled back. "Tibaut, why do you say that?"

The man's face split in two as he smiled. "'Cause I won't be with you! Be safe, my friends!" he said, embracing them all and limping back to the crowd.

Lailoken shook his head, grinning. "Tibaut's humor is often lost on me."

The group followed Driano's lead through the narrow streets until they passed the southern gate and the road to Woodpine.

"We've got days to go until we can rest properly. Conserve your energy," Lailoken said.

They travelled in silence, broken only by Driano's

complaints and insistence on Belthos reciting spells and lesser important things like village names and southern history. It was enough for Lailoken to retreat inside his own thoughts where Etain and the dragon-man Evros's words swirled.

By the time dusk was upon them, they'd made steady progress and were deep within the forest. Travelers were long gone off the road. They were afraid of bandits, a concern the slayers didn't share. Most gave them a wide clearance, especially with a Magus in tow.

"Let's make camp here," Darlonn said. They all agreed and quickly started a small fire, dropping their gear around it and spreading blankets out. The group was quiet and one by one, they laid down to sleep.

That night, they were awakened by a horrific scream.

Lailoken jumped from his slumber and grabbed his broadsword. The rest gathered their weapons and huddled next to each other, Driano forcing Belthos in front of him.

"What was that?" Ori asked.

"It sounded like an animal," Driano replied.

"It sounded like a dragon," Lailoken said.

Darlonn agreed. "I've heard that sound before, but it's odd that it's so far north. They must be stupid or brave to travel this far."

"Huh?" Driano asked.

Jor grinned. "You'll see."

The thing screamed again, a high-pitched call that sent shivers down Lailoken's back. He wasn't afraid, but his nerves grabbed hold of him. The thrill of the hunt was powerful.

"It's a Jade. Has to be. Their roars are nothing like the flying dragons," Lailoken said. "Come, let's kill the intruder. One less dragon is always a good thing."

He led them from their dying fire to the darkness beyond. "Be careful and stay quiet," he whispered. They traipsed through the late summer forest, twigs snapping and leather boots scuffling along the hard-packed dirt underneath.

Another scream came from their right. "It's closer. Keep your eyes open and be ready," Jor said.

"Can you tell how big it is by the sound?" Ori whispered.

"Not really. Their calls can be deceiving. No matter what, Jade dragons are much easier to kill than the others. They can't fly!" Tozgan replied. Lailoken nodded, though none could see the gesture.

The dragon screamed again, far too close for Lailoken's liking. A woman's shrill cry followed. He paused, the rest following his lead. "We're nearly upon it. Jor, take Ori to the left. We'll go right. Circle around, and when I give the signal, attack from your side. We'll do the same. One of us will get the kill!"

"You mean, I will," she said, clapping Ori on the back. "Come, we have a dragon to kill." They walked in the darkness, their footsteps giving away their location.

Lailoken went right, with Darlonn next to him and Tozgan close behind. Darlonn unsheathed his broadsword and was preparing for the attack. Tozgan drew his much smaller sword, only functional if they were in close quarters. Most likely, it wouldn't pierce the dragon's scales, but as a crossbowman, he wasn't expected to wield a sword.

Driano trailed them, keeping Belthos close to his side. "You have your bag? Tell me you have emeralds in there."

"Yes sir," Belthos replied, earning him rare praise from the Magus.

"Well done, lad. We'll sell these when we get to Woodpine. The Verdant Magus will pay handsomely."

"Magus, protect us with your enchantment. It should give us some safety from its poison."

Driano's stone glowed faintly, and the Magus wove a spell of protection over all the slayers. Lailoken felt a slight warmth as the spell covered him.

Lailoken moved a little farther to the right and saw the Jade dragon in a large clearing with a woman trapped in its claws. The half moon gave off enough light for him to see blood running down the woman's side. The Jade turned its head in Jor's direction and Lailoken used the opportunity to charge.

"Now!" he shouted. He raced from the trees with Darlonn and Tozgan behind him. Darlonn screamed something Lailoken couldn't understand. The dragon turned to them, dropping the woman, and Jor ran from the trees behind it.

Where's Ori? Lailoken thought.

The slayers converged on the Jade dragon. It stood twice as tall as any of them and swiped its long deadly claws at them frantically. They'd caught it off-guard and it was acting by instinct rather than intelligence. *Good*, Lailoken thought, *it's at our mercy*.

A crossbow bolt flew from the trees and sunk in the dragon's back. It screamed in agony.

Lailoken struck first, his sword slicing through the air in a downward arc. The Jade tried to parry the blow with its short arms. The sword clipped the forearm and sunk into its flesh, easily cutting through the thinner scales.

Jor stabbed the Jade in the back, causing it to scream wildly. It thrashed its arms feebly to remove the iron bolt. Lailoken slashed again, this time slicing along the Jade's belly. A long, deep gash opened and sprayed hot, thick blood on him. He was vaguely aware of Darlonn slamming into the Jade, sinking his blade into its heart. The Jade screamed again, wildly flailing arms in search of anything to lash out at. Darlonn pulled his sword free and plunged again as Jor held her sword firm inside the dragon's back. Lailoken pulled his sword free and sliced downward, catching the dragon's belly again, and carving a deep X into its abdomen.

"Press harder! Don't let up the fight!" he called. The dragon shrieked in pain. It had to know its life was at the end. Darlonn continued to strike with his blade, piercing its thick scaly hide. Soon, the Jade gave up the fight, and with a final slice, Lailoken cut along its neck, almost severing its head. Jor pushed forward and the Jade toppled over, nearly falling on Tozgan, who had yet to strike a blow at the thing.

Lailoken wiped his brow, brushing his long hair back. "Well done!" He pulled his blade free and ran it along his pants, cleaning it of the dragon's blood. He knelt down beside the woman lying on the ground, Jor joining him.

"My Menos, we were too late. She's gone," Lailoken said, bowing in a quick prayer.

"Hurry, Belthos! Give me the emeralds now!" Driano raced to the dragon with a fistful of emeralds and thrust them into the bleeding wound, coating his hands in the hot, sticky fluid. He chanted over the body, and a faint green glow covered his hands and the emeralds within as he invoked ancient spells to bind the gems with the dragon's blood. When he was done, the light dimmed and vanished.

"Wonderful kill, slayers! This will fetch a fair amount in Woodpine!" Driano smirked. "The Verdant Magus will pay well."

The group huddled around the dead dragon, catching their breath, and waiting for Driano to finish. There'd be no sleeping the rest of the night, with the excitement of the kill too powerful for slumber.

They piled stones and sticks on top of the woman, a quick burial for another Drakku victim.

THIRTEEN

Alushia penned the oxen for the night. They were getting more stubborn each day but she was more determined than they and would not let them run her. After the last one was safely within the pen, she closed the gate and trudged home with Brida at her side, her body sore and stiff from working the fields all day, and Brida sharing muted colors of brown and black through a mental bond. The fields were in terrible shape and if they stayed like that, the harvest would be worse than normal and that would mean a long, lean winter.

Her father promised help, but she sent the workers away. It was her land and her responsibility. If her father decided to leave and shirk his duties at home, she would not make someone else pay for it.

Arriving home moments before dark, she made a quick meal of barley and ale before cleaning up and laying down on her straw bed. It needed refilling but she was too tired to worry about it for now. Since her father's departure a week ago, she'd been working the fields alone and even though she was exhausted each night, she feared closing her eyes because of the terrible nightmares awaiting her. She tried to think of beautiful things like flowers and birds and the midsummer celebration to keep her mind focused to thwart the impending dark dreams. Tonight was no exception as she focused on a field of lilies, swaying in the breeze, and the warm scent of honeysuckle drifting over the plains. She scratched Brida's head. The large snowcat lay beside the bed.

Not long after, she fell asleep and the nightmare returned.

A large black dragon with tattered wings and smoky eyes streaked across the azure sky, bellowing horrifically and frightening her. The scene was a contrast in life. There were snow-capped mountains in the distance and wispy clouds drifting across the bright blue sky. The sun shone down on a land of vibrant greens interspersed with shades of red, orange, and purple. A forest to her left was alive with bird song. A stream flowed gently to her right, down a small hill and emptying somewhere past the horizon. An elk sipped from the stream, flicking its tail against the flies.

But then the dragon appeared in the sky, a dark cloud of evil against the backdrop of idyllic Tregaron life. It roared again and the elk looked up, water dripping from its chin, then darting across the field seeking shelter. The birds stopped singing, leaving the forest eerily silent.

The dragon soared in the air, drifting on a wind that wasn't there. It circled the scene, roaring and belching a plume of wretched smoke, the fumes so bad that Alushia could smell the rottenness coming from within.

"Go away! Leave this place!" she shouted. The dragon circled her, ignoring her words.

"Get away from here! You don't belong!"

The dragon shot high in the air and plummeted to the ground where it opened its fetid mouth and seemed to devour the very life on the ground, scooping up grass and rocks and cutting a swath across the stream that no longer existed. In its wake, a trail of black nothingness followed as though someone had scratched a large piece of charcoal across the surface. The dragon swallowed the landscape and went back for more, this time cutting through the forest and creating a trail of black across the trees.

"Stop! You must stop this madness! You shouldn't be here!"

Alushia ran toward the dragon, feeling like her feet were floating. As hard as she ran, she didn't gain ground. It was as though she was stuck in a pool of thick mud.

The dragon roared again, cutting black lines across the sky. A growing sense of dread filled Alushia, knowing that she could do nothing to stop the evil from spreading. The more of the dream the dragon ate, the more she felt powerless and wanted to weep. She fought the urge, fought against the evil within her mind and focused on something...

The mid-summer celebration.

The scene shifted to Kulketh, full of revelers and musicians enticing the crowd to dance. The Magus walked the crowds in search of any merrymakers out of control, yet still generously passing out ale, and even partaking themselves. Alushia danced with a boy she didn't know, the music lively and fun. The evil that threatened her mind moments ago was now lost and forgotten.

The dragon.

Screams to her right stopped her dancing and she watched as the dragon devoured the roof of a building and roared before it swooped down to the street and snatched townspeople within its rotten mouth. It flapped its enormous, tattered wings and an oppressive warmth spread over the revelers like a humid summer day.

"No! Not the people!" she screamed. The dragon roared its reply and continued to destroy all in its path. The evil feeling returned, Alushia's mind closing in on itself. When the dragon ate the musicians and the music was left hanging in the air, Alushia finally woke.

Perspiration beaded on her forehead. She turned into her sweat-soaked pillow. Brida's head popped up, her huge eyes staring at Alushia, furry ears twitching. Alushia tore off the rough sheet and sat up. She dangled her legs over the side of the bed. "What is it? Why do I have these dreams? What evil is this?" she asked Brida, stroking her head. The snowcat gave no impressions or colors to share.

Alushia was afraid to sleep. She forced herself awake 'til dawn when the day's work would start all over again.

After a quick meal of porridge, Alushia went back to the fields, letting out the oxen and checking for eggs in the chicken coop. She collected a few, as most were cracked and inedible, leaving them in a basket to bring home when the day was done. Then she went to the fields, tending to the rows of barley and wheat that seemed to deny growing from their seeds. Brida ran off, most likely gone for the day in search of game and adventure.

As the sun ascended in the sky and the heat increased, three mounted riders caught her attention.

She stood and wiped the sweat off her brow and waited for them to approach. She had only the knife on her belt for protection, and she was proficient in its use.

A wagon pulled by mules with men dressed in black flowing robes followed the riders. *A Magus*, she thought. The riders approached and halted, waiting for the wagon to catch up. The Magus stepped down from the wagon, assisted by a novice.

"Good day, Alushia!" the Magus said. It was the Kull Naga himself—Myrthyd.

"Good day. What brings you out here to my homestead?"

She could tell the riders were tower guards by their dress.

Alushia was concerned. "Is this about my father? Is he..." she paused. "Is he dead?" There had to be no other explanation why she'd receive a visit from the Kull Naga.

"Dead? No, not at all. At least, not that I know. He should be leading his slayers to the mountains. I expect they'll be in Woodpine by morrow's night. I've come here for you." His dark eyes leered at her, making her feel like an animal close to slaughter.

"Your fields...just like all the rest. I swear, I will find a cure for what ails our land."

"What can I do for you, Kull Naga? I'm busy at the moment and have a lot of work to do before nightfall."

Myrthyd scanned the field and nodded. "That you do. I thought I sent men to help you?"

Brida appeared from the fields, a low growl announcing her presence.

Alushia smiled. "You did, but I can handle my own. I'm capable of tending my own fields."

"Well, as that may be so, you should reconsider my offer. It would help you."

"I don't expect you've come to talk about why I refuse your assistance."

"No, not at all. It's about your dreams. Come, let's get out of this sun. You can take time out for me, right?" The stone around his neck glowed slightly, and she was overwhelmed with a desire to leave the sun and dirty fields and take shelter within her home, free of the heat and work.

"Of course. A break sounds lovely." Her words sounded false in her ears, but still she wanted to leave and accepted help from one of the guards who lifted her upon his horse and they rode back to her house with Brida loping after them.

She didn't remember entering her home, but there she was, seated at the kitchen table with two tower guards and Myrthyd, the Kull Naga of the Order. Myrthyd sat across from her, his gray eyes piercing her soul. *Had he always looked so menacing?* she wondered.

"Alushia, your father told me disturbing news of your nightmares. I'm so sorry they've plagued you. Can you tell me about them?" He cocked his head, his hard features betraying the false concern he tried to portray. Alushia's resolve strengthened.

"I don't want to talk about it. There's nothing to say. I don't know why we're here, but I need to tend my fields. Please excuse me, but I have to go."

Myrthyd turned his head again, tilting it to the other side. Alushia shifted in her seat, an overwhelming dread coming over her. Myrthyd's stone glowed again, and the need to work the fields dissipated. All she wanted was to talk to Myrthyd.

"So tell me about those dreams. It's important to me. I don't like the loved ones of my prized slayers dealing with such hardships."

Alushia couldn't help herself. She wanted to tell him everything.

And so she did.

When she finished, Myrthyd leaned back and crossed his arms, stroking his beard. "A black dragon with tattered wings and smoke for eyes?"

Alushia nodded. The vision was as real in her head now as it was in the dream. It frightened her to think about it, yet she was compelled to do so out of the burning desire to please Myrthyd.

"And it *ate* the dream, you say? How so?"

"I can't explain it fully. It was as if someone ran their finger over the ground. Only, it wasn't a finger. It was the dark dragon eating the images and leaving a trail of nothingness behind. It gave me the strangest feeling of terror, like my mind would soon turn to nothing...like the blackness left by the dragon. When I wake, I'm exhausted as if I had no rest at all."

"Interesting," he said, continuing to stroke his beard.

The need to share this with Myrthyd vanished and a sudden feeling of guilt and shame came over her. She had no idea why she told the Kull Naga about her dreams. Her face flushed with embarrassment. "I must get to the fields. It's mid-afternoon and there's so much to do."

"Of course, of course. I don't want to keep you. Alushia, please reconsider my offer for help. This place is too much to care for on your own. Please, think about it. I hate to see someone as young as you work so hard."

"Young as me? You're the same age as I!" she retorted.

Myrthyd stood, brushing off his robe as though their conversation left something dirty on him. "That we are. No matter. Refuse the help if you want. I'm only trying to take care of those my slayer deems worthy."

"Then what about my mother?" she grumbled under her breath.

"What was that?" he replied.

Alushia shook her head. "Nothing. Thank you for your visit and concern for me. I'll be fine on my own. I have been for years. This is no different."

The guards led the way, and soon all three were out the door. She listened as the men climbed into their saddles and the horses trotted away. With her eyes closed, Alushia tried to recall why Myrthyd had even come there and what their conversation was about. The events of the past few hours were cloudy in her head and left nothing but a shadow of darkness and fear.

"I can't waste more time dealing with that, whatever it was," she said to Brida. The snowcat yawned. There was work to be done, and daylight waited for no one.

FOURTEEN

Two days after killing the Jade dragon, Lailoken and the rest of the hunting party entered the gates of Woodpine and enjoyed a night of drinking and telling tales of past adventures at the Dancing Bear, the largest tavern in the city. Belthos was even given a mug or two of ale to the dismay of Driano. They shared tales of past hunts with each other, Tozgan with the most experience killing a variety of dragons, while Lailoken was the most prolific of all of them, despite hunting mainly Onyx dragons.

"Lai, we've been on the hunt for close to four years now," Jor said, her speech slurring, "Wh...why not give it up?"

Lailoken drank from his mug, slamming it down on the table. "Etain. I hunt for Etain. One day, I'll find the beasts that stole her and I'll finally end my days as a slayer."

"To Etain!" Darlonn said, raising his mug. A wide grin creased his dark face. The rest did the same and they toasted to her memory. After they drank, Lailoken collected himself.

"We must rest, for on the morrow we enter the mountains. The great hunt is here, my friends. We have a great foe waiting for us. We'll have a long journey ahead as we search for what might be the most powerful dragon we've ever seen, hidden in a cave on a mountain I've never heard of. Opaline. Opaline Mountain. Where is that?" He nearly fell off his chair, much to Jor's amusement. She laughed and almost fell out of her own seat as well.

"I may know a man who lives here that can help," Driano said over a mug of ale, his serious tone contrasting sharply with that of the group.

Lailoken arched an eyebrow. "Is that so?"

"I have connections."

"The Kull..." he said, pausing. He was ordered never to say a word of their true mission. But if he was going to ask them to lay down their lives out of trust, he felt better being honest with them. What could it hurt? Even Driano had a right to know. Myrthyd might get angry, but they were far from the Black Tower, and once they found what they were looking for, he needed to know they would be prepared for anything.

Lailoken glanced at the tables around them and leaned in closer, continuing.

"The Kull wants a gem hidden within the Dragonback. A kind of Blood Stone or something. It's hidden in a cave, protected by some kind of guardian. We're here to slay the guardian. We've been chosen because we're the best! Our mission," his voice dropped to a whisper, "is to retrieve this rock and bring it back. It is the key to reversing the blight upon our lands. Our crops will grow once more. Our people will not starve. More importantly, once this hunt is over, none of us will have to work again. We'll get a chance to grow fat and old, living off the money we earn."

Lailoken smiled and waved for another mug of ale.

The stunned group stared at him, Driano leaning closer.

"The Blood Stone?"

Lailoken nodded. "That's what he said."

Driano stroked his chin absently.

"We do this and we're set for life?" Jor asked, sloshing her ale.

"Aye, for life!" Lailoken replied raising his mug high.

"For life!" Jor replied, smashing her mug against Lailoken's.

"Come, let's get going, then. Before the both of you make fools of yourselves," Darlonn said.

"Let me ask around first and see if my friend is still here in Woodpine," Driano said.

"Another mug wouldn't hurt. More ale!" Jor shouted, the group cheering her call. Darlonn shook his head and smiled.

"Do what you must, Magus. You have until we finish this drink," Lailoken said.

Driano left the table and began asking around the tavern. Finally he ended at a table at the far end. A man looked past the Magus toward Lailoken and the group, making him squirm. They weren't supposed to share their hunt. Hopefully Driano could keep his mouth shut. He watched as the Magus pointed at them and nodded, reaching into his robe and handing the man a drac. The man grinned and left the tavern.

Driano returned to the table to find Lailoken nearly done with his ale.

"He is still here. My new friend is off to fetch him for us. It's best if we don't do this in here."

Driano led them out the tavern and across the dark

street near the boarded-up bakery.

"My new friend asked us to wait here."

"I don't like this," Darlonn said, reaching into his belt for his knife.

"I don't think we have a choice. If we can get any clue, it's better than what we have now," Driano replied.

Moments later, the man from the tavern approached, leading an older man in a tattered robe behind him.

"Here he is, like I promised," the man grumbled, his voice like rocks. Driano gave him a drac and the man left, whistling at his good fortune. When he was gone, they turned to the frightened old man.

"Frendule?" Driano asked. "Frendule, is that you?"

The old man's wild eyes darted back and forth, peering at the group. "Aye, Frendule, I am."

"You were exiled from the Black Tower years ago," Driano said.

"Driano? Are you him?"

The Magus nodded.

"I bear no ill will to you, Driano, nor the Order. I did what I thought right and still follow my wit. No matter, no matter."

The man's nervous tics caught Lailoken's eye. "Why are you afraid?" he asked, his words barely audible. His world was spinning and he saw two of the old man standing in front of him.

"I fear he's after me."

"Who?" Darlonn asked.

"Menos. He's angry with me. I went south across the mountains."

Lailoken laughed. "Menos would be angry with many Tregarons, if that's the case!"

"Aye, that be true, but I was one of his chosen."

"Frendule, do you know of a place called the Opaline Mountain? I assume it's a peak within the Dragonback, but which one? Surely someone as wise as you has heard of such a place," Driano asked, wasting no time.

Frendule's eyes widened.

"What do you ask? What do you seek? Terror! Terrible things. Menos preserve us!"

"Calm yourself, old friend. We seek—"

"We hunt a dragon," Lailoken interjected, aware enough to know Driano nearly shared their secret.

"A dragon? In the Opaline? You seek something worse," Frendule whispered.

"Please, my old friend, can you help us?"

He looked around and quietly spoke. "The Opaline Mountain. I know what you seek. There's only one reason to go there."

"You know?" Driano asked. "Tell us, man!"

"It's wrong. No man should have that power. None!"

"Stop the games. If you have something to share, share it. If not, let us be on our way," Darlonn said, a touch of anger in his voice.

"Come on, old man; no games," Lailoken added.

"It's no longer Opaline Mountain. It no longer shines bright. It's stained with the blood of the dead."

"No riddles! Tell us what you know," Driano said. He approached Frendule and grabbed his robe. "Tell us now."

"That's all, nothing more. I must go," he said, looking past Driano's angry face to the rest of the group. "I can't stay. I must leave now!" He wrestled his robe free of Driano's grip and scurried away, fading into the darkness

"Hey, wait!" Ori called and ran out after him. A few moments later, he reappeared. "He's gone. What did all that mean?"

"It means we have work to do in the morning, after these two sober up," Darlonn said. "Come, let's put this aside and find rest for the night."

Darlonn helped Lailoken to the Inn while Tozgan kept Jor upright until he could drop her off at her room. The slayers and the Magus retired to their rooms for the night.

FIFTEEN

The next morning rose with a crispness in the air. It was late summer but already the days were turning. It was an unusual break in the weather, but it was welcome, nonetheless. The stifling heat drained their energy and they needed everything they had if they were to endure what lay ahead.

Lailoken's head pounded. The ale from the previous night had flowed steadily, and for once, he let it. There were too many thoughts swirling in his mind and the ale numbed them all in a welcome respite. However, he was paying for it now. Jor looked to be in the same situation, moving slow with her head hung low. He entered the common room and sat at a table with his group, a warm cup of tea placed in front of him by the innkeeper.

"Let's get moving. We have a gem to find and dragons to slay," Lailoken said to the rest as they were in the common room eating warm bowls of porridge and enjoying imported fruit from the south. Most of Tregaron avoided trade with the south, but Woodpine, the last town before the mountains, had enjoyed a brisk trade with them since well before the reformation. The Verdant Tower defied the rest of the Order by their continued contact with the southern lands. They were also the chief supplier of available food for most of Tregaron because of the Green Magus's abilities with nature, something that had been pushed to its limits in the past few years.

"Where's Driano and Belthos?" Lailoken asked, rubbing his temple. *How much ale did I drink?* he wondered.

"Went to the Tower. I guess they're trying to sell those gems," Tozgan said.

"If they delay us—"

"We won't," Driano said entering the common room. "Though, if those damn Verdant Magus would pay fair price, I wouldn't have had to haggle as much as I did. No matter, it's done."

"Gather your things. We leave within the hour," Lailoken said. He drank the rest of his tea and went to his room, his stomach not agreeing much with anything at the moment. After he packed his bag and strapped on his sword, he met the rest of the group outside the inn.

"We go through the wall and into our destiny. Come, let's go." Lailoken led them across the slowly wakening town toward the large wooden wall that stretched from sea to sea across the southern border of Tregaron. Woodpine anchored the western end and Fearglen was at the eastern end. Guards from both towns patrolled the wall, expecting an invasion from the south at any time.

"You sure you can lead us?" Darlonn asked with a smile. "You were pretty drunk last night. Same with you, Jor. How's your head this morning?"

Jor growled her answer and Lailoken continued along the streets.

"I'm leading us now, aren't I?" Lailoken replied.

Darlonn laughed and said nothing more.

They approached the gate leading out to the mountains, and after Driano was forced to give up a few of the coins he'd earned from the sale of the gems, they were through the gate staring at the mountain range ahead.

"I swear, if I lose all my coins to this expedition, I'll make the Kull repay me with interest," Driano grumbled.

"I'm sure he'll have plenty to give," Lailoken said. "This way." He led them toward the main pass leading through the plain into the forest at the foot of the mountains. The snow-covered peaks rose high above them as they grew closer to entering the majestic region where dragons lurked and man hunted. Dragonfire Peak loomed high overhead, a beacon for weary slayers.

"This is our destination," Lailoken said, waving toward the mountains. They stretched east to west for as far as they could see.

Ori spoke. "How will we find a cave in that?" He pointed at the mountains looming before them.

"I never said it would be easy. It will be difficult, but we're the best and the best don't give up," Lailoken replied.

"Nor do we wait for a hangover to pass," Jor said, making Belthos laugh and earning a swift backhand from Driano.

"Where in that is Opaline Mountain?" Darlonn asked. "It could be any of those."

"According to Frendule, it's no longer called Opaline Mountain. He says it's stained with blood," Driano said.

"Dragonfire Peak," Tozgan whispered.

"You mean you believe that crazy old man?" Jor asked.

"Before he was exiled, that '*crazy old man*' was a librarian in the Verdant Tower. He knew our history better than most. He spent days in the library reading 'til he soiled his own clothes because he wouldn't leave," Driano said.

Belthos wrinkled his nose and shook his head.

"But why listen to him now? He doesn't seem to be in control of his mind. Did you see him?" Jor asked.

"True, he may not have all his faculties anymore, but from what I remember of the man, he had a head full of useless knowledge that might just have been useful to us. I think the young crossbowman is right. Dragonfire Peak is our most likely destination."

Lailoken ran a hand through his long hair. "Unless anyone objects, I think that might be the best place to start." None voiced dissent. "To Dragonfire Peak, then."

A wide-open field ran along the southern side of the wall creating a clear line of sight for those that patrolled it above. On the other side of the clearing was a forest stretching far beyond their view.

The dense forest took most of the day to travel and teemed with life. Rising from the green was a rocky path that twisted around the mountain's base. They entered the base of the mountain, the forest giving way to barren rock.

The treacherous path was lined with loose stones and sheer cliffs. The ground was hard and the air grew colder. It wasn't long before they were shivering from the vicious winds swirling through the towering mountains. Lailoken looked back and barely made out the wall on the other side of the forest. Driano grumbled and moaned, Lailoken scolding him several times to quit complaining.

"Would you rather be home sucking on the teat of a boar?" he called behind him. The man was relentless in his whining. *He could have sent me someone other than him,* Lailoken said to himself then gave up the thought. It was no use complaining or wishing for what he didn't have. Wishes didn't come true. Only actions with a purpose achieved anything.

Higher and higher they climbed, leaving the warmth and comfort of Tregaron behind for an unknown and frigid future.

Lailoken pushed them hard, not allowing many breaks. He wanted to reach a plain Jor spotted before nightfall. Otherwise, they'd have to navigate the tricky passages in the dark. Even with moonlight to guide them, it was far too dangerous to try their luck.

When they finally approached the plain, sunlight barely clung to the land. "Thank you, Menos," Lailoken whispered.

"I'll take Ori and find wood for a fire," Darlonn said.

Lailoken, Jor, Belthos, and Tozgan busied themselves with setting up camp while Driano watched the activity.

"You could always help you know," Jor grumbled.

"That's why I have a novice. He's learning our ways and takes care of trivial things such as this."

Darlonn and Ori returned and soon made a fire large enough to warm them. When it died down a little, Darlonn prepared a quick meal of porridge.

Afterwards, they sat around the fire warming themselves. They were quiet, as though the gravity of the situation was finally weighing on them. Lailoken stood, intending to break the mood with a joke when a terrible familiar sound interrupted him.

"A dragon," he whispered. The beast roared again and the slayers jumped to their feet and scrambled for their weapons.

"Careful, we may have company soon. Crossbowmen, to me. Everyone else, spread out. We may yet have a kill this day." Ori and Tozgan took their positions to either side of Lailoken as Darlonn went right and Jor, left.

The dragon roared again, circling them.

"Tozgan, be ready. Ori, watch your side. The moment we see it, fire. I won't let it get the better of us."

A streak of fire suddenly burst forth above them in the night sky.

"Driano, enchantment!" A slow warmth spread over them. Lailoken only hoped it prevented the dragon flames from burning them alive.

"Fire, now! Shoot the Garnet!" Lailoken yelled. Both crossbowmen let loose their missiles. Ori's went wide to the left and Tozgan's punctured the dragon's wing, causing it to spiral downward.

"Great shot! Ready your weapons for another!" Ori and Tozgan quickly reloaded their crossbows and cranked them back, preparing for another chance at glory. The dragon righted itself and sounded more furious than before. It roared and spit flame in the sky, twisting its head back and forth and turning the black sky into flame. Fortunately for the slayers, it illuminated its position.

"Fire now!"

Tozgan shot first, then Ori. This time, Tozgan's shot nicked the dragon's wing, but Ori's missile pierced the dragon's abdomen, the heavy bolt lodging within its thick hide.

The dragon bellowed a loud, painful roar, clutching at the wound. It fell from the sky in an enormous crash to the field before them.

"Now! Earn your glory! Go now!" Lailoken shouted. He raced toward the downed dragon as did Darlonn and Jor, ready to converge on the Garnet dragon to claim their prize.

Jor reached it first, her blade raised to strike when the dragon breathed flames at her, forcing her back. Darlonn was next, Lailoken barely able to tell what their plan of attack was. Darlonn slashed with his sword in a weak blow and the dragon shrugged it off. Racing around the flames, Jor followed with a vicious slice of her broadsword, and their tactic paid off. While the Garnet was busy deflecting Darlonn's strike, Jor's was left wide open and easily slit the dragon's hide along its back. The Garnet turned and exhaled fiery fury, narrowly missing Jor.

Lailoken drew closer to the dragon and it breathed an immense wall of fire between itself and the three slayers. Then, a brilliant flash of white erupted behind the flames and the dragon's roar ceased, replaced by the howling of a man.

"Stop, stop. I yield! I ask mercy! Stop this at once!" the man screamed in pain.

Darlonn turned to Lailoken. "It shifted?"

"I yield! Call off your attack. I'm yours!"

The flame wall dissipated and a naked boy lay on the ground, twisting and writhing in pain.

"Please, call off the hunt. I yield. I relent!" The naked boy turned to face the slayers.

"Who are you?" Lailoken asked.

"Please, stop the hunt! I mean no harm. I was curious, that's all." The boy, maybe thirteen, clutched his side where the bolt had driven into his flesh, though now in his human form it no longer protruded from his body but lay next to him still covered in thick blood.

"I ask again. Who are you? Say nothing and we will slaughter you."

Jor stood near the boy, her sword ready to sever his head from his body.

"My name...my name is Indrar, son of Etain."

Lailoken's anger boiled inside. Was the boy trying to ignite his fury? He was dangerously close.

"I don't know the names you speak of," Lailoken replied.

The boy pushed himself to sit upright, still clutching his side.

"I think you do," he replied.

Darlonn and Jor were in shock, staring at the dragon-boy. Driano stepped closer, the gem around his neck glowing faintly.

Indrar held out a bloody hand and a ball of flame ignited the night, hovering above them.

"Please don't make me. I don't want to harm you. Any of you. I was only curious. I meant no harm." His voice was weak and young.

"Wait!" Lailoken called, forcing Driano to halt and turn his way. "What did you mean by curious? Why'd you come for us?"

The boy shook on the ground, a large pool of blood growing around him.

"My father told me I'd find my mother's human mate in the mountains. He told me about...you."

Lailoken's fury blazed inside and it showed on his face. He felt the blood rush to his cheeks.

"How dare you say such blasphemy! My wife was no dragon! She was stolen by your kind!"

Indrar stood on shaky legs, his entire body exposed. If any of the slayers had a desire to slaughter the dragon-boy, he was in no shape to stop them. "I know you men of the north find it hard to reconcile humans with dragons, but it's not uncommon and it's not an abomination. I was hoping I'd find information about my half-sister Alushia."

Lailoken could no longer control his rage and rushed Indrar, his broadsword raised to strike. Indrar took a step back and held up his hands, creating a shield of flames. Lailoken nearly ran into it, stopping just as his beard singed and smoked.

"I'll tear you limb from limb! How dare you speak lies to me!"

"Sir, I mean no disrespect. I only mean to find the truth. I'm not here to sow discontent. Please, forgive me for angering you."

"Come out here and fight me! Die honorably!" Lailoken screamed, spit flying from his mouth. His arms shook; a vein stuck out on his forehead. The flames didn't fade, and his sword reflected their brightness in the dark.

"I cannot. I will not. Etain forbids us to harm you in any way. Even if I wanted to, I cannot touch you. One day, you'll understand all of this. You'll understand why we are who we are. And why Etain had to leave. I'm sorry, sir, I cannot tarry long."

"Coward!" Lailoken yelled.

The dragon-boy was engulfed in a brilliant white flame and when it dissipated, a Garnet dragon was before them. It roared loudly then streaked up into the sky, the sound of its large leathery wings beating against the wind as it flew away. The flames Indrar created popped then disappeared.

"Come back, you horrid beast! Come back here!" Lailoken yelled, but Indrar never turned from his path.

SIXTEEN

Myrthyd sat at his table with Drexon's tome before him, resting his head in his hands. The Nightwraith spell mocked him, unwilling to fully disclose its truth. He figured out most of it, at least believing he did so, and was confident that meditation and recitation would bring clarity.

What he gathered was this:

From dark crystal once hidden now found
Comes power unchecked, unbound.
Fill the blood with a dragon's soul
And own the dream, the dreamer whole.

There was a hidden crystal that gave the owner a great deal of power. *What kind of power? What did it do?* He thought he had a clue as to that as well. Filling it with a dragon's soul? That stumped him. How do you fill blood with the soul of a dragon? And then, how does that lead to owning a dragon and a dreamer?

Find the crystal among a dragon's back
Within a cavern dark and black.
Slay the keeper and take the gem
Power eternal; over dragon, over men.

This part of the spell was the most straightforward

to him. After he realized that it referred to the Dragonback Mountains, the verses were clear. The gem was
hidden in a cave with some sort of keeper to watch
over it. Slay the keeper, take the gem. Whoever kills
the keeper of this precious object will then obtain the
precious gem. He expected Lailoken to fulfill his part
and hand it over. The slayer was obedient to a fault.

He closed the book. He needed a break. The spell
alluded to a powerful magic and Myrthyd staked his
claim to it, forbidden or not. The council wouldn't
stop him now; no one would. His control over the
Drakku was to be absolute and nothing would stand in
his way.

A soft rapping at his door crashed his thoughts.

"Kull Naga, I hate to disturb your study, but you
said to let you know when the men arrived in Kulketh.
They're here, sir, at the Sailor," a novice named Kreel
called through the thick wooden door. Myrthyd's lips
curled into a sinister grin.

"Thank you, Kreel. You'll find your reward in your
room."

"Thank you, sir."

Myrthyd listened as Kreel's footsteps faded away.
He promised the novice a halfling to do what he
pleased with if he'd seek out cutthroats. He had a plan
for them. Kreel would have to kill his male halfling
when he was done, but he knew the boy would do the
right thing. He'd done it before.

Myrthyd set off for the Wandering Sailor, Kulketh's main tavern, with two guards in tow. Most who
frequented the place were animals and mindless thugs;
just the kind of men Mortha and Gregor were.

Myrthyd considered changing his robe to be more inconspicuous, but decided against it and wore his Kull Naga garb, letting the gem hang out from his cloak for all to recognize as he approached. It gave him quick access to whatever he wanted and made sure most of the horrid dirty people stayed far away.

If only he had a spell to wipe them out.

The streets of Kulketh were alive with activity as dusk approached. Lanterns and torches were lit along the streets casting chilling shadows in corners and alleys. When they noticed him with his guards, the people cleared a path and bowed as he walked by. Even at the young age of eighteen, he commanded a respect from the people that many older Kull Nagas before him had never had. He attributed part of that to his hardline stance against the halflings and the constant hunts conducted in the name of the Order.

There were a few men talking to scantily clad women outside the Wandering Sailor as Myrthyd approached. The women barely gave him notice while the men seemed nervous. They bowed slightly as he walked past. One of the guards opened the door for him and he entered the raucous room filled with music, laughter, and the sound of lies being told. Several gasps escaped patrons when they realized who had stepped in, but the activity didn't stop and the ale continued to flow.

"Excuse me, do you know Mortha and Gregor? Are they here?" he asked a grizzled old slayer named Goran. He'd lost an eye during a hunt and wore a blue dragon scale tied to a leather cord as a patch. No longer a dragonslayer, now he often spent his time slaying pints of ale.

"Kull! Good to see a lad such as yerself here. Mortha, you say? I think he back there messin' with some young lass who wants nothin' to do with him." He directed Myrthyd to the back of the tavern with his thumb. Seated at a table near the far wall was a young brute with dark brown hair teasing a girl that was maybe twelve years old. The girl looked like she'd been crying.

"Thank you, Goran." He tossed the man a half-drac and approached the cutthroat, the guards at his side.

"Please sir, leave me alone. My mum only wanted me to see about your boots, that's all. I don't want to—"

"Mortha," Myrthyd said. The girl took one look at him and ran off while the man's attention was distracted.

"Damn man, you see what you did? I lost my girl!"

Myrthyd's eyes narrowed. "You should leave her and others like her alone." His stone glowed faintly and Mortha made a tiny gesture of being startled.

"Yes, you're right. I should leave them alone. It's not good for me or them."

"Good man. May I sit?"

Mortha waved him to the table. No sooner had he sat when another man approached the table and took a seat.

"Gregor?" Myrthyd asked. The man nodded.

"I am Kull Naga Myrthyd," he began as though they didn't know by his robes and gem. "I'm here requesting your help with a delicate matter. Can we speak in private?"

"Yeah, sure thing," Mortha said. "There's a room in

the back that should be open."

Myrthyd followed the two toward a dark hallway leading to a room nearly as dark. With the flick of his fingers, a small ball of flame ignited and illuminated the dark room. Eyes glowing, Mortha and Gregor stepped back from the flame as though afraid it would consume them. Myrthyd grinned.

"Don't worry. It won't hurt you. Unless I let it." His voice was dark and stern, the perfect pitch to make them listen...and behave.

Myrthyd nodded to his guards standing outside the room to watch for intruders. It didn't matter if the guards heard the conversation or not, because Myrthyd had them in a constant state of compulsion and their wills were not their own.

"Wh-what is it that you'd li-like from us. Kull Naga?" Gregor asked.

Myrthyd cracked his neck and let the silence of the room make the men even more uncomfortable. "I have one of my Magus on a mission with the slayer Lailoken, but I fear my Magus is going to betray me."

"What business is that to us? Unless, of course, there's money in it," Mortha said.

Myrthyd smiled, the stone glowing around his neck.

"I want you two to track him down. He's in the south within the Dragonback Mountains. Do anything you can to kill him. Do this, and I will reward you with land and more dracs than you know what to do with."

The surprise on their faces told him his spell had worked.

"Land? And dracs?" Mortha asked.

"More dracs than you can imagine."

"I'm in!" Gregor said.

Mortha slowly nodded his head. "What assurances do we have the Order won't betray us? Killing a Magus is a serious crime."

Myrthyd crossed his arms and smiled. "Here, take this." He handed each man a small black stone with a crimson line embedded in it. "This is my word. Any Magus that sees you with these knows you're under my protection. I will be your surety. Do we have a deal?"

Mortha turned the stone over in his hand. "We're yours. Who's the lucky Magus?"

"Driano. Kill his novice Belthos too. You'll encounter resistance from the slayers. Do what you must with them. Bring me back the Blood Stone they should possess, and I'll double the offer."

He left as the two men giggled over their newfound luck. They'd be lucky if Lailoken didn't kill them first, but it was a risk worth taking. Driano couldn't be left to live, not after discovering the gem. Once those two brought the gem to him, he'd dispose of them. They weren't worth saving.

"Come to me in the morning and I'll give you all you need to get started."

The men looked to each other and then back to Myrthyd. "We'll be there," Mortha said.

***

Reinfrid sat at a table with his back to the wall watching as the Kull Naga met with the thugs. He hadn't been in the north long, but he knew the two men were easily bought.

What could the Kull want with those two? he thought. He sipped the ale, not listening to the words of his companions.

Something isn't right about this.

"Gentlemen, I think my time here is about over," he announced to the table. He didn't even know their names. He was only here to find out information regarding the north for his Queen.

"Reinfrid, have you gone soft on us?" one of the men asked.

"It seems you may be right," he replied.

The Kull disappeared down a dark hallway with his two guards close behind. Reinfrid sipped his ale, the mug nearly empty.

"Well good on you, then," another man said. "'Til next time." He raised his mug in a drunken salute and the other three men at the table did the same.

Reinfrid smiled. "I appreciate your support, gentlemen. Now I shall take my leave. Good evening to you all."

He downed the last of his ale, wiped his mouth, and stood. Scanning the hallway for the Kull Naga, all he caught sight of was the guards. Trying not to look too suspicious, he slowly made his way to the entrance and stepped outside, walked halfway down the block, and waited. It was nearly thirty minutes later when the Kull left with the guards ahead of him. The two thugs never did leave, and most likely stayed inside to drink the night away. He waited for them long into the night and when they finally left the tavern, he followed them to their homes. The men did nothing out of the ordinary, but at least Reinfrid had something to pique his interest.

There was a hunt on and he wondered if this had anything to do with that. He'd had so little time to observe how the northerners took to the hunt. If anything, the men were worthy of observation if only because of their meeting with the Kull.

***

The men arrived at the Tower early the next morning. They were at first turned away by the guards but were soon allowed passage as Myrthyd stepped in. Gregor's eyes were dark and tired. Mortha smelled of dirt and dung. Whatever they got into after they met didn't look like it went well.

Myrthyd quietly led them to his chambers, closing the heavy wooden door behind them.

"Are you gentlemen ready for adventure?" He wrinkled his nose when he caught their pungent scent.

"So what is this all about again?" Gregor asked.

Myrthyd's stone glowed faintly. "Did either of you tell anyone about our meeting last night?"

"No, but the entire tavern saw you come in and talk to us," Mortha said.

"We were shunned the rest of the night," Gregor added.

"But did you tell anyone what I asked of you?"

Mortha shook his head. "No. We kept the words to ourselves."

"Excellent. I trust the two of you understand to never mention this to anyone."

"Never," Mortha said. Gregor pointed at him and

nodded.

"Good." He unrolled a map of the Dragonback Mountains on the table in front of them. "I suppose Lailoken and his hunters are in this area," he said pointing at a small range in the center of the mountains. "He won't get too far from there by the time you reach him. If he doesn't have the gem, wait for that first. Then kill Driano."

"What about the hunters with him?" Mortha asked.

"They must not be allowed to return." Myrthyd waved his fingers at his side, forcing a small compulsion to settle on them. Since their meeting the night before, he decided they'd all need to die. Too many loose threads unraveled a blanket.

"None will ever see Kulketh again," Gregor said.

"I had the chamberlain prepare you something for the journey." Myrthyd pointed to the corner where two large leather bags with shoulder straps lay, as well as two swords with scabbards.

"They aren't fit precisely for you, but they'll do. Good luck, gentlemen. May Menos favor you."

They grabbed their goods and quickly left the room.

SEVENTEEN

Losing the young dragon-man stunned the slayers. They spent the rest of that day and the early part of the next sulking in their loss. Driano made sure to let them know his displeasure.

"I thought you were slayers. After all this time together, I wonder how equipped you are to deal with our foe. Sure, you killed the Jade and the Onyx, but your skills are lacking. Why did Myrthyd think you were the ones for this mission?" Driano snarled.

Jor threatened him. "I don't care who you are, My sword will taste your blood if you continue to doubt us. I'd rather live in exile after murdering you instead of living in Tregaron with you."

Driano arched his eyebrow. "Is that so? We're all going for the same prize. Maybe if you worked closer together, you'd be more successful."

"Maybe if you'd do something more than weave a spell on us to help, we'd get through this easier," Tozgan said.

"You know we can't. Why would you say such a thing?"

Tozgan shrugged. "Sure, if that's your excuse. I've seen it done. All you Magus aren't afraid to get in a fight with us."

"Then they're traitors to the Order and worth a traitor's death!"

"That's enough!" Lailoken said. "We're here together and we'll act like we belong together. No more
out of you, Driano, or you, Jor. We work together, got
it?" His long hair swung as he turned to each one. Jor's
face blazed red.

"If he doesn't learn to shut his complaining mouth,
I won't hold back," Jor replied.

"Well, now that we have that settled," Darlonn
said, forcing a smile on his lips, "can we get moving?
Honor waits for no one."

Most of the afternoon was spent in silent company
as they traversed the often-narrow mountain passes in
search of Opaline Mountain's hidden cave. Surprising-
ly, Driano shut his mouth, not once complaining about
the difficult terrain.

Ori spotted a valley not far ahead, calling their attention to it.

Lailoken wiped his brow. "When we reach the valley, we'll rest and find something to eat. Depending on
how light it is, we may camp there for the night and
resume our exploration tomorrow."

They followed his lead down the rocky path to the
snow-covered valley below. By the time they reached
the valley, it was near sunset. Shadows covered much
of the valley.

"We'll set up camp over there," Lailoken said,
pointing to a small stand of trees, "and leave by dawn's
light."

They quickly had the camp set up, a raging fire going, and were soon dining on dried fish and stale
bread.

After eating, they retired to their blankets around

the fire and rested as best they could in the cold night air.

When sunlight broke the darkness, Lailoken awakened the camp and they gathered their belongings, packing them as best they could with sleepy eyes, and were on their way up the adjacent mountain.

Halfway up the mountain, Tozgan spotted a dragon in the sky. "Look! Over there!" he shouted. They turned and circling above a nearby peak was a large Opal dragon.

"Dragonfire Peak," Driano said, pointing at the mountain where the dragon circled. The tip of the mountain colored a bright red.

"How many dragons do you think it took to stain the peak red?" Jor asked. The popular opinion was that dragon blood stained the ground and left the odd color.

"Not enough," Lailoken said, clapping her on the back.

As he watched the dragon circling in the sky, it tempered his excitement. "It's too far away to worry ourselves about." His heart raced at the sight of the dragon, but he calmed his anxiety, knowing it was probably out of his reach. The Opal really was too far for them to hunt, though the temptation was strong.

They continued their trek upwards, the path nothing more than narrow footholds in the hard stone, until they reached a wide clearing.

"Gather your strength and relax," Lailoken said.

They dropped their packs on the ground, also tossing crossbows and swords as they took a few moments to recover from the climb. The stone around Driano's neck glowed slightly as he rubbed his hands together.

Moments later, lightning streaked across the sky followed by a thunderous roar. The slayers looked up to see the Opal dragon diving at them, it's large, white leathery wings beating the air.

"Weapons!" Lailoken screamed. Ori and Tozgan struggled with their crossbows, trying to place the bolts and crank them back. The Opal roared again, spitting lightning from its mouth and striking the mountainside near them. A shower of rocks exploded, pelting the group. Driano's stone glowed bright and he raised his hands to create a shield. Lailoken covered his head and narrowly missed being struck with a rock large enough to cleave his skull open.

"Scatter! Don't let it get us. Prepare yourselves!" Lailoken yelled.

Darlonn and Jor snatched their weapons and ran in opposite directions just as the dragon swooped past them and angled its way back into the sky, circling around for another pass.

"Tozgan! Ori! Get those crossbows ready! We don't have much time!" Lailoken called out.

"Got it!" Tozgan yelled. Ori's crossbow was nocked and ready as well. They were to the right of Lailoken and the others, not in ideal position, but it would have to do under the circumstances. Driano backed away from the action, Belthos at his side.

"Wait for another pass!" Lailoken yelled.

The Opal roared and spit bolts of lightning across the sky. The loud noise made the slayers cower and cover their ears. Then it circled around and dove at them, breathing lighting at the ground.

"Now!" Lailoken yelled, hoping they would hear

him over the lightning's crackle. Two black crossbow bolts flew across the sky and both found their mark, striking the Opal in the side and forcing it to tumble in the air. It roared in pain and fell to the ground.

"Now!" Lailoken yelled and headed for the moaning dragon squirming on the ground. It tried to pluck the steel bolts from its side but was unable to reach them. Blood covered the snowy rocks. Lailoken was the first to reach the dragon and raised his broadsword high, but the dragon belched lightning at his feet. It created an immense crater in the hard dirt and knocked the slayer into the air, slamming him on his back. His sword flew from his hands.

"Attack!" he vaguely heard Darlonn yell, and the rest of the slayers joined him. Lailoken was dazed and unable to comprehend what was happening. He heard crack after crack of thunder as the dragon spit lightning at the slayers. Someone screamed.

"Ori?" he said weakly.

A warm sensation covered his body. *Driano*, he thought. The Magus was using his meager skill in healing to try and help him. Lailoken laid his head down on the cold ground and let the Magus do his thing.

Jor screamed somewhere to his left. Darlonn yelled for retreat. Belthos—*was* it Belthos? He wasn't sure—cried out for mercy. It sounded like chaos.

The dragon roared. Lailoken felt a whoosh of air and a dark figure passed over him. Lightning illuminated the afternoon sky. Thunder boomed. Then came the calm after the fight. The valley was stunned, as though unsure what to make of it.

Jor's bloodied face peered down at him.

"Are you all right? Are you hurt?" she asked. Her

voice sounded distant.

He wanted to answer but his voice had no strength.

"He'll be fine. Got hit in the head. He's a bit dazed right now," Driano said. Lailoken turned his head toward the Magus, noticing his stone glowing.

Jor looked away, her red hair flashing in front of him. Her eyes relaxed, the thrill of the fight now dissipated. "We make camp here," she said. "Ori, get a fire started. We need to clean ourselves of this filth." The slayer went to work building a small fire, producing a pot from his bag and filling it with snow, then warming it over the flames.

It took time, but eventually they cleaned most of the blood from themselves and their clothes, paying special attention to their swords and scrubbing them free of blood, then making sure they were dry before placing them back in their scabbards.

Lailoken did little to help, his head still pounding from the dragon's blast.

EIGHTEEN

Alushia worried about her father after Myrthyd's visit. There was something odd about the Kull, but what it was, she didn't know. It was just...different.

Her father had been on many hunts for as long as she could remember. She had more memories of watching him leave than of him doing anything else. There was the hunt when she was five, when thick snow covered Tregaron. The Kull Naga Shoran called for a hunt after three Onyx dragons were spotted east of Kulketh. Alushia was held back by her uncle while she watched her father trudge through the snow, never turning back.

There was the hunt when she was eight. The summer was thick and heavy, and a clan of Jade dragons had crossed the plains from the south and were spotted near the border. Her father left in the middle of the night and she woke to an empty house, her uncle arriving near midday after she'd felt the pang of loneliness during the morning hours.

But this latest hunt was one she had no concerns for. Until recently.

Myrthyd's arrival was unexpected and awkward. She still didn't understand exactly what he wanted, other than to talk about her dark dreams. It had been several days since she had one, but each dream left her feeling exhausted and on the edge of destruction, like her mind would soon succumb to the darkness that the dragon created as she helplessly watched.

"Stupid dreams," she muttered. She'd been out near the barn, gathering eggs and feeding the ox and swine. Brida was out in the fields chasing a hare, sensing the thrill of the chase as Brida sent impressions to her. She'd finished the fields the day before and had a few days to catch her breath and relax before heading back out and working dawn to dusk again. With as much rot as she expected, she had to work extra hard to grow enough food to eat.

That evening she fell asleep earlier than normal, the exhaustion from working in the fields catching up to her. She soon found herself high on a cliff overlooking the sea to the north.

Waves crashed on the beach below, smashing on the sand and rocks. The white-capped surf relentlessly slammed the shore and quickly retreated back to open waters. Gulls circled a dead fish washed up on the beach, their noisy calls barely audible over the waves. Far out to sea a large ship with white sails slowly crossed the horizon, no doubt a fishing boat returning to Bayfrost with the latest catch. She inhaled deeply, the salty air refreshing and alluring. The sun hung in the sky, ready for its moment to hide behind the horizon. The green grass was soft when she sat cross-legged to watch the serene view.

A large thud shook the ground behind her. When she turned around, she saw the black dragon with smoky eyes staring down at her, its large torn wings moving with the wind.

"Get away from me! Leave me be!" she shouted,

scrambling back from the dragon and drawing danger-ously close to the cliff's edge.

The dragon tilted its head ,and though the eyes were smoke, she felt them boring into her all the same. Her face flushed, turning her pale skin nearly as red as Jor's hair.

The dragon opened its mouth and she closed her eyes, waiting for it to devour her and turn her into nothing.

Then it spoke.

"You can see me?" it asked. Its voice was thick and heavy like honey on a hot day.

She opened her eyes and stared in disbelief at the dragon before her.

"You can see me?" it asked again.

"Ye-yes, I can."

"How long have you had the ability?"

"What ability? I'm not sure I understand." She grabbed her elbows, shaking. It never occurred to her to try and reason with her dream before. The fero-cious dream-eating beast seemed a little less intimidating now.

"How long have you seen me? How long have you had the ability to see me?"

Alushia shrugged. "I don't know. Since my father's last hunt, so maybe several months now."

The dragon bristled when she spoke of the hunt.

"The hunt, the slayer, the halfling." It tilted its head to the other side. Alushia was positive it was a male dragon, though how it was alive and speaking to her, she had no idea.

"Who are you? What are you? Why do you destroy my dreams?"

The dragon inhaled deep and slowly let out a rancid breath that stunk of sulphur and rotten meat.

"My penance for being weak. I'm trapped within a stone and cursed to devour halfling dreams."

Alushia scrunched her face. "The halflings? You're in a stone? But how can that be if you're in front of me?" *What kind of dream is this?* she thought, wondering if it was a dream within a dream.

The dragon roared. Alushia worried it was infuriated and would turn its anger on her. It settled down, the smoky eyes peering at her.

"My curse will destroy my kind. It will destroy you, too! All halflings will die. All halflings will live a life undead. Danger and death await from my curse. Hide the stone. Hide the Blood Stone from mankind. The power...the power is too much. No man should have the power it wields."

Alushia sat upright, the sense of danger coming from the dragon no longer imminent. It was calmer, more settled.

"Who are you?" she asked again.

"My name was once Avess," it said, the strain of answering apparent in the slow reply.

"Avess?"

The dragon roared, beating its wings. "No more! That name is dead now...dead like the body I inhabited."

"But what are you?"

"I am a cursed soul. A soul lost within a stone left to wander the living no more. My realm is within your mind, the minds of all halflings. My curse is to destroy until there is nothing left."

"I still don't know what you mean."

The dragon leapt in the air, beating its shredded wings and flew high into the sky.

"No wait! Come back! I want to know!"

Alushia ran after the dragon, calling for it to return, but it refused to change course.

Soon after, she woke.

A thin sheen of sweat covered her face and chest. The fire in the main room was almost dead and the dark night felt oppressive. Outside, owls and insects carried on in their nocturnal way, creating a chorus she'd come to find comfort in. Brida snored loudly in the corner of her room.

"What's going on?" she asked.

Sitting upright on her bed, the straw poking through and itching her, she swiped her face with her hands and tried to recall all she'd seen and heard in the dream.

The speaking dragon surprised her, and yet it felt...natural. She'd never been on a hunt before and only saw dragons from a distance. But to have it converse with her...to share thoughts with her was unexpected.

"Was it calling me a halfling? That's impossible!" Her small housecat jumped onto her lap, purring and rubbing her soft head on Alushia's belly. Alushia stroked the cat's head. Blackie, she called it because of its dark fur. There were at least ten cats running around the homestead other than Brida, and she gave up naming them all long ago. The cat continued to nuzzle her way closer to Alushia, her loud purring softening the oddness of the dream. She stood, Blackie jumping off her lap, and went to the main room of the house to get a drink.

It was near dawn and Alushia gave up the pretense of going back to sleep. Soon, the morning came and the animals needed tending to. It would've been nice to have help, but her pride wouldn't allow it. She grumbled but understood it was her decision when she left the home, and Blackie's, to go to the barn and start the day.

All day in summer's heat, Alushia's mind returned to the odd events of the night before. What did the dragon want? Why did it choose her to speak with? What did its words imply? They couldn't possibly be true, not about her, anyway. Her mother and father were both human. She'd never met her mother, but she knew without a doubt she wasn't a shifting dragon-woman. She would've been killed on sight in Tregaron and she wouldn't blame them for doing so. Those awful creatures were part of the problem in Rowyth. They fervently tried to subvert humanity with their species and it was just...wrong. Her father was clearly not a dragon-man. His entire life was spent hunting them and he was the best in Tregaron; maybe the greatest slayer of all. No, she was not a halfling. It must have been a lie, a trick at her expense. As she thought about it, she grew angrier.

"I hate those things," she said to the sow rolling in the mud. "If I had my way, I'd kill them with father. Lies. Nothing but lies." She tossed rotten lettuce in the pen and the swine hungrily gobbled it up, the fat sow in the mud late to the feeding and squealing at the others for her bit.

That night, Alushia fell asleep wanting to find the

black smoky-eyed dragon in her dreams. She had questions and fear was not going to stop her.

She was disappointed when she woke in the morning to find that the dragon did not visit her. Several nights passed without a dream at all and she was beginning to wonder if it was done with her. Then, on the fourth night after her last encounter, the dragon reappeared as she traipsed along a valley full of poppies bordered by pines on both sides. It was a pleasant dream that reminded her of her youth when she wasn't in charge of the homestead.

The dragon flew across the sky, leaving thin dark streaks as it nibbled on the dream. When it spotted her, it dove at her and landed in front of her. The large, terribly torn wings and the black body and those eyes, those smoky eyes almost made her run. She had learned to expect it, but the giant dragon in front of her still made her shiver with a touch of fear.

"Avess, I was wondering," she started. "I wondered if you'd ever return."

The dragon extended his wings wide. Holes and shredded membranes allowed the sky to shine through.

"My curse compels me to return. You're in grave danger. The Drakku are in a mortal struggle, and your father, the slayer and companion of Etain, is on a dark path."

"What about my father? How did you know my mother's name?" She stepped toward the dragon, anger growing within her.

"Etain is a powerful dragon. She rules over the Drakku."

"You lie! My mother was taken by dragons! She's

not one of you!"

Avess pulled his massive head back and inhaled. "I cannot lie about the truth. She lives, and she's a mighty dragon. Search yourself. You know something's different. My curse...my curse compels me to seek halflings. Without the Blood Stone, most humans cannot see me. You are a halfling."

"No!" she screamed. "It can't be! I am not one of you! I am not dragon-kind. Never! You lie, dragon!"

"No longer a dragon am I. My soul, imprisoned in the gem, will forever roam the dreams of halflings. If the gem falls into the hands of men, evil will descend upon the land. It must not be allowed."

"No longer a dragon? What are you?" Alushia asked. She didn't believe the thing. It shared one lie after another.

"Nightwraith," it whispered. "I am a Nightwraith, cursed to feed on the dreams of halflings. Their delicate taste is intoxicating and alluring. The difficulty comes when I must stop, and stop I will. If I devour it all, your mind will no longer be yours."

Alushia laughed. This fearsome beast no longer scared her. It was a liar; a creature of evil spreading false words. To what end, she didn't know.

"Take your lies and leave. I'm done with you."

Avess roared, the ground shaking. "I can devour you and turn you! Heed my warning! Man must not possess that gem. Your father must not succeed. Stop him. Do what you can to end this folly."

"I won't do anything for your kind." Alushia turned and walked away, Avess flapped his wings behind her and shot into the sky.

Before he left her dream, he flew by low and close to her. "I will stop him. The son of Etain will not succeed. His anger will not prevail."

"Son? Leave me, liar! Your words mean nothing to me!"

Avess roared and flew away, tremendous black streaks cutting across the sky.

When Alushia woke, her head pounded and a sickening sensation came over her.

What if he's telling the truth? she thought.

NINETEEN

Lailoken's head cleared and he broke camp the next day. The slayers hurried to pack their belongings before heading up the mountain.

"Look, there!" Ori called, pointing at the cave opening in the mountain above them.

"Might this be the place? Are we on Opaline Mountain?" Lailoken asked. It wasn't Dragonfire Peak, but maybe it was the mountain they sought. The slayers were giddy with anticipation. Driano huffed.

It took a couple hours for them to scale the mountain and land on the ledge in front of the large open cavern ahead of them.

"In here we might find the enemy. Be prepared for anything," Lailoken said. He'd pulled his sword from its scabbard on his back and slowly crept inwards. "Darlonn, get a torch ready. The darkness is not our friend."

The sound of flint and steel was followed by the crackle of flame as Darlonn illuminated the cavern, the flickering light exposing what lay hidden inside.

"Sir, let me lead. I've explored many caves in my time. They can be treacherous and our lives depend on careful movements," Ori said. Pleased at his initiative, Lailoken waved him to the head of the group. Darlonn followed, lighting the way.

"It stinks in here," Jor said. "What is that?"

"Mold? Rotten meat? Both?" Tozgan replied. Lailoken sniffed the air. The staleness was apparent, but so was the rotten scent Tozgan tried to place. Maybe they were in a dragon's lair. If they were lucky, they'd find the Blood Stone, though Lailoken didn't know how they'd find such a treasure in the dark cave. He didn't even know what exactly he was looking for.

"The path ahead splits into three," Driano said.

"Which one do we choose?" Jor asked.

Ori walked to the opening of each path and listened.

"We go this way," he said at last, pointing to the center path. The middle passage was narrower and Lailoken wondered if he had chosen the wrong one but deferred to Ori's instinct.

"We go that way, then," Lailoken said, a look of relief on Ori's face as he affirmed the man's guidance.

Ori led them in the cave, the walls closing in around them until there was barely enough room for them to walk upright. They had to bend over slightly, their packs scraping against the roof of the cave.

"Are you sure it's this way? We can barely fit. How's a dragon supposed to do the same?" Tozgan asked.

"And that stench is only getting worse," Jor said.

"I'm sure it's this way. My instincts are rarely wrong," Ori replied.

The tunnel narrowed even further until Ori shouted.

"We're here! Look at this!" The slayers ahead of Lailoken were standing upright in a large open chamber with a pool of dank water on the far end. The ledge along the right side was covered in bones and half-eaten elk bodies, some of the blood still fresh. The walls were blackened as though scorched by flame.

"We've made it to the dragon's lair!" Ori shouted, his voice echoing in the chamber.

"But where's the dragon? A Garnet by the looks of it, too," Driano said.

Lailoken scanned the chamber, wary of an ambush. Dragons were sneaky and would surprise them the first chance they got.

"Keep your eyes open, men; this might be a trap. If there is a dragon around here, it can't be far."

Ori carried the torch along the right wall, careful to avoid the carcasses. "It has to be a dragon. Nothing eats like this," he said. The torch cast dancing shadows on the wall, the bones and bodies gaining a more grotesque appearance in the flames.

"Over there!" Lailoken said, pointing near the pool of water ahead of them. The water occupied about a third of the chamber and to the left was a passageway, the only other way out.

Ori carefully walked across the front of the water, peering inside as he passed. When he came to the passageway, he turned back to the group. "Are you coming? I'm not going in here alone!"

Lailoken grinned. In their wonder, none had moved to follow. "Yes, we're right behind you."

Jor led the group toward the mysterious passageway. It went much farther back than they imagined.

"How long is this?" Jor asked.

"I can't tell, though I think I see light up ahead," Ori replied.

"Be ready for anything," Lailoken said.

"I hear something," Tozgan said. The men stopped and listened. They heard claws scratching the hard-packed dirt in front of them. After a few moments, Ori continued on.

"We may have our prey yet," Lailoken said. He wished he'd been in front of the line. There was no way around the others in the narrow confines of the tunnel. He had to hope they were ready to strike if needed. Myrthyd called it the keeper of the Stone, and it might be ahead of them. If it was a large dragon, Ori was not fit for such a fight.

"There's certainly something ahead of us. I hope you're all ready," Ori called back. Lailoken noticed the light growing larger as to illuminate a large cavern. They crept slowly through the tunnel until they were inside an imposing cavern. They were quiet, but it wouldn't have mattered. Their torch would've given them away—if there were something to give them away to.

The cavern's roof curved upward, ending at a large opening at the top where the blue skies peeked in. Inside the cavern, dark green lichen spread over the brown walls and reached toward the light above. It smelled of death; the rancid thick scent of meat and rot hanging in the air.

"What is this place? What is that awful stench?" Darlonn asked.

"A dragon's been here," Jor said. "It brings its food here to eat in private."

"But it's not here now," Driano said.

"Unfortunately not," Lailoken replied. "Come, let's get out and continue our quest."

Startled rats pulled themselves out of the rotting carcasses, running from the group.

"Why don't we stay here and wait for the dragon to return?" Driano asked.

Lailoken considered his question.

"We could wait for it to return with its prey and slaughter it while it eats. My guess is more than one dragon uses this cavern," Darlonn added, pointing to the floor. Green guard uniforms were piled in a heap.

"The Verdant Tower guards?" Driano said. "It's eaten Magus guards!"

"But what if it smells us? They have a heightened sense of smell," Ori said. He brushed back his long brown hair and leaned against the wall. "I don't wanna end up like them " he said, pointing at the uniforms, "I have dragons to kill."

"I agree with your man, Darlonn. Instead of living in the snow and cold, why don't we wait it out here? At least we can back track through the passageway. There's no way a dragon is getting in there," Driano said pointing from where they came. "That putrid smell might be a bother, though."

Lailoken offered a slight laugh. "True. Well, what do the rest of you think? Does Driano's plan have merit? Do you believe we can surprise the dragon when and if it returns?"

He looked to each person for affirmation, and one by one they nodded.

"I might slit his throat though if he complains about this place. I can't take his crying much longer," Jor said, glaring at Driano.

"Looks like we follow Driano's lead. Set up our gear in here and we'll enjoy the comforts of the cavern,"

Lailoken said.

They searched for wood to build a fire and huddled in the cave with the pool of water. At least there they'd be out of view if a dragon did return to the larger cavern, though Lailoken doubted one would ever return.

After they found enough wood to keep the fire burning through the night, they settled in.

Three days and nights they stayed without a single sound or sight of a dragon. Lailoken spent much of his time scouring the network of smaller tunnels in search of the Blood Stone to no avail.

The slayers grew anxious.

"How long are we going to stay here when the dragons are out there?" Jor asked. It was the morning of the third day and they were sitting around a small fire.

Lailoken sighed. "We won't be here much longer."

"I like this comfortable place to stay, but we've not had any sign of a dragon," Tozgan said.

"I swear, I feel it will return at any moment," Driano said trying to justify their stay.

"What do you know of dragons and their tendencies? What experience do you have in finding and killing them?" Jor grumbled. Belthos snickered, and quickly covered his mouth. Driano left the boy alone.

"We'll leave in the morning if no dragon returns," Lailoken said.

The mood lifted. Most were anxious to be gone, except for Driano. He sulked back to the larger cave after he ate, most likely to find anything to prove his point.

"Rest up. From here on, we'll be in harsher climes

and you'll need your strength. Relax and enjoy the last day of comfort you'll have in a while." Lailoken lit a torch and left them to perform a final search through the tunnels. There was one section he'd barely inspected, and this was his last chance to search.

He entered the larger cavern and found Driano looking out over the mountains from the large exit tunnel at the far end. Even from where he stood, he could see the snowy peaks beyond the Magus and the jagged rocks poking through. It almost looked like Driano was talking to someone, but as they were so high up, it wasn't likely. He was probably performing a spell or incantation.

To the left of Driano inside the cavern was a small passageway that Lailoken had explored on their first day, though he didn't get to finish the search. That was his plan for this day.

He entered the tunnel, the light from his torch illuminating the darkness, and found the one tunnel he had yet to explore.

Going inside, he hoped for a quick end to the hunt for the gem, but as the minutes became hours, he was certain it was not there. The tunnel twisted and turned, but in the end it led to nothing. He carefully retraced his steps until he found himself in the large cavern again. Stuck in the narrow passageway all day, he went to the exit to gain a moment of sublime freedom overlooking the mountain range. Driano was gone and Lailoken took his place, scouring the endless valleys and peaks outside.

It was a breathtaking view. Trees raced across the bottom of the mountains, a few stragglers daring to grow farther up. Rocky peaks jutted from the snow and clouds carefully surrounded many of the highest reaches. The outside air was cold and the wind picked up. He hadn't noticed how close they were earlier, but Dragonfire Peak was next to them.

For some reason, Lailoken's thoughts turned to his long-lost wife Etain. She was a beautiful woman with curly red hair. Her amazing smile and soft lips were alluring. When those dragons took her—it had to be dragons—they carried his heart away right with her. He'd never been the same since, and channeled his rage into the hunt, slaughtering each dragon as if it was the one who stole his wife. He hoped after all these years she was still alive, though that hope had faded some. The flame he carried for her dimmed, but it was still there.

The dragon guarding the Blood Stone would feel the full fury of his wrath. The anticipation of killing it grew with each day.

Turning from the ledge, he returned to the group and found them joking and laughing. A good sign. They'd been under stress as they waited for any sign of a dragon, and as the days dragged on and none appeared, it seemed more and more likely they were wasting time.

"Good to see you all in better spirits," Lailoken said.

Darlonn smiled. "We leave tomorrow and it would be great to find ourselves again. The hunt was invigorating."

"Tomorrow we continue our quest. There are more dragons awaiting the bite of our blades. Tregaron needs us. We will come through," Lailoken replied.

Most of the men nodded in agreement, but he did notice Driano looking away as though lost in thought. The on-again off-again nature of Driano sparked a tiny bit of doubt of the man's trustworthiness. Lailoken wanted to trust him and would have to let him prove it or prove otherwise. Either way, he'd be watching him carefully.

TWENTY

Myrthyd walked the halls of the Black Tower, praise heaped on him by the other Magus and novice and initiate Magus. No need for a touch of compulsion; they did so because they feared him and respected his power. He'd already shut down two councils convened to remove him, and the consistent executions gave the impression he was one not to be angered. Did they not see how important his work was? People were dying. They were hungry. At the last meeting he had with the steward, he was told about three grain bins that were lost to black mold. The situation was growing worse.

Tapestries hung throughout the tower told stories of ancient glory, of Magus leading slayers to the hunt, and the stones infused with dragon blood. Soon, a new tapestry, perhaps an entire hallway full of them, would tell his glory. Once he discerned the full effects of the Nightwraith spell, he expected the people of Rowyth to fall on their knees before him. Who else in their history had the foresight to eliminate the Drakku in order to bring their land back to life?

That slayer Lailoken had better come through for him, or Alushia might be headed for execution as a halfling. It was only right. Before then, he'd have that oaf Gregor kill Driano. Too many with the knowledge of what he was doing gave his enemies a chance to discern his intent.

Halflings like Alushia made Myrthyd cringe. He hated those abominations. It was unnatural for dragons and humans to mate, and their wretched offspring were worse. They were born of sin and evil. It was their fault fields were barren and his people were suffering. They deserved nothing short of death and he'd see to it that every last one of them were wiped from the face of the land.

As Myrthyd turned a corner, the group of Magus gathered down the hall to gossip noticed him and scattered like bugs exposed in the light.

The corridor to his room was dimly lit by ever-burning torches. There weren't any windows in this hallway. It was built in the central part of the tower's great wall with the purpose of hiding whatever was in it. For Myrthyd, that meant Drexon's ancient and forbidden spell book he discovered as a novice that aided his ascent through the Order ranks. The book opened many doors for him and gave him power most other Magus feared. When he coupled the words with gems empowered by the blood of vanquished dragons, his power was far greater than any living Magus. The one thing he lacked was the ability to thwart the Drakku menace once and for all. In doing so, he'd no longer have need of slayers and no longer be forced to give away land or dracs for their service. The more land the Order owned, the more powerful they'd grow. Not that he cared about the Order itself, but as the Kull Naga, he'd benefit the most from their unlimited and unchecked power over Tregaron. If he had his way, that would extend south across the Dragonback Mountains and he'd rule over all Rowyth.

If only that damn slayer would find the missing gem—and Myrthyd could puzzle out the rest of the spell—would he then control the most powerful creatures known to man.

And then no one would stop him.

As he neared the heavy wooden door to his room, he noticed the guard was gone and the door slightly ajar. Pulling in a flicker of magic in case he needed to defend himself, he slowly crept to the door and peered inside. He saw no one but it sounded like someone was leafing through a book. Puzzled, he opened the door as quietly as he could.

At his desk, Kreel was turning pages in Drexon's spell book. Fury rose inside him. The book had been hidden. He forced a tiny bolt of lightning across the room into Kreel's arm. The force of the bolt and its burn made him squeal.

"What are you doing in here?" Myrthyd asked. His voice was dark and menacing, the anger held in check by a thin veil of restraint.

"Kull Naga Myrthyd! I'm sorry. I-I was worried as your guard was gone. I feared something bad happened to you. I came in here to check on you and found this sitting on the desk." Kreel's face exposed his lies. The book had been hidden where only Myrthyd would find it and was not left out in the open. It was too dangerous for that.

"Kreel, you disappoint me. Your lies are terrible. Clearly you have no practice with them. Why are you here?" he asked through tight lips.

Kreel's expression became a dark, sinister grin. "I've come to learn what makes you more powerful than all the rest. It's not natural, and you aren't the best Magus we have. There's a secret, and I've found it."

Myrthyd thrust his hand forward and thin bolts of lightning slammed into Kreel. The novice screamed. Myrthyd used a spell to silence the sound and let the lightning flow into the novice. Smoke curled up from Kreel's head, the scent of burned flesh growing more intense. Finally Myrthyd relented. Kreel slumped to the floor.

"I will kill you, Kreel. No one gets away with this, especially not a novice who enjoys the pleasures of halflings." A thought occurred to him; something that would help solidify his hold over the Order. "You are a halfling, aren't you, Kreel?" Myrthyd's stone glowed and he cast a small amount of compulsion on the novice. His eyes registered the effect and Myrthyd knew he had him.

"A halfling? Yes. Yes sir, I am. I'm a filthy creature worthy of death." Kreel's expression turned to confusion. "Wait, I'm not a—"

Myrthyd's stone glowed again, making the spell stronger.

"Yes, Kull, I am a halfling and cannot hide it any longer."

"Stay here," Myrthyd replied. Kreel nodded and stood as still as a statue.

Myrthyd left and returned with two guards from the central hallway. "Gentlemen, this man has a confession."

"I what?" Kreel asked.

Myrthyd's stone glowed faintly and Kreel turned to the guards, lifting his hands to them in surrender.

"I am a halfling. Kull Naga Myrthyd has exposed my truth."

The guards, looking to each other in astonishment, tackled the novice and tied his hands together with a small length of rope. "By the order of the Kull Naga, you are under arrest and will be sentenced to death," one of the guards said. They pulled Kreel up and shoved him out the door.

"Set his execution for tomorrow." Myrthyd waved his hand. The guards nodded and led Kreel away.

The novice had served his purpose, but with his ambition came his end. Myrthyd could not afford for others to know his secret. He may be able to defend himself against a council and even kill a few Magus in the process, but with the entire Order after him, he'd not stand a chance. It didn't matter, though. Kreel would die for his treachery. Driano and the slayers would die for their roles in finding the gem.

The price they paid would be worth it. Their lives were easily traded for the greater good. With the power he'd possess from the stone, he'd be able to clear the curse on Tregaron, eliminating the Drakku and returning Tregaron to its former glory.

***

The next day, Tower bells sounded to alert Kulketh of the execution. No doubt it would come as a surprise to most because of how quickly it was arranged. The normal waiting period with a trial and ultimate judgement was disregarded at Myrthyd's orders with a slight touch of compulsion magic, a spell he came to rely on daily.

Guards escorted Kreel to the stage at his protestation. He argued vociferously for his innocence, but the damage was already done.

A crowd of dirty and hungry people shouted at him, cursing him for bringing misfortune to their lands.

Myrthyd made sure to send the two guards that arrested Kreel to a small council to share their testimony of what Kreel had said when they arrived in Myrthyd's room. The council approved the execution, though it was set to happen with or without their approval. Myrthyd had already set the events in motion, again compulsion aiding his cause.

Myrthyd walked farther behind them, watching as the crowd grew as the word spread that the criminal was none other than a novice Magus, which was a rare occurrence. He contained himself and kept a stoic face, though inside he was excited about the events unfolding. Executions solidified his power and brought both citizens and Magus to his side.

Kreel fought with the guards. One of them clubbed the novice with a small, thick wooden weapon, rendering him quiet and barely moving. He was alive, though, which would make for a fantastic execution.

The guards lifted Kreel up the steps and tied him to the charred pole at the center of the platform. The crowd cheered wildly. Kreel regained his senses.

"I'm innocent! I'm not a halfling!" he cried. The guards let him yell. Their job was done.

Myrthyd ascended the steps and stood on the edge of the platform, raising his arms. The sun beat down on him and the stink from the assembled people drifted upwards, filling his nostrils.

"My fellow citizens, it is with great sorrow that I am here this day. It is not common for us to have a Magus, or rather, a novice Magus, be exposed as a halfling in our midst. It is the work of the enemy to infiltrate our Order and cause chaos within." The crowd roared in choruses of boos and jeers.

"I'm innocent! I swear to you, I'm not a halfling! I've done everything you wanted me to do! It's that book! I know what it is! You can't hide forever!"

"Silence!" Myrthyd shouted. The crowd's roar dulled and Kreel dropped to his knees.

"Please, Kull! Spare me. I'm not a halfling."

"But yet, you confessed. To me and to Tower guards. Are we to take it you were lying, then?"

"No! I don't...I'm not a halfling. I was not in my right mind. I didn't confess."

"Yet you did. I heard it with my own ears, as did others, all of your own accord."

Myrthyd turned to the crowd. "The evil of halflings knows no bounds. Their lies and tricks will not be tolerated here. Tregaron belongs to humans. Rowyth belongs to humans. Death to the Drakku!"

The crowd roared approval. Myrthyd turned his attention to Kreel, whose face was streaked with tears.

"Please don't do this. You know I'm innocent."

Myrthyd opened his arms and two small balls of flame surrounded Kreel.

"No! Stop this!" he cried, straining against his binds.

Myrthyd motioned again and the balls of flame inched closer to Kreel, moving slowly. Myrthyd enjoyed making his victims squirm with the anticipation of their death. The crowd hushed as the flames moved closer to Kreel, who screamed and thrashed.

In Myrthyd's mind, he heard none of it. The young man, no more than a couple years younger than he, morphed into a conglomeration of himself and a brilliant red Garnet dragon. The wailing young man who at one time served him well was no more, but was Myrthyd himself, dressed in novice robes and screaming for his release. Myrthyd brought the flames down until they burned the hands of the vision before him. As he watched the flames engulf himself, he waited for the pain to come, but it never did. The dream-like version of himself suddenly vanished and the man turned back into Kreel, the novice clinging to the burnt pole in a vain attempt to escape the flames. Myrthyd opened his hands and the balls of flame grew. They settled on the screaming novice, scorching him and turning his skin pitch black. A sickening stench of burnt flesh emanated from him. His screams died and he slumped over the burnt pole, crumpling to the platform.

The two guards ran to him, checking for signs life, but Myrthyd knew there were none. It was punishment for his crime of viewing the forbidden book. It must remain a secret no matter what.

Myrthyd turned to the stunned crowd and they erupted in applause for the death of a halfling. Like him, they knew how harmful the Drakku were. The more he killed, the better off they'd be. But with the Blood Stone in his possession, maybe he'd not have to resort to such brutal measures.

TWENTY-ONE

When they left the cavern, Lailoken led the slayers toward Dragonfire Peak, the largest of the Dragonback Mountains. It was the next closest summit and their destination on the treacherous mountains.

Six hours after leaving the cavern, they came to a large clearing protected from the fierce winds by a mountainside on the north and a small stand of trees running along the western and eastern sides. The men made camp near a tree and unloaded their gear, taking a much-needed break from the harsh path they'd traveled.

No sooner had they dropped their bags than a loud roaring rained down from the sky. Lailoken's hairs stood on end and he scanned the cloud-covered sky for the foe. The Garnet dropped through the clouds and streaked downward, flames belching forth from its open mouth. It looked familiar.

"Indrar?" Lailoken asked aloud. None of the slayers replied, scrambling to get their weapons and returning to Lailoken's side.

"Our former foe has returned. This time, we don't stop until he's dead. Is that understood?" Lailoken asked, turning to the slayers. Jor was ready, her sword clasped tightly in her hands, while Ori and Tozgan prepared their crossbows. Darlonn nodded, his hand on the hilt of his sword. Driano and Belthos scurried to hide behind trees.

Indrar circled above, creating a ring of fire in the sky. His roar echoed across the clearing, the sound of his beating wings adding to their anxiety.

"The vile creature has returned for its death!" Lailoken had let it get away once. He wouldn't let that happen again.

"Driano, do what you came here for!" A warmth spread over Lailoken.

"Ori...Tozgan! To me!"

The two crossbowmen raced to his side. "Prepare your bolts. At my command, fire at the dragon." The men nodded and raised their crossbows. Above them, Indrar roared louder, fire arching across the sky. Lailoken's senses were on alert, his thoughts vanishing until only one remained: to kill the dragon.

Jor yelled at Indrar. "I'll kill you with my bare hands! Come down here, coward!"

Darlonn stood next to her, his sword clutched tight.

Indrar blasted fire toward the slayers and burst forth from the flames with talons extended, diving at the slayers.

"Now! Fire now!" Lailoken screamed. Tozgan and Ori let their bolts fly, but they both missed.

"To cover!" Lailoken cried out. Indrar engulfed the area in flames, scorching the earth around them. Lailoken smashed his fist to the ground. "Damn crossbowmen!"

"Get those bolts ready!" he yelled across the flaming field. He had no idea if they heard him or not. Indrar roared again, the sound of his wings beating the air as he flew by, making Lailoken stay hidden.

The flames died out, leaving behind a blackened trail and Indrar once again flew into the sky, roaring angrily at the slayers.

"We may yet get another chance! Everyone, be ready!" Lailoken called out. He felt the familiar warmth of Driano's spell covering his body. At least the Magus was prepared. He only hoped the rest were.

Lailoken sprung from his hiding spot onto the smoking grass. "Come here, Indrar! Face me, dragon!" He held his broadsword with both hands, ready for the dragon's attack.

Indrar circled above, roaring and belching flames, then dove from the sky, his aim straight for Lailoken.

"Ready the crossbows! He's coming again!"

Lailoken stood his ground, trusting his slayers were in position. Indrar came at him fast. Moments before colliding with Lailoken, the crossbowmen fired, each one striking the dragon's side. Indrar howled and rolled in the air, falling to the ground and landing with a massive thud next to Lailoken.

"Spare no mercy!" Lailoken screamed. He and Jor ran at the writhing dragon, Darlonn on their heels.

Ori and Tozgan followed, both men preparing another bolt to help their cause. Once Tozgan had his ready, he stopped, aimed, and fired. The bolt pierced Indrar through the wing and lodged in his leg. The dragon bellowed, flames bursting from his mouth. Tozgan rolled to the side, narrowly escaping certain fiery death.

Lailoken's anger grew more intense, his determination forged. Indrar would die.

The Garnet dragon writhed on the ground, its arms unable to pry the crossbow bolts free. An eruption of flame burst from its mouth and the dragon roared. In a white flash of light, the men were blinded and it disappeared. What lay before them was a boy, nude and bleeding. The crossbow bolts lay on the ground, but the wounds were sufficient to stall the eager dragon-boy.

"I let you go once. You will not enjoy the same fate this day," Lailoken said. He rushed to the groaning boy, intent on slaughtering him.

"Tozgan!" Ori shouted from his side. Lailoken glanced up to see him kneeling next to the crossbow-man. He appeared alive. That was all that mattered.

Lailoken rose his sword high and stood above the clearly wounded dragon-boy. "Your evil will never harm another human. This day, I claim your life for being the disgusting thing you are."

"No, wait!" Driano spoke.

"Let him be! He may have information we can use. We can hold him prisoner."

"But he's Drakku! They're responsible for what ails Tregaron!" Lailoken replied. His arms strained from holding the sword for so long that the veins on his forehead pulsed with each passing moment.

Indrar groaned, blood oozing from his wounds.

"I want him dead, but alive he's more valuable to us...for now," Driano replied. Lailoken lowered his sword and ran a hand through his long hair.

"What's your proposal, then? My confidence in you has been waning for some time."

"Wounded as he is, he lacks the strength to shift back to dragon form. We can interrogate him until he poses a threat, and then we kill him."

Lailoken grinned. Driano had his faults, but this idea had merit. Maybe Indrar knew something of the Blood Stone. It wouldn't take much for them to keep him prisoner until they had to kill him.

"No! He must die!" Jor shouted, pointing her sword at the boy on the ground.

"He will die, trust me. But until then, Driano is right. He knows things we don't. If we can extract that from him, we may finish our task much sooner than anticipated. Besides, he can't go anywhere, and if he tries to flee, we can stop him."

Jor's face reflected her disappointment. "If that's how it's going to be." She dropped to the ground next to Indrar and pulled out a large dagger.

"Jor, no!" Lailoken said.

"I'm not going to kill him. We'll leave that for later. I want to make sure he doesn't run." She grabbed Indrar's leg and dragged the blade across his Achilles, severing the tendon. Indrar screamed in agony as blood poured profusely from the cut.

"Now he'll find it harder to flee," Jor said. Darlonn went to console Ori. Lailoken said nothing. It was a cruel gesture and now they had to carry the dragon-boy, but Jor was correct.

"We have our prisoner, Jor. Tend to his wounds so he doesn't die on us. Not yet." Lailoken left the two of them and joined Darlonn with Ori, looking over Tozgan for any major injuries.

TWENTY-TWO

Indrar's wound bled profusely. He'd been given a spare cloak to stay warm. It had been a day since their encounter and they'd barely made it down the mountain on their trek to Dragonfire Peak. Jor's cut completely severed Indrar's tendon and at the same time seemed to prevent him from shifting back to dragon form, resulting in a lot of wailing and complaining from the dragon-boy. It grated on Lailoken's nerves.

"Shut up already! We know you're in pain. Deal with it. You're either in pain or dead. Which would you rather have?" Lailoken scolded Indrar. The whining tortured them and made Lailoken want to slit the boy's throat no matter what information he may possess. He saw him as dragon and nothing more.

"You idiots maimed me so much that I can't shift and be free of your ignorance. When I am, I'll burn you all, no matter what my mother's orders are. She'll have to live with it."

Lailoken rushed Indrar and knocked him to the ground. Darlonn was holding him up. Indrar screamed when Lailoken turned him to look into his eyes.

"Never speak my wife's name again! Her name is of no concern to you! I will find her and rescue her and slaughter every last dragon that dares cross my path. You will be one of them." Lailoken slammed Indrar's head to the ground and stood, leaving the young Drakku moaning in pain. Darlonn helped him up but not without landing a kick to the ribs.

"How much longer are we going to listen to him complain and cry?" Jor asked. "He's not been forthcoming with information and I tire of his sound."

Lailoken ran a hand through his long hair. Jor was right. They were getting nowhere fast. The thought of Indrar divulging useful information was good to begin with, but so far nothing had come of it. They might be better off without being slowed by his presence.

"I agree. He's becoming more of a burden than anything else. Indrar, for the last time, I ask you. Where are there caves among Dragonfire Peak that are inhabited by your kind? Where is the Blood Stone hidden? I'm done protecting you and allowing you to live. Speak the truth now and give us information, or we will slaughter you on the spot. I have no love for Drakku and would gladly see you bleed."

"I do have several rubies that could use his blood," Driano said.

Indrar turned to Darlonn then to Lailoken.

"You best speak or you will die," Darlonn said, raising fear on Indrar's face.

"On the north face of Dragonfire Peak," Indrar nodded to the mountain, "lies a cavern I've never been to. You might find what you seek there."

Ori stepped closer to Indrar, the dragon-boy a head taller than him. He pressed his finger into Indrar's face. "How do we know you aren't going to kill us if we go there?"

"You don't. You'll have to trust my word."

Ori slapped him, almost knocking him over. Darlonn strained to keep him upright.

"I don't trust him," Ori said, turning away and rejoining the others.

"What's he got to gain from treachery?" Darlonn asked. "He knows we have his life in our hands. He cannot escape. The moment we're attacked by his fellow dragons, we'll have slit his throat. His only chance of survival is to help us as best he can."

Lailoken nodded slowly. "We have no other choice but to trust his words, but hear me, Indrar. One false move...one hint of betrayal, and we'll kill you. Understood?"

Indrar nodded.

"We follow his lead," Lailoken said, motioning to Indrar. Darlonn helped Indrar hobble toward the base of the north side of Dragonfire Peak and the cave Indrar mentioned.

As they trekked through the desolate valley, dusk settled in and Lailoken ordered them to camp for the night. Jor and Ori set off in search of wood while Darlonn, Tozgan, and Lailoken erected shelters and kept an eye on Indrar. Driano attempted to help but was useless. Belthos helped arrange their gear. Not long after the first shelter was in place, a familiar roar echoed through the mountains, Lailoken's eyes lit up. Driano cowered. Indrar tried to stand but fell down in the attempt.

"A dragon?" Belthos asked, wincing as he awaited a backhand from Driano that never came.

"It seems we have company," Lailoken replied.

"He came," Indrar whispered. "You'll all die now."

The dragon's roar grew closer, flames streaked

across the sky from an unseen source. Then the giant Garnet dragon showed itself, its form blotting out much of the remaining light in the sky. It was above them, circling their camp and roaring madly.

"I'm here! I'm here!" Indrar yelled. Darlonn shoved him back and knocked him to the ground.

"Get out of the way!" Darlonn yelled at him.

The giant Garnet spread its wings and dove for the camp, breathing fire. Lailoken and Darlonn ran from the flames, both men clutching their swords as the flames separated them.

The dragon roared again, swooping upwards, circling, and dove for the ground, flames announcing his presence. Then it landed with a large thunderous sound that shook the ground. It roared, turning its head, and breathed flames all around it.

"Hurry before it gets Indrar!" Lailoken yelled.

You will release him to me, slayer! His life is not yours to take. Grymryg demands it! Lailoken heard in his head. He furrowed his brows.

"I will take what I want and you cannot stop me!"

Etain's commands grow weak. Grymryg knows better. Release him or I will slaughter all of you. Lailoken heard the slow deep voice in his mind.

"Never!" Lailoken yelled.

Jor and Ori had returned. Jor unsheathed her sword and rushed at the dragon with disregard to the flames in front of her. She ran through the fire, yelling.

"Jor!" Lailoken screamed. "No!" He turned toward Driano, the stone around his neck glowing as the Magus did what he could to protect them from the dragon's flames.

Jor ignored Lailoken and struck out at the giant dragon. It roared and swung its tail, knocking the slayer to the ground. Her sword flew from her hands as she rolled away. Tozgan was unarmed and stood at a distance with a look of shock on his face.

"Darlonn, do something!" Lailoken screamed. The slayer brandished his sword. Darlonn nodded and approached the dragon from the right, carefully maneuvering through the flames to gain distance on the dragon. Lailoken shifted to the left, hoping to catch the dragon between them. They were closing in when the dragon roared again, stomping its feet, and shaking the ground. Then it flapped its large leathery wings and breathed fire all around itself. The slayers jumped back to avoid a fiery death. Driano's enchantment might help slow the fury of the flames, but eventually they'd be burnt. It was a thin layer of protection that helped them survive long enough to do their job. Against an Onyx dragon, they'd be much more protected. The dragon stepped closer to Indrar, covering the injured boy with his massive body.

"Hurry! It's trying to take Indrar!" Lailoken called out.

But it was too late. The dragon jumped into the air, roaring, and flew away with the dragon-boy firmly in its grasp.

I told you to give him back. When we meet again, I will savor your death. The dragon's words were clear in Lailoken's head.

The remaining flames were fanned taller by the dragon's wind. As Lailoken watched the Garnet flee with Indrar, the flames began to slowly fade, leaving behind scorched ground and someone moaning in pain.

Jor.

Lailoken ran to where she writhed on the ground. She appeared to be fine besides having singed hair and slight burns on her arms.

"Did we get it?" she asked.

"No. It escaped with Indrar. We lost this fight." Jor slammed her fists on the ground. "Be easy, friend; you may have more injuries that I cannot see," Lailoken said.

He turned toward Driano. "Can you help with her wounds?"

Driano grumbled but approached, the stone hanging from his neck glowing.

Lailoken helped Jor up. The slayer winced from the pain, but she stood and dusted herself off.

With their source for knowledge gone in the air, Lailoken's anger raged inside.

"Clean up this mess and prepare yourselves. Our quest is now more important than ever," Lailoken said. Soon, they might all be dead and without the gem to show for it.

TWENTY-THREE

Myrthyd's execution of the novice stirred a hornet's nest within the Black Tower. Fear and anger tinged with rumors of an Order Council convened to depose him ran rampant. Even within the midst of this turmoil, Myrthyd walked the halls with a deadly dignity. Novices, apprentices, and even other Magus gave him a wide berth and bowed deep when he walked by. He merely returned their gestures with a slight nod of his head.

He retreated to his quarters intent on studying the tome to discover more spells useful in his quest to revitalize the land, conquer the south, and rid the world of halflings. He still hadn't puzzled out the entirety of the Nightwraith spell, though his desire to obtain the Blood Stone grew more intense every day. He was convinced it was the key to destroying the Drakku and their ill-gotten offspring. He trusted Lailoken to secure the gem. The man was relentless, but he also trusted his man Gregor to kill Driano and return the gem to him. No loose ends. They must all be tidied up.

Myrthyd sat at his desk, opened the ancient book, and began to read. Not more than a few pages in there was a loud knocking at his door. Annoyed, he quickly hid the book and opened the large wooden door to find a small group of Magus from all five Towers. The oldest living Magus, Magus Alfred from the Crimson

Tower, stood in front of the others.

"Alfred, how may I assist you?" Myrthyd asked. His dark grin barely masked his disgust of the other Magus.

"Kull Naga Myrthyd, it has come to our attention that, maybe, possibly..." The old man seemed unsure of his actions. Myrthyd glared at him. Alfred cleared his throat, adjusted his blood-red robes, and started again.

"It has come to our attention that you have discovered and used forbidden dark magic of the ancient Magus. Order decree dictates it is unlawful to ever study or use such magic as compulsion to enhance our station. We have evidence that you are working toward—"

"Are you accusing me, Alfred? Do I, the Kull Naga, stand accused of heresy? Would you have me on trial? For what? Rumors?" Myrthyd waved his hand slightly, casting compulsion on the men.

"We do so accuse you. It is also our accusation that you intend to bring Tregaron to war with the south, a war we do not agree with nor condone."

"A war? Don't you think it takes more than one man to wage a war? I don't have that kind of power! What I do want is to end the hunger plaguing our land. Tell me, when was the last time a bountiful harvest came in?" Myrthyd asked, spittle flying from his mouth. The compulsion he cast seemed not to affect the men, and especially not Alfred, who continued his accusations.

"It is not for me to decide. You have been summoned to a Questioning by a special council. On tomorrow's eve, you are to appear before this council in the Grand Hall of the Black Tower. Failure to arrive will be cause for immediate detention in the Tower dungeon. I do not intend on having to go that far with these orders." Alfred coughed into his sleeve, his long, dirty white hair covering his face. He pushed it back and waited for Myrthyd's reply.

"You dare question me? I will appear at this sham council, and when I do, may Menos have mercy on you all. I will not be second-guessed. Our time of peace with the south is over. The Drakku have run amok in our lands for too long, spreading their blight and wretched halflings. No more! I will face this council, and you will all regret this action!"

He slammed the wooden door behind him, leaving the group of Magus in the hall. Rage blossomed inside him, boiling and destructive. He wanted to unleash all his power and tear the Tower down, leaving only a pile of charred stones. Closing his eyes, Myrthyd sought the black void where he lived and let his anger flow into the nothingness around him. Soothed, he soon left the blackness and opened his eyes, returning to the present.

"Their council will not remove me from power. I earned this and I'm the one powerful enough to destroy the Drakku. They will see my logic or die as traitors," he said to the empty room. Too angry to study, he rested and prepared for the council the next day.

***

Myrthyd stood outside the immense black doors to the

Great Hall. Tower guards opened the doors and the talking and chatter inside ceased. It amazed him how over a hundred Magus with countless apprentices and novices could go silent so quickly. The hall was packed with Magus in mostly black robes, though there were some from the other Towers as well. Every last Black Magus seemed to have turned out to witness the Questioning of their young leader.

Myrthyd grinned. This was exactly what he wanted.

He strode to the stage in the center of the Hall like a prowling lion. His robes swished loudly in the quiet, echoey Hall. He approached the stage where one Magus from each of the five Towers were seated facing him at a large rectangular wooden table.

"I have come to your spectacle. What am I accused of?" he called out in a booming voice. Gasps rose from the audience. Magus Carleon from the White Tower raised his hand for silence from where he was seated at the table.

"Kull Naga Myrthyd," Magus Brin said. Brin was older than Myrthyd by maybe twenty years. His bright blue robe was pristine; not a touch of dirt on it. He was thin and wiry with thinning hair and a scraggly beard that looked like it was attached to a bony skull. Brin was one of the main opposing voices to Myrthyd's ascension to Kull. He, of course, would have to be there for Myrthyd's Questioning. His presence assured Myrthyd he'd go free from this, as he was the easiest to compel of the Magus in front of him.

Myrthyd clasped his hands in front of him. "How may I be of service?" he replied with a slight wave of his hand.

"We appreciate your time in attending these matters. As you can see, it's an issue large enough to affect the entire Order. Please, have a seat," Brin said, motioning to a chair on the opposite side of the table. Myrthyd waved him off.

"I prefer to stand, if that pleases the council." His disdain was growing and some of it came through in his tone, as Magus Jardyn's face told him. It didn't matter. He was determined to see his plan through. He'd bring Tregaron to health and feed the people, whatever the cost.

"No matter. We will proceed," Brin said.

Myrthyd scanned his accusers. Other than Brin and Jardyn, the other three were Magus Dornald from the Crimson Tower, Magus Morris from the Black Tower, and Magus Barr from the Verdant Tower. Dornald and Barr were older; not quite as old as Alfred, but close. Morris was quite a bit younger; maybe five years older than Myrthyd. His presence surprised him. Morris had always been a strong supporter of Myrthyd's, even without compulsion. The five men sat across from him with their neatly crossed arms resting on the table.

"Kull Naga Myrthyd, what is the purpose of slayer Lailoken's journey into the mountains?" Brin asked.

Myrthyd held his surprise in check. No one knew about his plan.

"He is leading a small band of hunters to slay dragons, of course. We must keep our land free of their influence. Their blood is needed for our stones."

"But Kull, why is he searching for the *Blood Stone*?" Dornald asked. He leaned forward, his eyes narrowing. Gasps rose from the crowd.

"The Blood Stone?" Myrthyd asked innocently. Whoever shared his plans would find themselves flayed alive when he found out! How dare they give him up like that!

"We have witnesses who testified to your obsession with Drexon's tome with spells intended to cause havoc and spread evil in the name of Tregaron. They also shared your plans to obtain the Blood Stone, a tool so forbidden and harmful that our predecessors hid it to protect the land and our people from certain destruction." More gasps rose from the crowd.

Myrthyd waved his hand again, this time more overtly, casting compulsion on the men in front of him.

"You can dismiss of the use of that horrid spell," Barr said. "It has no effect on us. Answer the accusation."

Myrthyd closed his eyes, found the dark black nothingness, and drew all the power he could from it, widening his cast of compulsion to fill the Hall. He felt the spell settle on those around him. He opened his eyes and stared at Barr.

"As Kull Naga, it is my duty to protect Tregaron from our enemies, and none are more cunning and devious than the southerners with their sinful love of Drakku. For centuries our order has been tasked with keeping them from our lands and infecting our way of life. It is more important now than ever to combat the infiltration of their ways. Have you not witnessed the daily swelling of the hungry and poor in your cities? For us to continue as we have since the reformation, we must make a stand. What I do, I do for all of us."

Myrthyd's voice grew louder and bolder, turning from the council to the assembled Magus around him. This was his moment. They'd all fall in line. A touch of compulsion didn't hurt, either.

"As we look back on this day, it won't be because I've revived ancient spells to assist in our glory. It will be because all of you decided it was time. We've had enough of halflings. Our slayers, as powerful and mighty as they are, cannot stop the influx of dragons. What I can do...what I've discovered... will change our course of history forever!"

Thunderous applause rained down on Myrthyd. He smiled, lifting his arms, soaking it in. When he turned back to the council, four of the five men were standing and clapping in agreement. Barr sat still with his arms crossed and scowled at him.

Brin held up his hands to quiet the crowd. "We hereby dismiss these charges against our wise and powerful Kull Naga. Furthermore, we support your use of Drexon's tome in hopes it provides the means to eliminate the Drakku threat for good. This council is dismissed."

Once again, the crowd roared its approval, shouts and applause filling the great hall. Myrthyd's moment was now. He had his entire Order on his side with the exception of a few, but they'd come around or find themselves dead for their disagreement. The future was his for the taking.

TWENTY-FOUR

Alushia spent day after day tending to the farm. The work was grueling and made her feel at least twice her age. Pains rose where they'd never been before, and her hands had become callused long ago. She'd never be one of those soft-skinned, princess-type women. She understood hard work and didn't shy away from it, even when she was completely exhausted from terrible nights with little sleep.

For close to a week fought sleep, worried the Nightwraith would visit her again and say things to confuse her. Dragons lied, which was the main reason why halflings existed. Was Avess lying to her? She didn't fear the Nightwraith. It seemed more interested in talking to her instead of hurting her. She grew tired of worrying, which she did to the detriment of her rest.

After the Nightwraith's last visit, Alushia almost believed its words. It made her think it was possible she was a halfling. She couldn't explain why, but she felt...different. As though maybe dragon blood did run through her veins. But if that were true, it meant she was everything she was taught to hate. She tried to dismiss it as too preposterous to believe, but an inkling of the thought stuck with her.

Alushia cooked herself a bland meal of gruel after the long day in the fields. Her energy was sapped with the day's heat. She kept Brida in the house, though her father forbade it. What did it matter; he was never there.

It had been too long since she slept through the night and soon after dinner, she passed out on her bed.

***

A snow-covered field stretched as far as she could see, white blanketing everything, and a cold, bitter wind swept across her face. Alushia shivered and pulled the hood of her thick wool coat closer to her face. At the edge of the horizon rose a mountain range with one peak covered in a pinkish color. "Dragonfire Peak," she whispered.

Behind her, the roar of a dragon made her spin around. Crossing the white sky was the black Nightwraith, carving large swaths of the sky and leaving long black streaks behind. The contrast in colors was startling and unsettling. It roared again and dropped from the sky, landing before Alushia and turning its smoky eyes on her.

"Avess," she called out in the wind. "We meet again. Are you here to fill my head with more of your lies?"

The Nightwraith inhaled deeply and let out a long loud sigh.

"What do I gain from treachery? My soul is trapped forever within the gem. How would lying to you gain me anything? I speak truth to you because I sense you know the right thing. You have your mother's blood and that of your father, and both of your parents have a strong sense of duty. You are no different."

Alushia turned from Avess, unable to believe what he said might be true.

"I do not come to cause confusion or hurt. I've come to warn you. To get you to see what must be done. Your mother needs your help."

"You know nothing of my mother!" Alushia screamed as she turned back to face Avess.

"I know her well. She leads the Drakku as Dragon Lord. She protects you and your father, though his prowess might convince some to disobey her."

"Why do you insist on this falsehood? Why do you continue lying to me? Why can't you be honest? This is why our people have hunted dragons for as long as we can remember. You deceive us and when you get a foothold, you destroy what you can."

Avess turned as though trying to get a better look at her. Heavy snow fell from the sky, large white flakes obscuring her vision.

"Do you have evidence of this? Have you ever seen a dragon do such terrible things? They've lived in harmony with mankind since the Reformation. Dragons do not seek to destroy. They seek to live in kinship with all. It was mankind lead by the Order who turned on the Drakku. The Order imprisoned me within the gem. They have stoked the flame of anger and fear for over a thousand years and Tregaron believes mankind is the gentle spirit and Drakku are the ruthless, evil ones. Have you ever heard of a dragon trapping a man's soul for eternity? Dragons are not the evil creatures."

"But how can I be the daughter of a dragon? That would make me an abomination!" Alushia protested.

When she spoke the words, she knew they weren't true. Something inside, something burning deep within her spoke to Avess' words.

"But how?" she whispered, sitting down on the cold snow. "How is it possible?"

"Etain is a magnificent dragon, one of the greatest alive. Her wisdom is beyond most."

Alushia turned up at Avess and the snow suddenly disappeared. The vast white plain turned to a pristine beach with waves lapping at the shore and birds fighting over a carcass near a large group of boulders.

"How, how can this be true? Why are you telling me these things?"

Avess sat back on his haunches, his wings folded neatly behind him and his smoky eyes fixed on her.

"The time is near. If your father fulfills his duty to the wicked Kull, I no longer run free. I will be under the power of the Kull Naga. Terrible things happen then; awful, horrible things. You will no longer exist if he turns me on you. Others like you will cease to control themselves. Soon a grand gray army, dead yet not, will be under his command. Other dragons will be forced into slavery. Like me, they will be imprisoned within the gem."

"I don't understand. None of this makes sense. You tell me my mother is a dragon and I am somehow a halfling? And my father's hunt will lead to war and destruction? How does that make me lose myself?" Alushia stood, digging her toes in the sand. "You're lying to me again, aren't you? Why? What benefit is there to you? My mother was kidnapped by dragons. She's most likely dead by now. I've realized that possibility long ago. It's just my father and me."

Avess rose, roaring louder than the surf behind her. "Why do you continue to argue with the truth? Have the Magus poisoned you that much? See inside yourself! When the time comes and you do nothing with the knowledge I share, the calamity of Rowyth is upon you!"

"How dare you—"

Avess leapt into the sky. "You will see the truth or die because of it!"

Then he flew higher, devouring the blue skies with abandon, roaring in a frenzy. His black tattered wings flapped hard against the sea-swept winds. He dove toward her, hovering in the air. "Only you can stop your father! He will listen to your words. Find it within yourself to do the right thing. I may not be able to stop if forced to devour your dreams. Your fate and that of all Rowyth rests in your hands. Do the right thing or suffer!" He roared once more and streaked off toward the sea, dipping down to the whitecapped waves and leaving a dark line behind him where he devoured the dream.

Alushia stood on the sand watching him leave and contemplated his words. She had no evidence, no direct connection to the words Avess spoke, yet something shook inside her. She felt a distant bubbling that threatened to crash to the front—she *was* a halfling. Dragon blood flowed inside her. The legacy of the past thousand years of Tregaron hatred fought with the reality of who she was.

***

When she woke, Alushia screamed in frustration. Her housecat ran for her life, hissing as she went. Brida lifted her head and laid it back down.

"No! Why is this happening? Why am I—" She dared not speak it aloud. That kind of heresy meant an execution.

She meditated on the revelation and the truth behind it for several days and then she fought them no more. She'd find her father and do whatever she could to stop him from finding the gem and giving it to Myrthyd. It went against everything she'd been taught, but deep inside, it felt right. If Avess had lied to her, it felt more real than anything in her life. She'd have to pay for the lie, but if it were true, her mission was more valuable and necessary than ever before. She had to find her father.

For her mother's sake.

TWENTY-FIVE

Lailoken's thoughts drifted to his family. He wondered how Alushia was holding up at the homestead and if she'd remembered to bring in the increasingly thin goats at night. At times she seemed scattered, but he had no choice but to trust her with the farm. Hunts were long, arduous affairs and without Etain or any siblings to help, she had to be in over her head. It pained him to think of her struggling with daily chores while he was gone. Was it fair to her?

Every day that went by, he always thought of Etain. Her disappearance soon after Alushia's birth, which he missed while on the hunt, was another needle stuck into his spine reminding him of his failure as a husband. He couldn't protect the most precious gift he'd ever had. Etain's kidnapping played in his mind as though he were there, and whenever he had the chance to run his sword through a dragon, he knew he was one step closer to securing her freedom. One day, he'd free her from dragon captivity.

"Is that it?" Driano asked, interrupting his thoughts.

Lailoken placed his hand above his eyes to block the sun's glare. "Yeah, I think that's the cave." Despite his antics and constant moaning, Lailoken believed Indrar when he shared information about the cave. At the time, the dragon-boy had no reason to lie. His choice was either tell the truth or die. Driano believed his old friend from Woodpine as well.

They may be walking into a trap, but if there were dragons in the cave—trap or no trap—they'd at least have the opportunity to slay the enemy and thin their ranks.

If it truly held the Blood Stone...

Tozgan moved slowly and refused assistance, gritting his teeth when the pain overwhelmed him. Unlike Indrar, he kept it to himself. Darlonn helped him through the dangerous passes, draping his arm around the man to hold him steady.

Jor was the last of the slayers, deep in thought and walking slowly behind Driano, Belthos, and Lailoken. She'd been that way since they left the cavern, a wary eye cast on Driano.

They climbed up Dragonfire Peak toward a black hole in the side close to halfway up. By Lailoken's calculations, it would take nearly an entire day to reach it. At their current speed, it might be longer.

"When we get there, be prepared for anything," Lailoken said.

Wind whipped through the mountains, carrying with it the scent of rain. An eagle flew above them, circling and leaving, its actions reminding Lailoken of a dragon. "If we come upon the enemy, all of you must be ready to carry the fight. I have no intention of allowing any dragon to gain the best of me," Lailoken said. "This might be the most fearsome dragon we've ever encountered. I know not what kind it is, whether a Garnet or Onyx or something else, but I expect it to be the fight of our lives."

Jor growled. "I'm done playing nice. Any scaly

beast dare show itself will find death at the tip of my blade."

"No dragon will be left alive if I can help it," Darlonn said, earning raised eyebrows from Lailoken. The man hadn't been one to boast, but the attitude was welcome. They'd need that kind of spirit to counter what may lay ahead.

Fighting the fierce wind that grew stronger the closer they got to the cave, they finally made it to the entrance.

"In there possibly lays the greatest gift we can imagine. If the Blood Stone is hidden within, we will soon rule over all Rowyth. Myrthyd's plan will be fulfilled and we shall finish the Drakku forever. Can you imagine a time when our crops finally yield something useful?" Lailoken said.

Driano grunted.

"What is it, Magus?" Jor asked. Her tone suggested she was ready for a fight.

"The problem, as I see it, is what happens when Myrthyd gains this power? What's to stop him? There's a reason the Order hid this gem. It's too powerful to control."

"It works on dragons, right? And the halflings?" Lailoken asked.

"Aye, that's what I'm told," Driano said. Belthos shifted his feet, eager to say something. Driano addressed him. "Yes, what is it?"

The boy's eyes widened.

"Well?"

"The Blood Stone is a farce. It doesn't exist. It's a tale told to scare Tregaron into submission."

The group was stunned, silence filling the void.

Jor burst out laughing. When she recovered, she smiled at Driano. "Let's not delay. I want to play in dragon blood today."

The day wore on and they neared the cavern. Ori unpacked the torches, lighting them, and handed one to Darlonn. "Here, we'll need these." He gave another to Jor and the last to Belthos.

"Let's see what's inside, shall we?" Lailoken asked. They followed him into the shadowy cave.

Not long after entering, something moved rocks ahead of them as though shuffling across the packed dirt.

"What's that?" Driano asked. "Did you hear that noise?"

"Be careful. Could be a trap," Jor replied.

Two steps further and they found the source of the sound.

Two Jade dragons twice the size of the slayers crashed toward them. They tossed a human arm and leg to the floor and ran, howling and spitting their poisonous venom at them.

"Run! Don't let that get on you!" Lailoken yelled. Belthos dropped his torch. He and Driano scattered, attempting to avoid the thick lines of poison, When they were hidden, Lailoken felt the warmth of protection come over him.

Lailoken flung himself to the cavern's wall and withdrew his sword, the fury of the hunt overcoming him. Darlonn and Jor did the same on the other side of the cavern while Ori ran back toward the mouth of the cave, dragging Tozgan with him.

"Split them up. We stand a better chance of surviving if we take them one at a time!" Lailoken commanded.

"Come on, you sick beasts! Have at me!" Jor yelled. One of the dragons raced her way, its arms flailing, and poison shooting from its mouth.

Lailoken rushed at the other dragon, ready to endure whatever it had for him.

"Die!" he heard Tozgan yell as a crossbow bolt slammed into the dragon's side, piercing its thick scales. The dragon howled, clutching for the bolt. Lailoken smiled and sliced at it, swooping downward and catching it along the leg. His blade sliced open the thin skin near its knee. The beast roared and another bolt struck its neck, entering near the back and hanging off it like a feather. Lailoken lunged forward, using his sword like a spear, and forced the blade into the dragon's belly. The dragon howled and swung its arms, knocking him to the ground and forcing him to let go of the sword. It pulled the blade free and flung it on the cavern floor out of Lailoken's reach.

"Got a few brains in you, eh?" Lailoken jumped up and rolled away from the poison the dragon spat at him. Tozgan shot another bolt, this one piercing the chest of the dragon. Its eyes widened and it stumbled. A few awkward steps to the right and it fell to the ground. Lailoken found his sword and rushed back to the flailing dragon. He raised his sword above his head with both hands and brought it down on its neck, nearly severing its head from its body. Blood splattered on his face and chest. He pulled the sword free and did it again, this time finishing the kill and separating the head from the body. Its legs and arms thrashed about for a few moments before ceasing. Its head rolled to the far wall and stopped, its face frozen in a mask of surprise with its tongue hanging out.

When he checked on the other fight, he saw Jor struggling and Darlonn attempting to help. The dragon backed up and kicked the head of its companion. When it saw it was lifeless, the dragon roared and disengaged from the fight, spitting poison in all directions to keep the slayers back. When it got near the entrance, it spun on Tozgan, swiping at his face. Tozgan fell to the ground to avoid the blow, giving the dragon enough room to run past him and out of the cave, scrambling down the mountainside howling as it left. Ori fired a shot and cursed when it went wide.

Lailoken turned and watched as Driano and Belthos knelt near the dead dragon. Driano's hands were inside the dragon, blood running over the stones he held there, the stone around his neck glowing. When he was done, he handed the stones to Belthos, who wiped them clean and stuffed them back in his bag.

"We're fortunate to have emeralds on us. When we return, those Verdant Magus will fight each other to get the prize," Driano said.

Lailoken wiped his forehead, brushing the hair from his face. He turned back to the darkness ahead of them. "Grab the torches. We have a gem to find."

TWENTY-SIX

From dark crystal once hidden now found
Comes power unchecked, unbound.
Fill the blood with a dragon's soul
And own the dream, the dreamer whole.

Find the crystal among a dragon's back
Within a cavern, dark and black.
Slay the keeper and take the gem
Power eternal, over dragon, over men.

The dragon soul you will bind,
A Nightwraith to destroy the mind.
The living will live among the dead,
When you control the visions within their head.

Vile offspring of a dragon's lie
Controlled by the onyx eye.
Within the fatal dragon fate,
Power of yours, a Nightwraith.

Since the council's failed attempt to overthrow him, Myrthyd spent much of his time in his room studying the ancient tome. No longer needing to hide his deeds from the rest of the Magus, he openly read aloud from it, causing more than one audible gasp from innocent novices.

As he sat in his chair reading over the Nightwraith spell once again, the apprentice charged with cleaning his bedroom piped up. The boy was raw and new to the order and knew no better.

"Kull Naga, is the spell referring to a halfling?" he asked from the other room.

"You will speak when spoken to—" *A halfling?* Had it been in front of him all this time?

Vile offspring of a dragon's lie
Controlled by the onyx eye.

"A halfling!" he shouted, jumping from his desk. "Boy, you're right! A halfling!"

The dragon soul you will bind,
A Nightwraith to destroy the mind.
The living will live among the dead,
When you control the visions within their head.

"The Nightwraith, the dragon trapped within the gem, destroys the dreams of the living. In turn, it makes them...undead?" Myrthyd said

"I've heard of that, sir. Back in my village."

"What village is that, son?" Myrthyd's elation tempered with the fact that he'd need to kill the boy to maintain the secrecy of this particular spell. Only he would know the truth of the spell.

"Esheron, along the eastern coast. My pap told tales of strange people that were dead but alive. They feasted on the flesh of the living. Called them undead, he did. I didn't pay no attention to his words, though. A story to scare us little ones straight, if you ask me." The apprentice, Davron, was half Myrthyd's age, yet his fortuitous hearing of the spell opened the mystery he'd failed to solve all this time.

"Davron, what else does this spell tell you?"

The boy entered the room, his face grimy and hair disheveled. His large brown eyes were tinged with innocence and his missing front tooth spoke to his upbringing and poor family. Like many in the streets of Kulketh, his eyes were sunken and his cheekbones had a thin layer of skin stretched over them.

"Well, sir, I mean Kull Naga," he clenched his fists at his side, scolding himself. "I believe the spell tells how the Magus controls the soul of a dragon by trapping it inside some gem, and that dragon can eat halfling dreams. That last line about '*the living will live among the dead when you control the visions within their head*' kinda seems like whoever controls the dragon soul will, in turn, control the undead."

Myrthyd leaned back in his chair and crossed his arms. "How did you get to be such a wise young soul?" He'd been reading the spell over and over again for months. The section about *the living will live among the dead* confounded him. Menos must be looking down on him to send the boy his way.

Davron shifted his feet. "Pap taught me how to see things that was hidden. Part of my talent when we—"

"Go on, boy, I asked you a question. When the Kull asks an apprentice a question, he better be prepared to answer it."

"I understand, sir. Kull. I understand, Kull Naga. It's just that my pap was poor and we needed food to live.

I meant nothing by it."

Myrthyd tilted his head to the side, not understanding what he meant.

"I'm sorry, Kull. I used my talent to steal things, to trick others when we needed what they had. I learned to see past the lies people told us so we'd be able to con them out of food and money, and one time, I even got a cat. But we ate him."

Myrthyd's stomach rolled. This boy would never be missed. His 'pap' probably sent him to the tower to earn a few dracs off the boy's enhanced talent when he returned. This was the symptom that pointed to the Drakku. Hunger and thievery brought on by the Drakku curse upon their lands caused this boy to be what he was. Unfortunately for Davron, he would never make it back to that dirty hovel of Esheron.

"I see. What else can you tell me about the spell? What else do you see?"

The boy twisted his mouth and looked up at the stone ceiling as though in deep thought. "Not much, I guess," he finally said. "Sounds like you've got a way to trap dragons and control the undead. Pretty neat powers, if you ask me." The boy smiled. Myrthyd patted him on the head.

"Good lad. Now," he said with a wave of his hand, "go up to the third-floor study. The window is unlocked. If it isn't, try the fourth floor and so on until you find an open window. When you do, jump. You'll be able to float. I promise."

"I will?"

"Of course," he replied with another wave of his hand. "It's part of all Magus training. I think you have the power already. You only need to test it out to make sure it works. We all have."

The boy's eyes lit up and excitement made him quiver. "Can I go now? Can I try my powers now?"

"Yes," he replied in a slow, menacing tone.

"Thank you, Kull! I won't let you down."

"You couldn't if you wanted to. Go along now. Test those powers."

The boy ran from the room to the nearest window. Myrthyd's skill with compulsion had been growing stronger as he used it. Now, instead of enhancing someone's natural desire, he was able to make them do things they'd never do, such as jump from a window to their death. The boy had served his purpose and knew too much. He was better off dead anyway. He'd never make it to novice.

Not too long after, Myrthyd heard screams coming from within the tower.

Apparently, the boy had found an open window.

He returned to Drexon's tome, unconcerned with the activity going on inside the tower and the screams and wailing of Magus when they realized what happened.

"How does the most powerful Magus in Tregaron fail to see what an uneducated oaf of a child can see?" he said out loud. "Is the boy right?" He read over the spell again and everything the boy had said made perfect sense. If he possessed the gem and somehow trapped a dragon soul within, he'd have dominion over the thing—the Nightwraith, as the spell called it, and that Nightwraith devoured the dreams of halflings. And if it ate enough, it destroyed their mind, making them 'undead' and completely under his control as master of the gem. It was all clear to him. The power of the gem was more than he imagined when he sent the slayer after it. To possess it meant absolute power. He had to have it at all costs.

"Should I send more?" he asked. If he sent more seekers after it, he'd have a better chance to find it. But then if he did, he also had more loose threads to clip. He wanted the gem, but he didn't want more attention to his plans. He'd conquer Rowyth on his own if he had to. The heathen of the south would submit or die. Either way, all the Drakku would suffer at his hands. Dragons, halflings, and now...Nightwraiths. All would be subject to him.

A knock on his door snapped him out of his thoughts. "Kull Naga Myrthyd, I apologize about interrupting your studies," a novice named Peekon said through the closed wooden door, "but we have a crisis, sir. One of the apprentices jumped from the fifth-floor study to his death. The entire tower is in a panic."

"I'll be there in a moment." He rubbed his hands together in anticipation of holding the Blood Stone, the source of his soon-to-be conquest and end of the Drakku. Then, he'd heal the lands of the disaster they brought and return Tregaron to its former glory.

CHAPTER

TWENTY-SEVEN

When Alushia left the homestead with Brida, she packed a backpack with supplies and hired a boy from Kulketh to send a message to her uncle to look after the farm. She waited until she was ready to leave the city before having the boy deliver the message in case her uncle came looking for her. She didn't have time for that.

After her most recent dream and conversation with Avess, her mind swirled with thoughts she never would have considered months ago. Now, she was opening her mind to the reality that maybe...just maybe, she was a halfling.

Growing up with an absent father, she spent much of her time alone, with only Brida to keep her company. Early on, her uncle would often spend the time with her, watching over her and the farm, but he was an aloof man and not much for children even though he had three of his own. Watching over her was more a chore and he made it known. Instead of clinging to him like a father, she avoided him and went off on her own through the fields and played in the wooded areas near the homestead.

More times than she remembered, she found herself playing with random animals that were unafraid of her. It was as though she understood them and they her. A special bond connected her to the animals, but at the time she didn't think much about it. Recognizing it now, however, she thought it was because of her halfling nature; of the dragon blood within her that the animals sensed and accepted her as one of them. She previously understood it to be her gentle nature appealing to the animals, but now she doubted that was it.

Once, she was playing by a stream and didn't see a young snowcat sipping from the cool water when she approached. Normally, those large cats were aggressive and often mauled people to death. When she startled it, the thing hissed and raised its nose in the air, audibly sniffing. Then the hiss turned to purring and it approached her. She was afraid it was going to strike her, and knowing she'd never outrun it, she stood stiff, hoping it would pass by. Instead, it stepped closer and sniffed her face. She shivered, still expecting the thing to maul her. It purred louder and rubbed its head against her side, nearly knocking her over. She giggled and it purred louder, rubbing its head along her other side. Stroking its chin, the giant white cat rolled over onto its back while she gently and carefully rubbed its belly. The snowcat acted like the housecat she had back at the homestead. She thought it strange at the time, but it gave her a sensation of comfort.

She brought it home and named it Brida and their strong bond began to grow.

She was never taught the effect halflings had on other animals. Halflings were to be despised and hated. Killed, even. They were a scourge on their people, tainting the race with their vile, mixed blood. She'd been witness to many executions in Kulketh. The Order was adamant about making sure the people viewed the events, especially since Myrthyd's ascension. The Kull was ruthless in his quest to destroy all halflings and demanded to do so publicly, claiming they were part of the reason so many were suffering.

Her father was no better.

Alushia remembered Lailoken's tales of hunting dragons and the excitement in his eyes as he recounted tales of the hunt and finding halflings trying to disguise themselves in Tregaron. He helped hunt them as well, bringing them back to the Tower for judgement. Would he do the same with her?

She stopped on the worn dirt road to consider what he might do to her once he found out. The thought that he'd turn her in never crossed her mind. Going to stop him from his mission was all that mattered if Avess were to be believed. But would her father turn her over to that wicked Myrthyd, or would he come to terms with the truth?

"Doesn't matter. I have to stop him. That gem cannot fall into Myrthyd's hands," she said to Brida and looked around when she realized she spoke it aloud. If anyone heard her words and reported back to Myrthyd, she'd have more trouble than she intended.

The road was clear and she continued on, losing herself in her thoughts.

Traveling alone wasn't common practice. There were too many bandits along the route and other natural dangers to fear. Alushia worried about these, though if an animal should come at her, she had Brida to protect her.

Three days and nights they travelled, hiding along the side of the road when other travelers were in sight.

A woman alone was an invitation for problems, though the large snowcat at her side would be a deterrent to most. She could defend herself well enough, but only if she needed to. She preferred to avoid confrontation if at all possible. The visible short sword and the dagger hidden within her sleeve had tasted blood before and might very well do so again if needed, but still, it didn't hurt to be extra cautious.

On the fourth day on the road, it was nearing dusk when she heard voices ahead of her. Brida had run off in search of food, leaving her alone. She wasn't paying attention earlier and didn't notice the small band of people. Hiding in a thick stand of trees off the side of the road, she waited until she thought the travelers had passed. After their voices faded, she waited a few minutes more before coming out. When she did, she was confronted by two men and a woman. They were dirty and stunk of animal dung. The woman was missing an eye and the empty eye socket yawned obscenely, causing her once beautiful face to contort into an ugly grimace. The two men were both thin and looked barely alive. Their clothes hung loosely on their skeletal frames.

"Aye, look what we have here," one of the men said. His dirty blond hair was matted with something brown. He wore wool pants and a dark blue shirt with questionable brown and red stains.

"A pretty little one, she is," the woman replied, brushing her brown hair back from her face. Her once-white tunic was now a dingy gray. Her leather sandals looked new compared to everything else.

"Me thinks she's lost. Not a good thing for a little

girl," the other man said. He was slightly taller than his companions and twigs and leaves stuck in his long brown hair. He wore a torn tunic and holey leather boots.

"I'm not lost and I don't mean any trouble with you," Alushia replied.

"I think she needs our help, don't you, Trenton?" the taller man asked the other man.

"I was just telling Gerthe we needed a new woman around here, wasn't I, Gerthe?"

The woman nodded. "She's a pretty one, too. Rolan, think we can keep her?" she said to the tall man.

Rolan grinned, exposing a huge gap in the front of his mouth where his teeth had rotted away. "She won't be no trouble at all, will ya, little girl?"

Alushia pleaded with them. "Please, I mean no harm. I don't want to cause any problems. Just let me be on my way. That's all."

"Where ya going?" Rolan asked.

Alushia paused, unsure she wanted to give away her true purpose. "To Woodpine. I have family there."

"They ain't ever gonna find you, girl," Gerthe said. The one-eyed woman lunged at her, knocking her to the ground. Alushia rolled with Gerthe's weight and pinned the woman to the ground.

"Don't make me do this!" she yelled at her.

"Get her, Gerthe! Don't let no little girl get the best of ya!" Trenton called out. The men goaded their friend and it seemed to give Gerthe a second wind. She struggled against Alushia's grip and broke free, toppling her. Gerthe jumped up and kicked Alushia in the ribs.

"No little pretty thing gets the best of me!" she

screamed. Gerthe produced a large blade from under her tunic and flashed a wicked grin. "I want one of them pretty eyes. Then no one will want to touch you ever again. You might even be good enough to eat. Food is scarce out here, ya know."

Alushia pushed herself away from the woman but ran straight into one of the men. She looked up to see Rolan. He sneered and grabbed her arms to prevent her from going any further as Gerthe slowly stepped closer, grinning madly.

"Come on, Gerthe, take it! Take it quick! I want my turn!" Rolan said, encouraging his friend.

Alushia's angered swelled. A fire blazed inside her like never before. Her eyes flashed red.

"Did you see that?" Gerthe said, backing away. "Her eyes! They...they changed!"

"Have you been drinking ale already. Take the eye!" Rolan said.

Alushia felt the warmth surge through her and Rolan let go, yelping.

"My hands! She burnt my hands!" he yelled.

Brida growled behind them, and they all turned. The snowcat dropped the hare in her mouth, snarling at the attackers.

"A snowcat?" Trenton cried. He turned to run, but Brida was faster, pouncing on him and tearing into his flesh with her large claws.

Alushia seized the moment and pulled out her dagger, lunging at Gerthe, distracted by Brida's vicious attack. Alushia plunged the blade in the woman's chest, the metal slipping within her flesh, and puncturing the soft organs underneath. Gerthe screamed and flung her arms at Alushia, striking her on the head. Alushia fell back, Rolan grabbing her and holding a knife to her throat.

"Call off the snowcat or I'll kill you!"

Alushia struggled, the warmth returning to her. She felt her skin grow hotter, forcing Rolan to let go again.

"She's burning me!"

Alushia spun and slammed into him, forcing him to the ground and landing on top. Brida pounced in their direction. "No!" Alushia said. "Get her first."

Brida leapt to Gerthe, the woman screaming as Brida finished what Alushia had started.

"What are you?" Rolan asked.

"A woman you should've left alone." Alushia drew her dagger across his throat. A fountain of blood spurted and splashed on Alushia. She stood, leaving him to die on the ground. When she turned to Brida, the white cat's face was red with blood, flesh hanging from her mouth.

"Thank you, girl." Alushia looked around at the mess they created and felt sorry for the people. She didn't want to kill them, but they'd left her no choice. Fortunately, she had Brida with her. "Let's go, girl," she said to the large snowcat. She grabbed her pack and sought the nearest stream to clean up and rest, Brida at her side.

The next morning, sore and weary, the pair set off toward the south. "We can stay in Woodpine. My father will return there from the mountains on his way back to Kulketh. If he has the gem, we can stop him there. I worry that if we go into the mountains, we'll never find him."

Brida grunted as though she understood, making

Alushia smile. They were far from safe, but the two together were a pair to recon with.

As the day progressed, Alushia thought about the attack and how her skin grew hot, as though on fire. It had never happened before and surprised her; even frightened her. *What was that? Was that proof of my dragon blood?* she thought. Asking someone about it would create unwanted attention and possible execution. If she ever met Avess again, she'd ask him. Until then, it would be her secret.

TWENTY-EIGHT

Lailoken stood with the slayers in the dark cavern, Etain's lovely face suddenly flashing in his mind. Indrar's lies came back to him, making him more eager to slay what lay ahead and force the end of the Drakku. Their deceit and treachery knew no bounds. He'd be the one to deliver their salvation from dragon lies by acquiring the Blood Stone. Matched with Myrthyd's power, they'd have the means to eliminate dragons and their horrid halflings forever. Hunger would be eliminated and their fields would once again produce their fruits. Their quest was close to an end and so were the Drakku.

If they were in the right cave.

Indrar's words at the point of death carried weight for Lailoken, though his lies about Etain were something he'd never accept.

Etain might not be alive. Surely, she would've tried to return to her family if she were. To claim she was a dragon was preposterous. That would mean in her human form, she seduced him to capture his humanity and give birth to their halfling Alushia. It was all a lie. Every last word, deception on the part of Indrar, but why?

Why would Indrar lie to him? What did he gain from it, other than a moment's respite when Lailoken was ready to slay him? Was it all a ruse to escape? Was there something more to the lie? How did he know who Etain was, anyway? Had she been captured by the dragons and held captive? They'd all die for it. Every last one of those flying evil creatures would lose their life because of his fury.

Lailoken looked to his fellow slayers. "We are about to embark on a journey that ends in death. I for one do not intend to die." The slayers nodded their assent, Jor talking up their prowess to the group.

"We're stronger and smarter than any dragon. Those things run on instinct. We've got intellect to guide our way. We've got training to bolster our wit. Those things have strength without direction. They fight out of animalistic urges and nothing more. We can do it! We can kill what lies ahead. I want one of their eyes to parade around Tregaron so that everyone will know Jor is a true slayer!" She nodded toward Lailoken's sword with the dragon eye embedded in the pommel. When the speech ended, he sheathed the sword.

The others voiced their agreement. Lailoken understood her bravado and had witnessed it first-hand. She believed every word she spoke, and from the looks of the rest of the slayers, so did they. Driano was the only one who appeared unsettled, but he always did.

"You three stay here," Lailoken said to the two Magus and Tozgan. "We'll scout deeper ahead. Be prepared for dragons attempting to enter the cave."

"We'll get a fire going," Driano said. Since their time in the mountains, the man's demeanor had changed subtly. Instead of an instant backhand to

Belthos, he gave the boy the tiniest bit of respect, and it made Lailoken not hate him as much.

Belthos along with Tozgan went in search of wood and Driano used his powers to keep himself warm, his gem glowing.

Lailoken scanned the cavern. The dead Jade dragon lay to the side of the cave, its blood clotting on the dirt beneath it.

One less evil beast to deal with, Lailoken thought as he lit a torch. *May Menos guide those souls to rest*, he prayed. Human body parts were strewn around the cave in a horrific display of the Drakku's evil.

"Come, let's find what's inside." He led them deeper into the blackness ahead.

The cave echoed with the voices of the men discussing wood and the fire. The howling wind at the mouth of the cave created an otherworldly sound that made Lailoken turn around several times in fear of a surprise attack. Darlonn, Jor, and Ori were behind him. Nothing would get past them.

He hoped.

The cave itself narrowed a bit before dropping down and to the left. He followed carefully, hoping the flame didn't go out before he could return to the entrance. Soon the voices of their friends were silent. He had no idea how far they'd gotten, but the darkness around them seemed bleaker in the light of the flickering torch. He moved deeper and farther away from the entrance of the seemingly endless cave.

"I don't like this," Jor said, breaking their silence.

"Are you afraid of the dark?" Darlonn asked, a hint of humor in his voice.

"Of the dark? No. Of what's hidden in the

dark...yes. What could possibly be hiding in here, guarding a magical stone? It certainly can't be anything commonplace. How would it live in here?"

"Maybe it's some kind of spirit?" asked Ori.

Darlonn laughed. "If it is, our swords are useless. I don't fear anything that I can see through."

"Ori, spirits aren't real. In all my travels, they've never been proven," Lailoken said. "Most likely, it's an old tale to warn off intruders like us, to prevent us from even trying to find the gem. For all we know, it's nothing more than a rock of no significance."

"Then why are we here? I'm not excited about dying for something with 'no significance,'" Jor replied.

"Fine. It's a magnificent gem that if nothing else will fetch us a lot of dracs, especially if Driano infuses his magic into it," Lailoken replied. *And, because of Etain. He promised...*

That seemed to end the discussion and the group fell silent again, continuing into the ever-increasing darkness of the cavern.

They'd been gone at least an hour when the long narrow path widened. The cave also widened to reveal an enormous dome that appeared to occupy the entire inside of the mountain.

In the distance, bright green and blue glowing orbs of light illuminated the cavern. Their warm glow gave the illusion of stars painted on the ceiling. They marveled at the strange sight, the torch almost unnecessary under their light. An orb on the wall caught Lailoken's eye and he approached it carefully. "What is this?"

"I've never seen anything like it," Darlonn said.

"Me neither," Ori replied.

It glowed a wondrous shade of blue. Moss-like in appearance, it had a mesmerizing glow. "These are spectacular," Jor said.

"*I know.*"

Lailoken's heart jumped into his throat. Swords were unsheathed and Ori squeaked. They spun. Standing only a short distance from them was the older dragon-man with eyes glowing red.

"You! Your days are over!" Lailoken dropped the torch and clutched his sword. The dragon-man laughed.

"You still don't believe me, do you? Why is it so hard to hear the truth? Your wife Etain lives. She commands my brethren. Her power is known amongst my kind and we honor her with our loyalty. Your daughter Alushia is a halfling. One day she, too, will come to know the truth and no longer will we have to do this pathetic dance. We aren't evil, Lailoken; we never were. Your Magus would say different, but then again, they were the rebellious ones Deavos tried to bring to the side of right."

Jor and Darlonn were stunned and their mouths fell open at the words spoken. Ori pulled back from the group, unslinging his crossbow and knocking an iron bolt.

Lailoken roared and rushed the dragon-man. In a poof of red smoke, he transformed into his dragon form, flapping his large leathery wings and soaring high into the cavern. He was the same dragon that saved Indrar. If this dragon was here, Indrar was probably not far behind.

The dragon belched fire, overpowering the ethereal

glow of the plants on the walls.

Why must you be so hard headed? the dragon's voice came slow and deep in Lailoken's mind. *I want nothing but to reunite you with Etain. You must come to terms with the truth. Don't force me to act in anger.*

"Come to me and fight! One of us will die this day!"

The dragon roared. *If only I could!* He spit fire at the ground far enough away not to harm them.

I'm sworn to protect you, but the rest of them are mine, the dragon said in his mind. Lailoken cast a glance at his friends and his heart beat faster.

"No, leave them be!"

"Who are you talking to?" Jor asked. It hadn't occurred to Lailoken that they didn't hear the dragon. *What does that mean?* he wondered.

A roar behind them made Lailoken spin around. An immense Opal dragon appeared like a ghost above them, flapping its tattered translucent wings. It howled and screeched.

You have awoken Chepon, the Lady of the Skies. I hope you are prepared to die, slayer, the Garnet said in Lailoken's mind. Chepon flew across the cavern, roaring hideously.

"Evros, you dare enter my lair!" Chepon said.

"Evros?" Jor asked. She turned to Lailoken. "Did that dragon...speak?"

"I heard the name!" Ori said, "I heard it say words."

The Garnet roared back. *Chepon, I do not come to steal your treasure. I have come to rid the world of this slayer.* Lailoken heard the words but wasn't sure if the rest had.

"I yield to no man and to no dragon! Be gone, Evros, or face my wrath."

The Garnet—Evros—howled and spit flames at the ceiling, burning the glowing plants. Then in a furious beat of its wings, it flew out the way the slayers entered, leaving them alone with the great Opal hovering above. It twisted in the air and landed a good distance from them. She glowed like the plants on the walls and he could see through her form.

"Why are you here in my home, slayer?"

"To rid Rowyth of the Drakku! I will not rest until you're all dead!"

"To kill you and others like you!" Jor yelled.

Chepon laughed, a deep chortle that lacked the power of Evros's voice.

"Death? Do you not see me? Death does not hold me. Your sword will not find flesh to pierce here."

"My daughter dreamt of one like you devouring her dreams. She felt anger and hate, but you would know, wouldn't you? It was you!"

"I am no Nightwraith. That kind of evil must never be let loose on the world."

Lailoken scrunched his face. "Your words will not spare you."

"Enough!" she boomed. "Evros was right about you. Etain lives still. Your daughter...is a halfling. Accept these truths and live a better life. Deny them at your own peril."

"Why spread these lies?" Darlonn demanded.

Is this the guardian that Myrthyd spoke of? Lailoken thought. If so, the Blood Stone must be somewhere in the cave.

"You're the one," Lailoken said. "You created the Nightwraiths, didn't you?"

Chepon roared and flexed her wings, extending them wide. "Those abominations are not to be trifled with. They bring nothing but death on our kind and consume the lives of the halflings. They are horrible. Never must they exist again." She roared and spewed streaks of lighting in the cavern, the brilliant light followed by booming thunder. The slayers dropped to the ground, covering their ears.

"You lie! Your kind are liars!" Lailoken screamed at her.

Chepon flew around the cavern, spitting lightning and creating cracks of thunder with each bolt. The slayers covered their ears from the overpowering sound. The ground shook with each thunder boom.

"Leave now!" Chepon bellowed above him.

Ori stood and let a bolt fly. It was on target but passed safely through the dragon's ghostly form.

"Your weapons do nothing to me. I am more powerful than any of you will ever understand. Leave this place now or suffer my wrath."

"You won't scare us away. We've slaughtered worse than you," Jor said.

"You'll no longer slay any of my kind. Prepare for death," Chepon said. The Opal lunged into the air, circled them, and blasted the wall with lightning.

"Your time is over now," Lailoken growled, clutching his sword and standing at the ready. The fight had come at last.

TWENTY-NINE

Lailoken bowed his head and prayed to Menos, but then Chepon roared and it echoed throughout the chamber, forcing his eyes open. Jor and Darlonn fanned out, preparing for the fight. Ori hid behind a rock formation, cranking his crossbow and nocking another bolt.

How are we going to slay this thing? Lailoken wondered. The dragon apparition flew above them, circling as though preparing to attack. Which of their weapons could hurt something that didn't have physical form? An unsettling fear crept over him. This was unlike any dragon he'd ever encountered.

"Lai, over there!" Jor shouted, pointing out a faintly glowing altar at the far end of the cavern. "Do you think that's it?" From where he stood, it was difficult to see exactly what it was.

"Let's advance," he replied. Darlonn followed them along the back wall of the cavern.

Chepon spit lightning on the ground, the bolt crackling and creating a loud explosion when it struck ahead of them. Rocks flew in the air and the slayers were knocked to the ground.

"Leave this place now! You must not continue!" Chepon bellowed.

Lailoken and Darlonn crept next to Jor. She turned to them. "Is that thing talking to us? Since when do they talk?" Lailoken had heard their voices before, but always in his mind. He was not about to share that with them.

"It must be something different," Darlonn said. Lailoken nodded, keeping his thoughts to himself.

"You'll never leave this place alive!" Chepon yelled. Lightning erupted from her mouth, flashing around the cavern. The sound was so loud that their ears rang and momentarily deafened them.

Darlonn said something that Jor and Lailoken couldn't hear. Frustrated, he pointed toward the altar. Three Jade dragons were ambling toward them. The flightless beasts stumbled over each other in their mad dash toward the slayers who unsheathed their swords and prepared for the fight.

Jor moved to the right and Darlonn to the left. The slayers held firm, waiting for the dragons to advance.

Jor slipped further to the right and one of the dragons broke from the others and came after her. Darlonn did the same on the left and easily enticed a dragon to follow him. So far, the dragons were acting according to instinct and it made the fight a little easier for all the slayers.

Darlonn shouted to engage his dragon, his voice finally breaking through the ringing from the crack of thunder. Lailoken caught a glimpse of Darlonn swirling and slicing as he did his best to kill the dragon. Jor was doing likewise but he didn't get to see much as the final dragon was upon him.

"Come on, then; let's have at it," Lailoken growled. Overhead, Chepon urged on the smaller dragons.

"Don't let them pass! They must be stopped!" She

released bolt after bolt of lightning, striking the sides of the cavern and raining rocks down on them, making a conscious effort not to strike the slayers with the deadly emission. Lailoken had a moment to consider it before the Jade swiped at him.

Crouching beneath the awkward attack, Lailoken rolled to the left and jumped up, brandishing his sword for an attack. The Jade was slightly off balance from the failed strike. Lailoken lunged at it and gracefully sliced at its exposed belly. He felt resistance as his blade dragged through the rough green hide. He held firm, every muscle in his arms and back burning and crying in pain. The sword broke free and left a deep gash in its stomach that spurted thick blood. The Jade roared and swiped at him, striking his shoulder and knocking him to the ground, sending him rolling into a large rock. His sword flew from his hands and clanged on the ground behind him as he slammed to a halt.

Jor and Darlonn seemed to be having a better go of it by the sounds of their shouting.

"Come on, you ugly son of a goat! Is that all you've got?" Jor called out. Lailoken didn't have time to enjoy her taunts. The Jade had followed him, though noticeably stumbling. It flung its short limbs at him and missed, striking the rocks around him instead.

Chepon spit lighting behind the Jade, goading it to attack. "Get him! Do not let him live!" the ghostly dragon screamed. Yet still, Lailoken noticed, the dragon did not strike any of the slayers directly.

The Jade almost fell over when the lightning hit behind it. The dragon roared and swatted in Chepon's direction and then turned back to Lailoken. He looked around for his sword and caught a glint of light off the blade, but it was out of reach. He scrambled to his feet and ran for the sword. The Jade roared and spit a stream of poison at him. He avoided the saliva and fell to the ground, forcing himself back up until he finally reached the dragon-eyed blade. He spun around and held it in both hands. "Now it's time to die."

The Jade shuffled toward him, the wound in its belly noticeably slowing it down. Not taking any chances, Lailoken ran toward it with the intent to kill. It spit poison at him. The stringy spittle clung to his exposed skin, leaking into his nostrils with every inhale.

No, I can't! I have to rid myself of the poison. It was in his eyes, too, making his vision blurry. The Jade was a shapeless green blob in front of him. Without Driano's spell to cover them, the slayers were exposed.

Lailoken spit out as much of the vile substance as possible. The Jade rushed into him, striking him with his claws and trying to tear through his leather armor. Lailoken backed away as he felt a sickness come over him.

Inside and out, he felt nothing but pain. He'd taken down many Jade dragons before, but somehow fell victim to this one. It wasn't an overly clever dragon and he should've overpowered it.

Chepon belched lightning in the cavern, a thunderous boom following. Lailoken's hearing dulled once again.

Poison surged within him. His eyesight was all but gone, and his hearing dimmed. The fight had taken a turn he was not prepared for. Leaving Driano at the entrance was a mistake, no matter the man's constant complaining.

The Jade swung its thick arm and knocked Lailoken to the cavern floor. He slammed into a large rock; his back bent and twisted awkwardly. He cried out. "Menos preserve me!" His legs felt numb. His stomach churned like he'd had too much ale and was ready to come back up. Furiously wiping his eyes to clear the poison away, he only made it worse.

"Kill him! Don't let them live! They must never possess the Stone!" Chepon roared. Her voice was strong and powerful, breaking through Lailoken's dulled hearing.

"No! We must have it! Our people...our land..." Lailoken's voice weakened as the poison surged through him.

In a brief but powerful vision, he saw his wife smiling at him. He caught the scent of her perfume. Her long red hair flowed in a breeze. "It was for you," he whispered. Then the scene changed and he saw Alushia tending the fields, Brida at her side bounding after insects and small animals.

His heart broke knowing he'd left her to raise herself. Without Etain to help, he did the best he could. The growing crop crisis and increasing Drakku infiltration meant he was called away from her more than he wanted. Because of that, he barely knew her. Now as she was an adult, he regretted the life he led. What kind of father was he to leave her by herself all that time?

The thoughts were chased away when the Jade stumbled toward him and clawed at him. He had the briefest moment of recognition and instinctively rolled to the side. He felt a claw graze his arm but nothing more.

He rubbed his eyes again and could make out more than an oddly shaped green dragon. The poison had weakened, though his stomach was still twisting on itself and making it difficult to focus.

Chepon let loose a burst of lightning toward the far end of the cavern.

"Darlonn! Jor!"

Lailoken scrambled along the rocky floor to look for something...anything to defend himself against the Jade. Grabbing hold of a fist-sized rock, he flung it in the direction of the dragon. He found several more loose stones and continued his assault, hoping to catch the dragon's eye or deepen the pain in its abdomen.

The dragon roared and shambled toward him. Lailoken turned to flee, but the poison had finally taken its toll. Wracked by spasms, he emptied his stomach, falling to the ground and shaking violently. The poison burned his insides, a sensation like he'd never experienced in his life. Five nights of drinking ale never made him feel worse than he did from the poison.

His eyes watered as he continued to expel the wretched poison.

The dragon slammed its claws into his back, their sharp points piercing his leather armor. Their tips dug into his flesh and he screamed in pain.

Then his vision slowly cleared, his tears washing away the poison. They still burned, and most of what he could see was still covered in a slight haze, but shapes morphed into rocks and dirt.

Chepon let out a bolt of lightning and a flash of light burst from the ground nearby. The Jade roared and pulled back its claws to strike. Lailoken fought the urge to vomit again and scrambled along the floor toward where he noticed the flash of light. The gaping wound on the Jade's stomach took a toll and it was slow to react to him.

As Lailoken got closer, he realized what the object was. *Thank Menos*, he thought.

It was his sword.

Grasping his sword, he stood on shaky legs to prepare to fight the Jade.

Lailoken swiftly slid to the side as it swung at him and spewed poison. He swung his sword up, catching it in the belly again. His muscles tensed as he held the sword against the dragon's flesh. His insides were on fire, ready to expel their contents again. The Jade swung both limbs down and struck Lailoken's shoulders. The blow stung and he staggered, still holding the sword tight.

"No more!" he yelled, pulling his sword free. He shifted on his feet, trying to hold it together, then plunged forward. The tip of his sword pierced the dragon's hide and slipped inside its belly. The dragon roared from the injury. Lailoken twisted the blade, opening the wound. He pulled his bloody sword free, and before the dragon had a chance to retaliate, he plunged it into its stomach again. The dragon's roar weakened and it stumbled back a step before falling backwards. It slammed to the hard ground, life leaving its body.

THIRTY

Chepon roared madly, illuminating the cavern with endless bolts of lightning. The thunder crashed deafeningly, and soon Lailoken could only feel the power of the thunder as his hearing went nearly silent again. Still stunned by the poison and his stomach turning on him, he held his sword ready to strike.

Chepon screamed above them. "No! They must not be allowed to live! Kill them all!" A flurry of lightning followed, the jagged bolts lighting up the dark cavern. Thunder shook the ground as the fearsome Opal dragon spirit unleashed a torrent of anger-fueled lightning.

Lailoken cowered from the falling debris let loose by the lightning, and when he looked up, he caught a faint outline of Jor racing toward the altar they saw at the back of the cavern. Chepon didn't seem to notice her, but when she finally did, it was too late.

Jor screamed victoriously and raised both hands in the air, clutching something black with a faint red glow, pulsating and deadly.

"No! You cannot! Leave that be! You know not what you do!"

Chepon roared louder than the thunder she had created. The dragon spewed lightning at Jor but still didn't hit her directly. Jor danced from the bolts, barely safe from the blasts.

"This way!" Lailoken called out. "Hurry!"

Darlonn was covered in blood and rubbing his eyes furiously, but he had slain his dragon and was racing toward Jor as best he could.

Ori prepared his crossbow for another shot.

Chepon continued to belch lightning around Jor, slowing her progress.

"Come on, Jor!" Darlonn called. He avoided large rocks set loose by the furious lightning strikes coming from Chepon. The Opal dragon's anger burned hot as it attempted to stop Jor's progress. Darlonn finally reached her, and together they made careful strides back to Lailoken.

"Ori, go to the entrance. Make sure we have a way out!" Lailoken yelled. The crossbowman nodded and ran toward the tunnel where they had come in.

"Lai, stop her!" Darlonn yelled, pointing at Chepon. "We have the Blood Stone!"

What could he do? The dragon was a spirit, a phantom without physical form.

"Chepon!" he yelled, trying to attract the dragon's attention. "Come down here and fight me!"

Chepon ignored him, focusing on the cavern walls above Jor and Darlonn, spitting deadly lightning bolts that exploded on the rocky surface.

Darlonn fell over a large rock in front of him. Jor stopped to help him up and Chepon let loose a torrent of lightning above them. A shower of rocks rained down on Darlonn, forcing Jor to jump out of the way. When the lightning stopped and the dust cleared, Darlonn was half-buried under debris.

Blood oozed from Darlonn's head. He was barely alive.

"Darlonn!" Jor screamed, running to him. She set the Blood Stone on the ground and dropped to her knees, frantically trying to clear the rubble.

"You will die for that!" Lailoken yelled. He ran across the cavern, his ears ringing and the shapes around him still not nearly as clear as they once were. The cavern grew darker, lit only by the glow of the mysterious plants on the walls. He followed the sound of his friends. The lightning had stopped.

Chepon circled above them, laughing. "You cannot kill that which is already dead! You cannot stop me! You shall never leave this place!"

Lailoken joined Jor and they worked furiously to uncover Darlonn.

"Don't. Waste. Time. Your time," he said between shallow breaths. "Not. Going. To make it. Legs." Darlonn's face was covered in blood, either from the gaping wound on his head or his fight with the dragon, Lailoken did not know which. His beard was stained dark crimson. He moved an arm from under the pile of rocks and screamed. Jor hurried to free it and she gasped.

"Your arm," she said at last. A bone jutted from the skin on his forearm.

"Get out," he said. "Leave. Take. Blood Stone. Live."

Chepon roared above them. The lightning ceased as her anger suppressed.

Lailoken reached out and held back Jor's hand. "He's right," he said softly. "We must go."

"But we don't leave our own behind!"

"Go. Please go," Darlonn said.

"Goodbye, my friend. Your death will not be in vain. Your actions will be remembered always,"

Lailoken said, holding Darlonn's head in his hand. The dying man nodded, the effort forcing a grimace on his face.

"When my time comes, I will find you," Jor said. She wiped away tears and kissed his forehead. "Good-bye, my friend."

Chepon's anger returned, sending lightning crashing against a far wall when Lailoken lifted the Blood Stone from the dirt floor.

"Leave the gem! Leave this place! One of you is dead and the rest will join him!"

"You will not stop us!" Jor growled. Lailoken pulled her away and left Darlonn moaning in pain.

It took all his strength to leave his friend. They'd been through so much and to abandon him when he needed help most was a devastating blow. Lailoken's insides twisted as the poison continued to crawl through his body and he fell to one knee. He closed his eyes, unsure if he could continue. Then the gem vibrated in his hands, radiating a warmth that almost made him drop it. "By Menos," he said. "Did this vibrate when you touched it?"

"What? The gem?" Jor shook her head.

His hands went numb from its touch, the vibrations growing stronger. "My hands," he said. Forcing himself upright, fighting against the sourness inside him, he clung to the Blood Stone.

Chepon's anger flared. The ghostly dragon swooped at the pair closer than she'd been throughout the entire fight. Jor unsheathed her sword and prepared herself. Chepon roared and aimed for them. Jor stood in front of Lailoken and sliced with her sword when the dragon flew above their heads, but it went right through the dragon. Jor fell forward and crashed to the ground.

The dragon circled back and dove for Lailoken. He cradled the gem in his hands and he was intent on not dropping it. Darlonn was willing to give his life for it. This was the reason they were here.

Chepon flew at him and he faltered to the ground clutching the Blood Stone as the poison gripped his insides. The dragon passed overhead and flew back to the top of the glowing cavern.

"Leave the gem! Leave and live!" she cried.

Jor sheathed her sword. It was useless against the spectral dragon. She helped Lailoken to his feet. "Our only chance is to flee. We cannot kill it. We have the gem! We must go."

"I agree. Come! Hurry before—"

Chepon blasted the ground around them with lightning, the thunder vibrating their bodies. Then she dove at them again. Jor rolled away and hid beside a large rock. Lailoken stumbled and fell to his knees. He faced the giant dragon as it came down at him, clutching the gem close to his chest. He felt it vibrate furiously against his body, the heat moving up his arms and into his body. Mixing with the poison, it sent a fresh sensation of sickness within him.

It was then he knew. The spell Myrthyd recited. The words came crashing back.

Chepon's mouth was open as if to eat him, and he held the gem out to her in an offering to rid the world of this menacing keeper of the gem. The pulsating red of the Blood Stone grew intense and bright. The heat seared through his arms. Chepon noticed, but it was too late.

As she closed in on him, the gem's light intensified until the cavern glowed blood red. Just as Chepon was on him, the gem's glow was blinding and bright.

The dragon cried a pitiful, painful sound. The light pulsated and the cries of agony from the ghostly dragon filled the cavern, louder and more powerful than any thunder and seemed to go on without end. Lailoken held firm, the gem growing hot and vibrating madly.

Chepon howled a hideous sound. In a flash of intense light, she disappeared. Thin curls of smoke rose from the gem.

Lailoken stood still. "Am I...dead?" He was sure the dragon had killed him and he'd soon meet Darlonn.

The sickness returned with a fury, forcing him to drop to the ground and expel what little he had left inside. Each convulsion wrenched his muscles and sent piercing lines of agony through him. When the episode passed, he wiped his mouth and cleared his eyes.

A calm quiet settled around him. After a few moments, Jor spoke. "If you're dead, then I'm in death with you."

The Blood Stone pulsated in his hands and he looked down at it. A faint blue glow darted from one side of the black facets to the other, trapped in the confines of the gem.

"Where'd the dragon go?" Jor asked, stepping next to him. She helped him to his feet.

"I...I don't know. I think—" he looked down at the gem. "I think she's in here." It sounded absurd, but he knew it was true. The Blood Stone was now Chepon's prison.

"How did that happen? What did you do?"

He shook his head. "I just...knew. I can't explain. I only knew it would work. Somehow."

Jor exhaled and clapped him on the back. "I don't care what or why. Let's get this thing out of here and be done with it."

"I was hoping you'd say that," Ori said, approaching from behind. The two slayers turned and the cross-bowman grinned. "Where's Darlonn?" Jor lowered her head and Lailoken placed an unsteady hand on Ori's shoulder.

"He didn't make it. He died for this," he said holding the gem up, the glowing light inside struggling against the smooth black walls.

Jor took Ori back to Darlonn and soon both slayers were weeping. Lailoken knew in his heart his friend was gone. He watched from where he stood as the two kneeled and prayed to Menos for Darlonn.

THIRTY-ONE

Ori lit a torch and led the solemn party through the now quiet tunnels back to the entrance where they'd left Driano, Belthos, and Tozgan. Lailoken didn't say much as they traversed the winding path, his focus on the slightly vibrating gem in his grasp and forcing his insides to obey his will. The heat from the gem had diminished, but the blue glow continued its manic dance inside the black gem.

"This gem better be worth it," Jor said, finally breaking the silence. "Darlonn died for it. Don't let it be for nothing."

"I can't explain it. There's something about this gem. Didn't you feel it when you held it?"

"Nothing. It was a dead rock like any other, except it did that strange glowing thing like it was a beating heart. Like it is now." She pointed to it.

"But you felt nothing?"

"No. Are you well?"

"Shhh. I hear something," Ori said. He pulled his short sword from its sheath and crouched. Lailoken was aware of the disturbance as well. Could it be the Garnet come back to exact revenge on them for entrapping Chepon?

Jor unsheathed her sword and stepped in front of Ori. "Protect him and the gem. Anything happens to me, you must defend it at all costs." He nodded and fell back next to Lailoken.

They waited as the sound grew closer. A faint light illuminated the tunnel ahead to the right. The gem's vibrations grew stronger. *It had to be the Garnet*, Lailoken thought. He held the gem in front of him, hoping to repeat the sequence that trapped Chepon.

Suddenly the tunnel was bathed in light from two torches. It wasn't the Garnet, but two men.

"Driano? Tozgan?" Jor asked. Lailoken didn't think it was them. They were larger than the Magus and the crossbowman.

"Aye. We be they," one of the men said with a laugh. They walked closer and their features were exposed.

"Who are you?" Jor growled.

"Looks like we got a feisty one!" one of the men said. "Come on, Mortha. This must be them."

"My pleasure, Gregor." The two men blocked the tunnel. Mortha pulled a large battle axe from a strap on his back and Gregor dropped the torch and pulled a warhammer with a large spike at the end from the strap on his back.

"We'll take that gem," Gregor said.

"You'll do no such thing!" Jor replied. She crouched and brandished her sword. "I'll die before I let you have that."

"If that's what ye want," Mortha replied.

The large man strode forward. "Give it over and don't make me kill such a fine thing as yourself."

Jor screamed and ran toward him. "Never!"

Mortha swung his axe and missed. Jor somersaulted and landed on her feet. She swung her sword, the blade slicing into his leather boot and sending blood slowly flowing out. Mortha yelled and staggered back.

"You vicious wench!" He regained his footing and braced himself before swinging his axe again. This time Jor could barely stop the blow with her sword. She stumbled backwards from his massive weight advantage.

Ori crouched next to Lailoken and cranked his crossbow, loading a bolt.

"Give me your sword," Lailoken asked him. Ori held the crossbow and gave over his short sword.

Lailoken held the gem in his left hand and the sword in his right. It wasn't ideal, but there was no way he'd drop the gem.

The one with the hammer joined his partner. "Come on, Mortha! She ain't that hard to kill!"

Jor darted across the tunnel to avoid the hammer blow. She was a blur of long red hair.

Lailoken fought the sickness as he approached Gregor, but before he engaged him, a crossbow bolt screamed past his face and lodged into Gregor's eye. The man screamed and fell backwards, his body convulsing as his blood pooled on the tunnel floor. Lailoken looked back to Ori, who grinned broadly. He turned to help Jor with the last man standing.

Mortha swung his impressive axe. Jor deflected the blow, harmlessly pushing it aside. Mortha pulled back, hoping to catch her on the backswing. The dull side of the axe blade struck her in the chest, knocking her breath away. She fell to the floor clutching her chest and heaving.

"Get to her, Ori!" Lailoken screamed. He lunged at the larger man. At first, Mortha blocked Lailoken's sword and swung a fist at the slayer.

"Myrthyd said ya might be difficult. No matter; we'll still get that gem and then kill that Magus."

Magus? Does he mean Myrthyd? Maybe it's Driano. He didn't have time to dwell on it. Mortha swung his heavy axe with intent to cleave Lailoken in two. The slayer twisted away at the last second. Mortha's axe clanged loudly, striking the hard dirt. He then whipped it back and slammed the handle against Lailoken's back. The blow struck deeply, forcing Lailoken to crumble in pain. He clung to the Blood Stone. He felt the immense power within it and feared what it could do. Mortha might kill him, but he'd never give up the Blood Stone willingly to the man.

"The great slayer forced to look like a little babe. How did you ever kill all those dragons?" Mortha pulled the axe over his head, too sure of his advantage, and Lailoken caught the larger man in the belly with the short sword. Like a dragon, the larger man moved slow and was even slower to react. Lailoken twisted the sword in his guts and pulled it free, blood pouring from the wound. Mortha screamed.

"I'm gonna kill you for that!"

"Not if I can help it," Lailoken replied, rising to his feet. He danced to the side, narrowly missing the clumsy man's fist, and sliced open his belly. His guts spilled out. Mortha dropped his axe and clutched at his intestines in a failed attempt to delay his death. He fell to his knees, looked up at Lailoken, and slammed to the ground. With what little life clung to him, the man convulsed. Finally, he gave up the struggle and his breathing slowed.

"Jor, are you alright?" Lailoken asked. He dropped to his knees next to Ori, who attempted to assess the damage, though Jor was having none of it.

"Get your hands off me. If you value the ability to grab something, you better remove your hands from me now," she growled. Despite their awful circumstances, Lailoken couldn't help but laugh.

"That's the Jor I know!"

She slapped Ori's hand away and forced herself to stand, rubbing the spot on her chest where the axe had struck. "That'll leave a bruise," she said. "Who were they?"

"I thought I heard that dumb one," Ori said, pointing to Mortha, barely clinging to life, "say something about Myrthyd. Do you think the Kull Naga has anything to do with this?"

Lailoken wiped his face with his hand, exasperated. Were they only on a fool's errand for a madman who wanted them killed? "I don't know. Before we return anything to him, we ought to discover what his true intentions are."

"If these men made it this far, do you think they did anything to the others?" Jor asked.

"By Menos, I hope not!" Lailoken replied. "Come! Our journey is not over."

They grabbed the torches from the floor and left the bodies to find their way back to the cave's entrance.

"Where are they?" Ori asked when they'd finally made it. There was a small fire in the central part of the cave and the two dead Jade dragons beside the walls, but the men were gone.

"Who...who's there?" a weak voice called out.

Jor instinctively grasped her sword, but Lailoken waived her off.

"It's us, Belthos. Lailoken, Jor, and Ori."

From behind the headless dragon, Belthos timidly stepped forward. "Lailoken?"

"Where's Driano and Tozgan?"

"The men, sir. The men came in and..." The novice's face turned bright red. "I think they killed them. I hid."

"Do you know for sure?" Jor asked. She frantically searched around the dragon bodies.

"N-n-no. I was scared."

"So they might still be alive," Lailoken said. "Search the cave. Look outside. Even in death, they should be here." His stomach felt sour, but the twisting pain of earlier had eased up, making it tolerable.

Ori helped Belthos relax while the two slayers went out into the cold, dark night in search of their friends.

"Driano! Tozgan!" Lailoken yelled. The wind picked up, sending a chill over him.

"Stupid novice," he heard a muffled voice say.

"Jor, over here!" Lailoken called. Jor ran to his side and they followed the sound of the voice to a large bush at the cave's entrance. Lailoken held up a torch and peered behind it to find Driano and Tozgan seated on a small ledge overlooking the valley below.

"What the...how did you get down there?" Jor asked.

Tozgan turned upwards. "Jor! Lailoken!"

"Would the two of you mind to pull us out of here?" Driano asked. "The damn novice pushed us out of the way trying to escape the dragon that flew out of there. We heard some men come through and threaten him. For his sake, I hope they got him."

Jor laughed hard, clutching her chest. "He's alive inside the cave."

"He'll wish he wasn't," Driano grumbled.

"Enough! Leave the boy alone, or we leave you down there!" Lailoken barked. He'd had it with the older Magus. As far as he was concerned, the Magus could stay there. So far, he'd offered little help on this journey.

Driano glared up at him. "Fine. But he'll be your problem, not mine."

Jor left and returned with rope and lowered it down. Driano nudged himself in front of Tozgan, who let the Magus go first. After they'd lifted Tozgan out, they returned to the cave.

"Where's Darlonn?" Driano asked when they were all situated.

Jor looked down. "He didn't make it."

Driano stood and approached her, placing a hand on her shoulder. "I am sorry for your loss. He was a good man and a great companion."

"His death was not in vain. We did get what we came for," Lailoken said, producing the Blood Stone from an inside pocket.

Driano's eyes widened and he approached carefully. "It does exit," he said quietly. "I can feel the power within. It's real." He reached out and touched it, closing his eyes and breathing in deep. "By Menos, it's amazing. The terror, the power, the—" he opened his eyes and snatched his hand away.

"What is it?" Jor asked.

"It's evil. I felt...evil. It was like something black

threatened to consume me. It wanted to destroy me. I can't fully explain it other than that it's evil. This is not right."

Lailoken watched as the blue glow inside suddenly dashed back and forth.

"It's alive," Driano said, shrinking away from the gem. "We cannot. We mustn't."

"What are you saying?" Lailoken asked, but he knew what scared the Magus.

"We cannot give this to Myrthyd. It's not meant for man to have."

Lailoken nodded. He felt the same way. He couldn't explain it, but he understood Driano's reservations. Still, they couldn't leave it. They had to find a way to destroy it. His friend died so they'd get it, and he wasn't about to toss it away.

In the morning, they gathered their things and left the cavern for the long trip back to Woodpine and then to Kulketh. As they were leaving, Lailoken and Jor stopped at the cavern's entrance and turned back, Dragonfire Peak looming high above them.

"Goodbye, my friend. 'Til we meet again," Lailoken said. Jor closed her eyes and nodded, then turned back to the rest of the group.

Their hunt was near the end.

THIRTY-TWO

The last message Myrthyd received from Gregor's snowdove was promising. He mentioned they found the cave, though the slayers had yet to show. They were lying in wait until they arrived.

That was two weeks ago.

There should have been another message by now and that worried him. The men should have disposed of that wretched Driano and his novice, and if they had any sense, the slayers also.

His patience wore thin. The call of the Blood Stone was powerful. He felt like he understood the spell now and unleashing the Nightwraith was all he thought about.

Alushia must be a halfling. There's no other explanation, he thought. Her dark dreams. The feeling he had when he was near her that screamed she was different. It was similar to when he executed halflings. When they were on the platform, he sensed their uneasiness and their dread. It was a bond he couldn't describe. Instead of accusing Alushia of his suspicions, he kept his concerns to himself. *She'll be useful to me yet.*

He sat in his chair in the Great Hall taking visitors from all over Kulketh. The recent drought on top of the previous year's drought was causing chaos amongst the people. The Drakku menace was allowed to live for far too long, and this was their punishment. The Drakku would be dealt with. Halflings would be eliminated and used for his glory. It crushed him to listen to story after story of families without food having to make difficult choices about their lives. More than once he heard about Garnet dragons torching farms and homes.

"Kull Naga, what is your decision in this matter?" It was Magus Renfro, a wiry man twice Myrthyd's age yet still with a full head of hair. He was an enjoyable man and a great drinking companion.

"What? The question again?' Myrthyd asked.

"Neron the steward of Opren to the north requests fifty bushels of wheat for his community. With the recent burning of their fields—"

"Fine. Give him what he asks."

"Thank you, sir," Neron said. The man backed away, bowing as he left.

As the day wore on and his attention drifted further, Myrthyd dismissed the remaining petitioners. "Renfro, tell them to come back in a week. I'm done here."

"Yes sir," the Magus said and did as he was told. Those in line grumbled and complained, but Myrthyd's mind was elsewhere. He made a decision earlier in the day that he had to carry out.

He was going to the Dragonback Mountains to get the Blood Stone himself. At the very least, he'd intercept either Driano and his companions or Gregor and Mortha. He hoped it would be the two hired men, as they'd be easier to kill and dispose of. The others would be much more difficult to eliminate, but he would do so.

Under the pretext of visiting the Verdant Tower, which he hadn't done yet during his reign, he arranged an escort of five Tower Guards led by his head guardsman Tukra, to protect him on the long and perilous three-day journey south.

The next morning, Myrthyd left the Black Tower at the light of dawn in a donkey-drawn carriage guided by Tukra. The other four rode horses, and the animals acted up when Myrthyd neared them.

After the first long day of riding, they set up camp under a stand of willow trees. The horses grazed on wild grass.

Tukra set up a tent for Myrthyd. "Got excellent weather for this journey, sir. I expect we'll not see a drop of rain."

Myrthyd nodded. "That's true, Tukra, but that's also part of the problem."

The guard turned to him. His face was dirty, one of his eyes barely poking out of his twisted flesh, and paused his task of tying down the tent. "Problem, sir?"

"Have you not noticed? Our people are starving. Crops are failing. A scourge has come across our land. We need the rain, Tukra. We need it to nourish our fields."

"Your point is well made, sir. My farm doesn't yield as much as it used to, though we get by. My wife and our five children work hard to get what we need. My livestock aren't quite as plump as a few years ago, but we've learned to adapt."

"That's it, though!" Myrthyd waved his hands frantically as he paced. "We've adapted! Why do we need to adapt to a terrible situation? Why can't we be

252 *Jason J. Nugent*

vibrant and abundant again? Why do we roll over and allow this to happen?"

Tukra wiped his hands on his trousers and stood. He let go of the rope and it slithered like a snake as the tent wall waved gently in the breeze. "Roll over? I don't think so, sir."

Myrthyd's eyes narrowed. He considered casting compulsion on the man but forced the thought away. He needed to know what his people thought to gauge what his next moves should be.

"Why not, then?"

"The way I see it, good fortune comes and goes. Menos watches over us and sometimes turns his eye away. Eventually it will return."

Myrthyd's pacing quickened. Is this how his people felt? Ready to accept the problems hoisted on them from the Drakku?

"Menos cares about us. Menos guides me. But Menos does not turn his eye from us. The Drakku have done this to us. Don't you see it?"

Tukra nodded. "Of course, sir. Drakku blood has done much harm to us. But—"

"But what? They are the true cause of our problems, not Menos!"

Tukra's face turned down. He went quiet and then returned to his work. "I'll have this up in a moment sir," he called over his shoulder.

Myrthyd crossed the camp to let the moment drift away. He'd gotten too caught up with Tukra. The man was only expressing what he thought to be the truth. Did more of his people believe the same thing? They had to know it was all because of the Drakku.

The evidence was clear!

A roar in the distance caught his attention. The guards must have heard it, too, as they all dropped what they were doing, grabbed their swords, and circled around Myrthyd.

"There!" one of the guards said.

Myrthyd turned to the sky and saw a Garnet dragon crossing the fading light of day. He felt the dragon and sensed its presence. It was much like being near Alushia. The dragon emitted a blast of flame that illuminated its grotesque shape. A sneer crept across Myrthyd's face. "Our enemy. It comes to taunt me."

"What are we to do?" Tukra asked.

None of the guards were slayers or had experience against them, as far as Myrthyd knew. If only he had the Blood Stone, he'd have a weapon to rid Rowyth of the beast.

"Stay close and prepare for an attack. I can offer some protection." The stone around his neck glowed as he settled the spell on the men around him, hoping it was enough to save them.

The dragon roared again, spiraling in the sky. Then it let out a blast of flame, igniting trees and the fields around it. Flames reached high in the sky. The Garnet roared and shot off to the south, leaving a trail of smoke behind it.

Myrthyd let the spell dissipate and the men relaxed.

"Do you see? We must get rid of them before they burn it all!" Myrthyd's anger grew bright as the fields that were now engulfed in flames. His task was clear.

He watched as orange and yellow flames died

down, the scorched fields left behind.

It took a few minutes before the guards returned to their work, Myrthyd nudging them with a touch of compulsion.

Tukra gathered his men. "We'll watch through the night. The Kull cannot be harmed. Is that understood?" They nodded.

Myrthyd entered his tent and laid down to rest knowing his men would alert him if the dragon returned. The disturbing sensation he felt with the dragon in the sky unsettled him. What did it mean? How could he sense the thing? Was it something made up in his mind?

"Soon I will have the means to destroy you. I will return Tregaron to its glory. And when I do, we'll rid Rowyth of the Drakku for good." He closed his eyes and forced his thoughts into the black nothingness as he sought rest.

When Myrthyd woke, he left the tent and approached the small fire in the middle of the camp where the guards warmed themselves.

"Any sign of our foe?"

"No, sir. The night was calm," Tukra said stifling a yawn. The guards grumbled in their tiredness.

"Have you all been up?"

Tukra nodded.

"Aye, sir. We lot didn't sleep much overnight, but we'll be ready for anything."

"That, you will," Myrthyd said with a slight wave of his hand, casting a spell of endurance on the man. It was another spell he discovered while reading Drexon's tome. He didn't quite understand why it was a forbidden spell if it helped soldiers with a boost of strength. It was another spell he added to his collection of lost abilities that he was slowly unlocking.

He pushed them hard that day, casting endurance and compulsion on all the men, forcing them to their limits and covering a lot of ground. Had he cast those spells when they set off, he expected they'd make the journey to Woodpine in two days instead of three, if the animals held up. He'd have to test it out on their return.

Constantly he scanned the skies, expecting to see the Garnet return. They must hurry; the Blood Stone awaited. It had to. There was no room for failure. Menos was on his side. He was sure of it.

THIRTY-THREE

By the time they approached Woodpine with its wooden walls, the men were exhausted and the horses and donkey seemed beat.

They were greeted at the gate by a small retinue of Verdant Magus who had been alerted to the coming of the Kull Naga by snowdove.

"Kull Naga Myrthyd, so good to see you. We welcome you to our city. The Tower is yours," a short man in dark green robes said with a deep bow, nearly kissing the dirt ground.

"You must be—"

"Magus Menathon, the Keeper of the Verdant Tower," the man said. He held out a hand to Myrthyd and helped him out of the carriage.

"Menathon, I appreciate your kind welcome. My men and I will require rooms and food. It's been a while since we had a good meal."

"Of course. Whatever you require. We are here to serve. Come, this way." He held out a hand and gestured for Myrthyd to accompany him. They walked side by side through the dirty streets of Woodpine.

At every corner people begged for food. Near a tavern, Myrthyd's heart broke when he witnessed a boy with a grimy face wearing tattered clothes begging a woman walking by. Instead of helping, she smacked him on the head and kept walking.

"Do you see that, Menathon? Look what the Drakku have done to our people."

Menathon turned to look.

"That boy has been reduced to nothing because he has no food. Look at that family over there," he said, pointing toward another corner. "It's deplorable. How are your stores holding up? Can you feed them?"

"We're running low, and even with our powers assisting us, we cannot break the rot and drought. I fear we don't have much time left before the situation grows dire."

"Isn't it already? When there are this many people starving, how can you survive? I've even witnessed Garnet dragons setting fields on fire! Something has to change."

Menathan said nothing and they continued toward the Tower.

The guards that accompanied Menathon led Myrthyd's guards to an entrance on the side of the Tower. Menathon and two other Magus who Myrthyd didn't know led him to the Tower's main entrance. Once inside, two lines of Magus, novices, and apprentices lined either side of them, cheering him.

"Welcome, sir."
"We are here to serve."
"He's much younger than I thought."

Myrthyd listened to all their concerns and comments, not once stopping to acknowledge them. Menathon wiped his brow several times on the sleeve of his dark green robe.

"Right this way, sir," he said, his voice shaky. Making others uncomfortable seemed to be what Myrthyd did best, and he quite enjoyed the spectacle. It made it easier to get them to see reason.

Menathon droned on about advances in gardening techniques by the Tower and the discovery of new poisons. "By accident!" he claimed, and their continued vigilance of the Dragonback Mountains.

"We spotted our first griffon only two weeks ago. Quite the surprise to our guards. It didn't do anything but fly along the mountains roaring before heading back south."

"A griffon? This far north?" Myrthyd asked. He stopped walking and cocked his head.

"It's been a long time since one travelled this far, but it was alone and we figure it was curious to see how the true people live."

"Interesting. Or it could be wanting to witness what the Drakku are doing to us. If this ever happens again, I must know of it immediately."

"As you wish," Menathon said, bowing.

"Here we are. Your rooms while our guest."

"Thank you, Menathon. If the rest of your Tower is as welcoming as you, we shall truly praise Menos for your hospitality. I'll be needing rest and silence for the day. Please make sure I am not disturbed until dinner time."

"Of course. I'll have guards posted at each end of the hall to repel any who would seek an audience with you. I'll send an escort when dinner is served. I'm sure the entire Tower will turn out for this. Good day. Until later." Menathon held the door open and waited for Myrthyd to enter, closing it gently and leaving him be.

Several hours later, a soft knock on his door told him Menathon had returned. He opened the door and the Magus grinned back at him.

"Kull Naga, I hope I'm not disturbing you. It is time for the feast, and the Tower is overjoyed to have you as our guest. This way." He held out his arm and Myrthyd followed his lead.

The Tower was unusually empty on their walk to the Great Hall. Menathon was right; the entire Tower must have crammed into the Great Hall for his visit. That suited him well. If he needed to coerce them into action, that made it much easier.

As they approached the grand wooden doors to the Great Hall, two Tower guards bowed and opened the doors. Menathon entered first and the crowd silenced. He smiled and addressed the assembled Magus.

"My fellow Magus, novices, apprentices, and friends. I present to you Kull Naga Myrthyd, leader of the Order of Eschar!"

The crowd erupted in applause. Myrthyd stepped forward and waved to those inside. He was escorted by Tukra and his own Tower guards to the dais at the front of the Hall where a large table with other high-ranking Verdant Magus sat. When he reached the dais, he turned to the Hall and raised his hands. The crowd grew silent.

"Thank you for the kind reception. I'm honored and humbled by your greetings." They cheered wildly at hearing his words. He was here for the Blood Stone but bringing them to his side in preparation for what was to come had to start now. His plans were grand, and the more he convinced them to see his reason, the easier it would be when the time came.

"I come to enjoy your company and to unite our Towers. Our people are hurting. They die of starvation and our crops fail. The Drakku destroy our land!" The applause ceased, replaced by an uneasy quietness. He wasn't going to make this easy on them. They needed to see the truth.

"It is my hope to remove the source of our plague." Some of the Magus at his table shifted, murmuring to each other. "The Drakku have long lived among our people and their blood permeates throughout. It is my ardent belief that they have brought our lands to ruin. Have you not seen their effects? How many beggars line your streets? How much harder must you work to help those in need? Your skills are tested daily. The time has come. With the Towers united, we shall overcome this menace once and for all. With the Towers united, we can work together for a greater future. Can I count on your support? Can I trust in you as you trust in me?"

He was prepared to cast compulsion on the Hall if they refused his logic. It was a drastic step, but he'd do what needed to be done.

A Verdant Magus from a table midway through the hall stood and applauded. "We support you, Kull! You can count on us!"

Myrthyd had no idea who the man was but was grateful for his show of support. Soon, other Verdant Magus joined him in a series of affirmations and applause. The entire hall descended into a call of support. Not a single Magus remained seated.

Myrthyd smiled. He hadn't had to nudge them. They supported him so willingly and that was more valuable than blind obedience forced by a spell.

He raised his arms high. "Please, let us eat and enjoy each other's company."

The crowd cheered his words.

He sat at the head of the table and all in the room waited until he was served first before they enjoyed their meal. Musicians set up in the corner of the Hall began playing and a joyous, festive atmosphere filled the area. Ale flowed freely and soon Magus upon Magus approached the head table to have a word with the Kull Naga.

Myrthyd smiled and nodded, not caring what they said or petitioned him for. He was here solely to acquire the Blood Stone. He'd stay as long as needed until he possessed the greatest weapon ever created by the Order.

THIRTY-FOUR

"Now Brida, stay close by. I wish you could come with me, but they don't allow animals like you inside the city," Alushia said to her snowcat. The large white cat hung her head and slowly stalked away. Alushia felt that Brida understood her; she had ever since they met, though in the past few weeks it had grown stronger.

Alushia turned from the sulking snowcat and entered Woodpine, hoping to find her father and stop him from delivering the Blood Stone to Myrthyd.

It was late afternoon and already the three taverns in the city were full. Music drifted across the busy streets and people were anxious. It was like the midsummer celebrations she knew back home but well past time for that. More than once she had to force her way through a throng of poor, destitute people that clamored at her for a coin or piece of bread. They were worse than in Kulketh! She found an inn that didn't look too rundown and entered.

"Aye. How can I 'elp ya?" the old man behind the counter asked. He was tall and fat. Sweat pasted his thinning white hair to his scalp and ran down his cheeks and. One eye was nearly closed and the other was milky white.

"I'd like a room, please," Alushia replied.

"Don't we all, dear...don't we all? All I got is a little

space upstairs. Seems like everyone and their brother come into town on account of the Kull's visit. I swear, people ain't got no sense at times. Ya want it or not?"

"The Kull? He's here?"

"Look, dear, I got a house full o' strangers arguing over every little thing. I ain't got time to chat. You want the room?"

"Oh. Yes, yes please." She felt her skin warm at the mention of Myrthyd and had to control herself to temper her anger.

"This way, then," the old man said. "My name's Rufus. Call on me if ya need anything. Got it?"

"Yes, sir."

She followed him up creaky stairs and all the way down a narrow hall and waited while he unlocked a door on the left side.

"Here ya go. Ain't much, but ya can have it. Dinner is at six, breakfast is at six, and lunch is at—"

"Six?" she answered with a giggle. Rufus didn't smile.

"Lunch is at noon. Enjoy your stay," he grumbled and left to attend a man and his partner at the end of the hall. The two men were complaining about rats and Rufus grumbled.

"I'll be kickin' yer arses out of my inn unless you stop talking nonsense about the vermin. People'd be lucky to eat 'em."

Alushia closed the door and went to the small lumpy bed. Dust puffed from the mattress when she sat on it.

Myrthyd is here. He must know that my father retrieved the gem, or maybe he's close to getting it. I might have to go into the mountains to stop Father. She closed her eyes and focused. She'd been driven this far by a feeling, a notion that dragon blood filled her veins and the mysterious ghoul of a dragon named Avess spoke truth to her. Why was she so accepting of these truths when she was raised to abhor halflings? Avess hadn't appeared to her in over a week. Was it all a figment of her imagination? Did she leave her homestead for nothing? Something deep inside made her think that wasn't true. Too many coincidences pointed to the truth: she *was* a halfling. Her mother *was* a dragon. She could never speak those words aloud. Ever.

That evening after a meal of bland soup and stale bread, Alushia left the inn in search of Myrthyd. She wove her way through the people-filled streets until she approached the Verdant Tower. Guards blocked her entrance.

"What business do you have with the Tower?" one of the guards asked. He was a muscular man with piercing blue eyes and looked to be close to her own age.

"I've come to see the Kull Naga. He's a friend of mine."

The other guard--shorter, rounder, and older-- laughed. "You think we're gonna let anyone who claims to be a friend of the Kull pass through these doors? You hear her, Ryn?"

The first guard, the one with the blue eyes that she couldn't tear her gaze from, smiled. "I do, Blart. She can pass." The older guard protested, but Ryn opened the door and allowed her passage.

Alushia didn't move at first. Ryn captivated her.

"Are you gonna stand there all night? I swear, Ryn,

if you don't stop all the ladies staring at you, I'm gonna pluck out your eyes myself!"

Ryn shook his head and waved Alushia in. Once inside, she turned back to the guards and caught Ryn smiling at her. Then he closed the door. Alushia felt her skin grow warm, but it wasn't from anger or the dragon blood boiling within her. It was a reaction to the man; one she'd never felt before. Looking around inside the tower, she wondered why she was even there. Then it struck her. She was there to find Myrthyd and see if she could discern anything from him.

Magus and their visitors milled around the central hall. There weren't as many as she expected. Music drifted through the hall and pulled her attention toward its source. She walked along the stone hallway, gazing at the tapestries hung on either side depicting the Dragonback Mountains and slayers doing the bidding of the Order, always with a Magus looking on with approval. As she neared the end of the hall, the music swelled. Magus in dark green robes floated in and out of the imposing wooden doors, and at one point she glimpsed inside. The hall was filled with Magus. A long line headed for the main table where she thought she saw the Kull Naga himself. She didn't want to be seen, so stayed to the side and listened to the conversations around her.

"Can you believe he showed without a warning? I think he's here to spy on the Verdant Tower. I never trusted him," a male novice said to a female novice. It startled Alushia at first until she remembered that only the Black Tower never accepted females. All the rest were mixed, but she'd never seen a female Magus.

The two male novices on the other side of her were drinking ale and growing louder and more boisterous. "Claims to a gem of some sort, I hear. What's it do? Only Menos knows," one novice said.

The other replied, "I hear he's got that slayer Lailoken out hunting for it. Why would he send a slayer on a treasure hunt? Don't make sense to me. I think there's more to it. Seen them griffons? Bad signs happening. Bad signs, I say."

Alushia carefully moved toward the door to the Great Hall, wary of being seen by Myrthyd. She wanted to discover what he knew about her father but without attracting his attention.

"Hey, what are you doing?" someone called. She turned and Blart was pointing at her. "Yes, you! What are you doing?" Alushia's skin warmed. All eyes turned toward her.

"Me? I'm here to see the Kull. He's a friend."

Blart ambled in her direction. "Then why are you slinking around like a cat hiding from the master of the house? What are you doing?"

"Nothing. I'm just—"

"She's fine, Blart. Leave the girl alone." *Ryn!* "She's not done anything to earn your ire. Let her be. If you keep on shouting like that, they won't let us in and our replacements will want us to return." He ushered Blart through the doors and winked at Alushia. Her heart leapt in her chest. Who was this man that stirred these primal feelings?

Blart reluctantly let Ryn guide him to the feast. Alushia watched the two heap their plates with vegetables and slices of pork from the five roasted hogs on the serving table. It was more food than she'd seen in a long time and would have been better used for the people outside the Tower.

By the time she stopped staring at the two of them, she realized Myrthyd was gone. Fearing he might find her, she scurried away through the doors now guarded by Blart and Ryn's replacements and kept going until she was back at the inn. It was silly of her to act as though Myrthyd even cared she was there, but the fear at being noticed gnawed at her. Something about the Kull scared her; even more so since his last visit and their discussion about Avess.

THIRTY-FIVE

Lailoken kept the Blood Stone in a pocket normally reserved for dracs inside his heavy fur cloak. This was much more precious than a few bits of gold. But who was it important to?

If Myrthyd got his hands on the gem, he was certain something evil was to come of it. Even before Driano's declaration, he knew it held a sinister power. Ever since he held it, danger and dread hung over him. It made no sense. He was a dragonslayer by nature, sworn to hunt for their blood. The Order required it for their stones. They were forbidden from slaying the things themselves, a prohibition Lailoken never understood. If they needed the blood so bad, they should do the deed.

"Come on, this way. I really want to enjoy a good mug of ale and a warm bed," Jor said. She led them through the mountains toward the main pass to Woodpine. They were two days removed from Dragonfire Peak, or Opaline Mountain as it must have once been called, and they were slowly trekking through narrow passes and snowy ledges. The wind swirled around them and even with Driano's magically created heat, they were still frozen to the bone.

"Aren't we close to the road yet?" Belthos asked. Since the cavern, he realized he would never be a Magus. If Driano ever made it back to the Black Tower, he'd renounce the boy and that would be it. Belthos recognized this and broke from his usually subdued self, Driano's threats no longer meaningful.

Lailoken watched Driano tense as if to smack the boy. The last time he'd done that, Jor nearly gutted him because Belthos was no longer his novice. It wouldn't be official until they returned, but in the mountainous wilds, the relationship was severed.

"Not quite," Ori said. He and Tozgan were at the back of the group, Tozgan still sore from their earlier encounter. Despite the vicious blow from the man in the tunnel, Jor carried on like nothing hurt. Lailoken assumed she did, but he also knew Jor wouldn't dwell on pain and let it consume her.

The day wore on, Belthos continuing to ask if they were close. Lailoken almost wished the boy was still under Driano's thumb and kept quiet.

Near late afternoon, a loud roar echoed through the mountains. Jor froze, holding up a hand for the others to do the same. Lailoken scanned the skies for the dragon. Then cresting over a nearby peak, something appeared, but it wasn't a dragon.

"What is that?" Belthos asked.

"By Menos, it can't be!" Driano replied. Lailoken knew exactly what it was.

"I've not seen one of those in a long, long time," Tozgan said.

"Griffons," Lailoken added. "Another halfling."

They watched as the griffon flew across the sky, soon joined by three more. They roared and sounded like dragons, but they were much smaller; half their size. The griffons flew north.

"Are they coming to Tregaron?" Jor asked.

"When was the last time a griffon bothered to cross these mountains into our land?" Ori asked.

Lailoken felt the gem within his cloak vibrate and warm. He pulled it free and the bluish ball inside dashed back and forth, madly careening this way and that. He looked up at the griffons and back to the gem. "None of this is right."

Driano clapped him on the shoulder, careful to keep his distance from the gem. "I fear we've un- leashed a horror on this world unlike anything it has ever known."

"Then why don't we get rid of it?" Jor asked. "If this thing is so wrong, why do we still have it?"

"Darlonn died for this. Myrthyd wants it so bad that he sent sell-swords to take it. We must find a way to destroy it so it no longer entices evil to surface," Lailoken replied.

"How do you know so much about it? You're a slayer!" Ori said.

"Lailoken is right. This is an instrument of evil," Driano said.

"But I don't understand," Jor said. "How is it you both have come to the conclusion that the gem is evil? I held it. It didn't feel like anything special to me. I didn't get a sense that the world was coming to an end. It's just a gem, forged over time by the pressures of the rocks around it. Nothing more. And why call it evil? Aren't we sworn to kill dragons?"

Lailoken shrugged. "I wish I knew why or how I know. It's a feeling...a deep, horrific feeling that some- thing bad is going to happen."

Jor shook her head. "You make no sense. Where's

the Lai I knew before we came out here? Next, you're gonna tell me you don't slay dragons anymore."

The griffons roared again, cutting off the conversation. They crossed over a northern mountain and were gone.

"Can we get food soon? I'm starving," Belthos said. The urge to smack the boy was strong with Lailoken. He was coming to understand why Driano was so hard on him.

Jor spotted a clearing near the bottom of the mountain. "We'll get there and stay the night. We're close now. It won't be long."

They pushed through the narrow passes and made camp for the night, the group unusually quiet through the dark, cold night.

When they set off the following morning, the skies were dark and a storm was threatening. The forest at the bottom of the mountains was close. The thick brush and dark green leaves were just on the horizon from where they stood.

"Let's hope we get there before this storm does," Lailoken said.

"Pah! What's a little rain?" Jor asked with a smile. Lailoken smiled in reply.

Since the day before, the tension was heavy in the group, but once morning's light awakened them, it dissipated some. Maybe it was spotting the forest and knowing they were close to done in the mountains; maybe it was something else. Whatever the cause, Lailoken welcomed it.

Thunder boomed beyond them. Lailoken turned, half expecting to find an Opal dragon, maybe even

Chepon, racing toward them. Then it hit him that the Opal guardian of the gem was now trapped inside his cloak. The bluish streak that darted across the gem *was* Chepon. It had to be. What else could explain what had happened?

Jor hurried the pace. "I don't want that storm to ruin this good mood!" she called over the loud rumbling thunder. Even Driano moved with a quickness he rarely exhibited. Before long, they were at the edge of the forest and the storms appeared to have moved west.

"Through here and we're almost home. At least we'll be in a city where I can get some ale. And food. And a nice place to sleep," Jor said.

"'Tis true I could use ale, as well," Lailoken replied. He'd not had a drop in weeks, and the thought of it made his mouth water.

"What do we do when we get back? I was promised a lot of dracs for this gem. If you decide to destroy it, then what? Where's my money?" Tozgan asked.

"I will pay you what you earned," Driano said before Lailoken could reply. "I will make sure you're all compensated for your time and efforts."

"What about Darlonn? What are you gonna do for him?" Jor asked, turning on the Magus and holding her finger at his chest.

"His passing was an unfortunate event. We all knew coming here was a risk. Every hunt is," Driano said. "But we must go on."

"Easy for a Magus to say; you don't kill dragons. You play in their blood with your precious gems to make yourselves more powerful. Try doing the dirty work sometime," Jor grumbled.

"Jor, enough. This has been difficult on all of us.

The sooner we get back, the sooner we put this behind us," Lailoken said.

Jor turned to him. "You're taking his side now?"

"No, but we have to work together and not accuse each other of things we have no control over. What's done is done. I'll forever carry Darlonn's death with me. He was one of the finest slayers I ever knew, and one of my closest friends."

"Yeah, sure," Jor replied in a soft voice. "Let's get going, then."

She shifted the pack on her shoulder, heading toward the path leading to Woodpine. The rest of the group stood quietly watching her leave. Finally she turned back.

"Are you idiots coming or not?"

Lailoken smiled and he caught a flash of one cross Jor's face. They'd be fine. Eventually.

THIRTY-SIX

Myrthyd sat meditating in his cozy room. He'd read through the Nightwraith spell more times than he could count, nearly memorizing the entire passage, the words flashing in his mind as though burned into his brain. A small candle the only source of light, he opened his eyes and watched the flame flicker.

"Soon, I will be the flame that ignites Rowyth to a greater inferno. My conquest of the southern lands begins with the Blood Stone." Obsessed by the promise of power, Myrthyd's every waking moment was consumed by thoughts of the gem. Why had the Order of old hidden such a powerful tool? Why had they resisted using it to further their cause? "Because they were weak and unambitious. When an orphaned child becomes Kull Naga, what else can he do to attain power?" he asked the flame.

A light knock on his door interrupted his thoughts.

"Kull Naga?" the voice of a sweet young boy called. "Kull Naga? Are you...are you awake?" the boy called through the thick wooden door.

"Come in," he replied.

Slowly the heavy door opened and a young apprentice, new to the order by the looks of him, crept inside.

"K-K-Kull Naga? I hate to disturb you, sir. Magus Menathon sent me. The guards report griffons have flown over the wall into Tregaron."

"Griffons? Are you sure, boy?"

The boy, no older than ten, averted eye contact and studied the stone floor instead. "Yes, sir. Griffons."

Myrthyd stroked his scraggly bearded chin. "Not a promising sign at all." *But proves the need for the Blood Stone*, he thought. This might be a serendipitous moment for him.

"Thank you, boy. Let Magus Menathon know I'm concerned about this development."

"Yes, sir. I will. He's also told me to tell you that a small party of warriors are nearing the wall. They come from the forest."

Could it be that Lailoken has found the Blood Stone?

"Are you sure that was the message? Tell me, boy! I must know!"

"Yes, sir. Magus Menathon made me repeat it to him. He believes it is your slayer Lailoken, as we have no slayers in the mountains."

Myrthyd rubbed his hands together and grinned. "Thank you, boy. You may leave me." The boy bowed and scurried out of the room.

With the glee of a boy after his first kiss, Myrthyd gathered his cloak and gems, soon to be replaced by a powerful weapon, and called to his two guards at either end of the hall.

"Come. It's time we collect what we came for." They followed him through the maze of stone halls, interested verdant Magus watching the small retinue, and bowing as they passed. It was mid-morning and most should be in training or studies, though there seemed to be an exceptionally large number of Magus and novices throughout the Tower not where they should be.

I'll need to enforce order on this Tower, Myrthyd thought as he passed one too many Magus lounging. *Order will come to all the Towers.*

By the time he left the southern entrance, he'd collected the other guards from the Black Tower and they swiftly crossed the Tower grounds headed for the gate to the Dragonback Mountains. He left Tukra behind to stave off questions. His guards said nothing. The compulsion spell was now automatic for him and they blindly followed him, even if he said nothing to them. What began as a tool to assist others in making a decision had become second nature for him and he used it more often than not.

The wall dominated the southern border. It was almost as tall as the Verdant Tower and men walked along the top with their attention to the south. Small fires burned at regular intervals along the top where guards huddled for warmth.

Townsfolk gave them a wide berth, their black armor and long flowing black robe a sign that they were not from Woodpine; the lightning bolts embroidered on the back of Myrthyd's robe also a clear sign of who he was. Whispers and gestures aimed at them persisted, but it only made Myrthyd smile, knowing one day he'd be calling on them to march south through the mountains.

When they reached the gate on the far southern end of the city, the Verdant guards attempted to block their passage.

"Halt! What business do you have in the mountains?"

Myrthyd approached the guard, who immediately

recognized him.

"My apologies, Kull, I wasn't sure who was hurrying this way." The guard bowed.

"I forgive your insolence this time. What news have you of griffons and a hunting party?"

"Yesterday evening while the feast was going on, we spotted four griffons crossing the mountains and go northwest. My guess is they were headed for the western sea. I haven't seen griffons cross these mountains since I was a boy."

Human halflings were an abomination. Griffons, the halflings created by dragon and lion were a disgusting mating of species. They were brainless, grunt-like animals with the intellect of a rock. The last thing Tregaron needed was more Drakku influence.

Myrthyd narrowed his eyes. "What about the slayers?"

"They are a few hours away at best. We've spotted them through the forest and they're headed in our direction."

"Good, good," Myrthyd said. He turned back to his guards and then to the gate. "Let us pass. We must meet with them. We shall forge our way ahead and greet them back to the city."

"But Kull, I would ask that you reconsider. It's dangerous beyond the wall. Many creatures stalk unknown in the forest. Dragons roam free. Exiled Tregarons turn wild out there. It's not safe."

The gem hanging around Myrthyd's neck glowed slightly. "You will let us pass."

The guard smiled. "Men, open the gate and allow them to pass." The four guards slid back the heavy iron locks. They pulled on one of the large wooden gates, each slat thick as a hundred-year-old tree. It took all of them to open the door. It creaked and groaned but opened enough to allow them passage.

"Thank you," Myrthyd said. The guards bowed and ushered them through the long tunnel cut through the stone wall until they came to an iron gate manned by two more guards.

They attempted to intercept them, but with a wave of his hand, the guards instead opened the iron gate, raising it high enough for them to pass.

"May Menos guard your travels," one of the guards said. Myrthyd acknowledged him with a slight nod and proceeded through the final gate into the plain on the other side. The forest stretched across the horizon.

"In there we will find our slayers, and then we can go home," he said to his guards. They said nothing, the compulsion spell so ingrained they were incapable of independent thought.

"Come, let's find our men." Myrthyd followed the worn path leading across the open expanse toward the forest. The Dragonback Mountains dominated the view beyond, their snowcapped peaks rising high above the green forest. In the distance, Dragonfire Peak was barely visible, though the pink-hued top poked above the rest, piercing the sky.

Excitement grew inside him, the thought of holding the Blood Stone a powerful attraction. He recited the spell repeatedly in his mind, preparing for the moment when he merged the gem with his magic. The amount of dragon blood the gem needed to be created must have been immense. He imagined the slaughter it must have taken to imbue the gem with their power. *Soon,* he thought. *Soon I will possess this power.*

They walked for close to an hour. Chilled winds whipped down from the mountains and across the plain, stirring Myrthyd's robe. He pulled it close around his neck.

"Sir, I think I see them!" one of his guards said. The man pointed into the forest and Myrthyd followed his gaze.

Then he saw them. A small band of slayers and that irksome Magus Driano. Anger ignited inside him. Those fool sell-swords failed. He'd have to dispose of Driano himself.

"Do not let that Magus live," Myrthyd told his guards. All four of them unsheathed their swords as they crossed the flat plain.

"As you wish," they said in unison. He had no fear others would hear him out here. The guards were under his complete control.

CHAPTER

THIRTY-SEVEN

Alushia returned to the inn, giving a curt nod to Rufus as she silently retired to her room. She lit a candle and sat on the uncomfortable bed. Brida prowled outside the walls of Woodpine, and Alushia missed her. She could use Brida's company now. Myrthyd was up to something horrific; she felt it in her bones. The growing sensation of dread made her worry that her father was in trouble.

"Why is this happening? Why? Who am I?" she said to the quiet room. Her world had taken a turn she never expected, and it disgusted her how much it bothered her. "I can run a farm, but I can't come to grips with this?"

Lying down on the bed, she watched the candle burn. Wax ran down the side, congealing in slowly hardening pools on the metal holder. The flame held her attention and she stared at it, trying to rid herself of all that had happened.

***

Dark gray clouds chased the blue away. They grew darker in the west, a sign of an impending storm. Alushia pulled her cloak tighter around her face as the wind picked up. It carried a chill and she shivered as it pierced her thick clothing. Her leather boots crunched on the snow and she worried how far the nearest shelter might be.

Snow fell from the sky and pelted her face, stinging and forcing her to pull the cloak even tighter around her face. She didn't recognize the place and wondered where she'd gone to. Suddenly, a loud roar carried across the wind, a sound she recognized immediately.

"Avess," she hissed.

The large black dragon with tattered wings and smoky eyes raced across the sky, devouring the dark gray clouds and leaving behind black streaks of nothingness. Avess dove to the ground, opening his enormous mouth and scooping up not only snow, but the world itself. Then he shot upwards, circling around, and landed in front of her.

The snow stopped. The wind died down. Mountains rose behind Avess, snowcapped and proud.

"What are you doing here?" Alushia asked. It had been some time since Avess visited her.

The Nightwraith inhaled deep, his smoky eyes growing more intense.

"Evil comes. The end comes. All must be stopped. I fear...I fear for you. I fear for all the halflings. The Drakku are in danger. It cannot happen. It cannot be allowed."

"What? What cannot be allowed? The gem?"

The Nightwraith roared, his head pointing to the sky.

"The evil one is close. Your father has the gem. They cannot...they must not meet. The gem is not for man. Decreed long ago. Evil the only result."

Alushia cocked her head. Avess's words were

pointed and stunted.

"What can I do? I'm here in Woodpine. How am I to stop this? Myrthyd is here, ready for my father's return."

"I cannot stop what I'm forced to do. You must...you must end this. Don't let it. Too powerful. Will is held. My will is not my own."

"Avess, your words are confusing. What can I do? How am I to stop this? I have no power over Myrthyd. My father will complete his task. He's a man of honor."

"You. Only you. It is decreed. You...must end this. Destroy the gem. You alone."

"I don't understand! How am I to do this?"

Avess whipped his head to the east, his mouth dropping open. "No," the massive creature whispered. "No."

He roared and flapped his tattered wings, leaping to the sky and circling above.

"Only you!" he shouted.

"I don't understand! Tell me why! Tell me what I must do!"

Avess ignored her and flew away, occasionally turning to the east like he was flying away from something. Alushia saw nothing but gray clouds and snow-covered land.

"Come back! I need to know!" she shouted. Avess flew away, taking small bites out of the sky as he left.

***

Alushia woke in a cold sweat. "What...was that?" she said. The candle had gone out long ago and the room was dark. Quiet. Alone.

She wiped her brow and sat on the edge of the bed, the visions and Avess's strange behavior confusing her. A light knock on her door scared her.

At first, she ignored the sound, thinking maybe she made it up. *Who could be here this late?* Again, a light knock on her door.

"Alushia?" a man's voice asked. She didn't recognize it. "Alushia, are you awake?" The voice was louder and she thought maybe it was—

Alushia grabbed her knife and quietly stepped to the door. The person knocked again. "Alushia? It's me, Ryn. I come with news."

Ryn? Why would he be here? She struggled with the idea of letting him in or staying quiet. The man was a mystery to her and she didn't know a thing about him. For all she knew, he was here to harm her.

"Alushia, your mother Etain sent me. She said to mention Avess."

Alushia's heart leapt in her chest. *Her mother? Avess?* No one knew the Nightwraith's name, not even her father! What was this madness?

Against her better judgment and because Ryn called out names only she knew, Alushia opened the door. Holding the knife in front of her, she waved him in. "Don't try anything or I'll slit your throat." Ryn nodded and cautiously stepped past her into the dark room. He flicked his fingers and a small ball of flame appeared from nowhere, illuminating the room.

"What are you?"

Ryn grinned at her.

"I'm a friend of your mother's. One of her servants, to be exact, but we won't get into details."

Alushia moved closer, holding the knife pointed at his chest. "How dare you use my mother to gain entrance to my room!"

Ryn held his hands up. The flaming ball flickered and his deep blue eyes glowed. "I use no one. She sent me to find you and your father. A terrible calamity is soon to come if we don't act fast."

"Avess. Tell me what that is?" she asked, knowing full well who it was.

"A poor soul trapped within a gem. The gem your father currently possesses, and if I'm correct, the gem he intends to deliver to Myrthyd. That must not happen."

"But how—"

"Like your mother, what you see is not exactly who I am. I mean, it is, but it isn't. I can't get into too much now. You have to trust me. We need to stop your father."

"Why would I trust you? I don't know you."

"No one knows who Avess is. At least, none among men. How would I know him?" Ryn crossed his arms over his sculpted chest. His muscular arms strained against his sleeves.

"None of this makes sense. Why is this happening? What's it mean? What am I?"

"Now that is a different question. I think you might have a clue by now about who you are. I dare not speak it aloud. This land isn't kind to those like you."

"Like...me?" she quietly replied, dropping her hand to her side, the knife falling to the floor. "By Menos, what is this?" she asked, taking a seat on the edge of the bed.

"It's the moment we destroy the most evil, sinister,

and powerful item known to the Drakku. The Blood Stone has been hidden for centuries. No man has set foot in that cave since the Reformation, and now that your father has, if we don't act it could be the end of not only the Drakku, but every last person in Rowyth."

Alushia turned up to face him. "Everyone? How can that be? It's only a gem."

"If Myrthyd gains that gem, he will access a power so terrible that it will make the ground shudder. He will have the ability to capture the souls of living dragons and enslave them to his will, turning them into beings like Avess. Then, under his command, they will devour the dreams of halflings, human and otherwise, turning them into the living undead...a horde to control and overrun every last living creature. It's a fate we must avoid. Gray-souls are dangerous. It could spell the end of Rowyth."

Ryn's voice was gentle and matter of fact, as though the details were rehearsed and recalled by rote.

"I don't understand. How can all this come from a gem? None of this makes sense."

Ryn turned from her and wiped his face with his hands. "I'm sorry, Alushia, but the world is not what you thought it was. It's not always black and white. It's not mankind versus Drakku. We all live together and flourish together. This path Myrthyd seeks leads to the end. We cannot let that happen."

"How do you know so much? Why tell me? I'm just the daughter of a slayer and a mother who's been gone most of my life."

"It's precisely because you are their daughter that you must know. Your mother Etain is a powerful dragon trying to unite the Drakku as one and create peace with humans. Opposition exists, but she's determined to win them over. You are the key."

Months ago, Alushia would have raged against such accusations, but with what she'd experienced since her father's departure, she was willing to listen to even the outlandish.

"I'm but a slayer's daughter. I see no way I should affect things."

"We don't have time for it all now. We must go. Your father is closer to Woodpine, and Myrthyd will want to get his hands on the Blood Stone. We must get to your father first and stop this."

Brida, she thought. "What about Brida? I can't leave without her."

"That giant prowling monster outside the city walls? I'm sure she'll be waiting for us. She's had most of the guards on edge since you arrived!"

Alushia giggled, the first moment of levity since Ryn entered her room. "Fine. Let's go save the world, or something like that, right?"

"Exactly!" Ryn replied. They gathered her things and quickly left the inn, the old innkeeper Rufus smiling when Ryn dropped off a couple gold dracs, which was more than enough for the stay.

THIRTY-EIGHT

Ryn led Alushia through the streets as the sun poked over the horizon, passing many dirty people sleeping on the ground along the way. They headed for the north gate to find Brida.

Brida pounced on Alushia when they had moved away from Woodpine's walls. The large snowcat wrestled her to the ground.

"Brida! I've missed you. I hated to leave you out here, but I had to." The snowcat purred loudly, rubbing her head forcefully against Alushia's torso, nearly winding her.

Ryn stood back. "Are you sure she's safe?" he asked. "I'm usually fine with animals, but she's...huge!"

Alushia laughed, trying to see over Brida's head. "Yeah, she's perfectly fine unless you mean to harm me. Otherwise, she's just like a housecat, only bigger." The snowcat dropped to the ground and rolled in the dirt. Her white coat became dingy gray.

Alushia stood and brushed herself off. "Brida, this is Ryn. He claims to want to help us stop Father from giving the gem to Myrthyd. Think we ought to trust him?"

The snowcat rolled to her feet and shook the dust from herself. She peered at Ryn, then to Alushia, and slowly prowled closer to the guard.

"Wait a minute! I'm here to help!" he said, holding

up his hands and taking a few steps back. "Call her off! I don't want to—"

"Brida! He's with us. Keep an eye on him, but he's on our side...I think."

Brida sniffed the air, shook her head, then returned to Alushia, rubbing her legs, and almost knocking her over.

"It's settled. Don't harm me, and Brida will leave you alone. Do something to me, and you'll have to answer to her."

"Understood. As I've told you, I'm here on your mother's orders. Your life isn't what you think it is. You are so much more than a slayer's daughter. Come. We have a long day's journey ahead."

Ryn took the lead, Alushia and Brida following. The man was taller than she. His brown hair was cut short and she couldn't help but take in his muscular frame. He wore a dark green leather vest over a dark green shirt and pants tucked into black leather boots. A sword hung from his waist and when he turned to make sure she was still behind him, she noticed his bright blue eyes every time.

He led them southwest, staying far from the city. The wall around it was barely visible to their left. Brida kept pace, never leaving Alushia's side, even when tempted by a nearby elk.

Distant roars caught the cat's attention. She stopped and cocked her head, then looked up to the sky.

"What is it, girl?" Alushia asked. She felt the sensations Brida passed to her. Wonder and curiosity. Ryn stopped and followed the snowcat's gaze upward.

"There!" he said, pointing at the sky. Four griffons flew southward in formation. "Oh no."

"What?" Alushia asked.

"The time has come. Myrthyd must be near the gem. We're out of time."

"We can't be! We'll make it—"

"I'm sorry to do this. Just jump on. I'll get Brida."

"You'll what?"

Ryn looked to the ground and a faint glow surrounded him. Then he exploded in a ball of brilliant blue light. When Alushia opened her eyes, a Garnet dragon stood in his place. It was as tall as a two-story building; maybe taller. Its wingspan was huge, and its deep blue eyes were much like..."*Ryn?* Is that you?"

Months ago, she would have been terrified at the sight of a dragon, but circumstances had changed now. She had changed. Or maybe she was always the same, but only realized her truth during her moments with Avess.

The dragon roared, and in her head, she heard its voice deep and slow.

I am he. Come. Get on my back. We'll get there in time. The griffons are a sign. We must hurry!

"Griffons? How are they a sign? You don't make sense!"

They're scouts. Powerful and nimble. Like me, they serve your mother.

Alushia shook her head. It was too much!

Brida took a few steps back.

"What about her?" Alushia asked.

I'll take care of her. He dropped one wing to the ground for her to climb. The thick hide felt unusual. She crawled up his back toward his long neck.

Hold tight.

He flapped his wings and rose. Alushia clung to his neck, her arms straining from her grip. He laughed in her mind. *It's ok. You'll be fine.*

He then approached Brida. She was shrinking back and he grabbed her gently in his long claws. *She'll be safe. I promise.* Then with a power she could feel through his body, he flapped his wings harder and they rose high in the air.

Ryn darted southward through the clouds. The view for Alushia was extraordinary; a sight she never imagined she would see.

Below them and to the left, Alushia saw all of Woodpine and the Verdant Tower rising above the city. The people cluttering the streets looked like tiny insects. Far to the south, she could see a giant wall stretch across the land. It seemed to go on forever.

"There's the wall!" she shouted, pointing it out and then quickly returning her hand on Ryn's neck.

There were other creatures in the sky ahead of them. It was hard to tell by the way they darted back and forth in the sky, but they looked like dragons. Four of them. The four griffons were also closing in on them, like a meeting in the sky.

"Look! More dragons!" she shouted.

Seek inside. Do you feel it?

"Inside?"

She closed her eyes and tried to block out the sound of the passing wind and the beating wings.

"*Mother?*" she whispered.

Fire raced across the sky where the dragons danced. The griffons roared, and even at this distance, they sounded clear. As they drew closer, she noticed there were only three Garnet dragons, one much larger than the other two. A spark inside ignited and she knew. In that moment, clarity enveloped her. *Mother.* The massive Garnet was her mother, Etain. Her mother was alive!

You feel it now, don't you? It's true! Ryn spoke in her mind. Alushia almost let loose her hold on his neck. Everything else paled in significance. The gem. Her father. Myrthyd. She'd found the one thing she'd wanted her entire life—her mother. Though she flew in the air and had large, yellowing talons, Alushia thought she was the most magnificent sight she'd ever seen in her life.

Ryn flew faster until they were close to the Garnet dragons. Suddenly, a flurry of voices crashed into Alushia's mind. Then she singled out the one female voice, ignoring the rest.

Alushia, my dear, she heard in her head. *Oh, how my heart has longed for you! I leap for joy at your safety.*

"Mother?" she replied out loud. "But how? Why?"

All will be revealed in time. Your father is about to make a mistake, and we must not allow this. He's a good man.

At her words, the other dragons erupted in angry roars.

Despite what they think, he's a good man. We must stop him.

Alushia was at a loss for words, the moment overwhelming her. The dragons roared and she heard her mother command them.

Do not harm the slayer or those with him! They are under my protection! The young one in black must not be harmed. Do not hurt him. Not yet. I may be able to reason with him still.

One of the Garnet dragons roared displeasure. *He's evil, Etain! He must be stopped!* Alushia heard.

I know. But he's also my son.

THIRTY-NINE

Lailoken felt the warmth of the gem in his pocket. It vibrated and hummed. The temptation to pull it out and marvel at the dashing lights inside was strong. Knowing he held the soul of one or more dragons sent a shiver down his spine. He'd killed dragons; that was his duty. But to hold their souls captive was another thing. Even Driano had his doubts, and he was a Magus in need of dragon blood to enhance his power.

A loud roar overhead halted the group.

"Dragons?" Jor asked. The trees were thick and it was difficult to see the sky.

"It has to be. The griffon roars are much different. Not as deep or deadly," Lailoken replied. The sight of griffons was an omen and he'd been trying to work it out since they first flew by. Now with dragons over-head, the omen proved right.

"Something's not right. I have a bad feeling about this," Jor said.

"We're slayers. We don't back away from such danger," Lailoken replied. Though in truth, he agreed with her. Something wasn't right. Griffons and dragons heading north across the mountains into Tregaron wasn't common. He had the feeling the Blood Stone had something to do with it.

Belthos peered through the trees. "I think I see something." Running off the path, he stopped when a small clearing afforded him an unobstructed view above. "There!" he shouted, pointing upwards. "Garnets. Three of them! One is twice the size of the others!"

Lailoken sprinted after him, Jor and the rest trailing behind. When they got there and looked up, three Garnet dragons spewed flames and intertwined with one another in a deadly sky dance. Belthos was right. One of the dragons was a Garnet with long red wings and a tail longer than the height of three people.

Lailoken stared in awe at the dragons, the thought of killing them never crossing his mind. Instead, he felt a peace; a connection to them he'd never felt before. "What are you?" he whispered.

"Are you daft? Those are dragons! I bet the blood of that large Garnet holds immense power," Driano said.

"It would be hard to kill, but I'd try. One of those claws would look great hanging on my wall," Jor said.

Much to his surprise, Lailoken couldn't muster the rage that fueled him to action. "No, we can't. We—"

The dragons raced away, the trees obscuring their view again.

"Are you all right, Lai?" Jor asked. She approached him and placed her hand on his shoulder. He barely registered the touch or her words.

"Huh?" he asked after several moments.

"What's gotten into you? Have you lost your nerve?"

"No. You were correct when you said something isn't right. Be on your guard, all of you. We approach danger and I will not allow us to die in vain." The feeling of peace left him and his senses returned.

"Come on, then. I want out of this forest before we all lose our minds," Jor said. She guided them back to the path headed for Woodpine.

Tozgan and Ori moved slow. Tozgan's injury hindered him more than he let on.

Driano had resumed a cordial dialogue with Belthos. Lailoken assumed it was more out of boredom than anything else. Belthos engaged the conversation quite a bit, his past shyness and cowering all but gone.

Lailoken walked with Jor, trying hard to ignore the warmth from the gem.

"I'm done with this," Lailoken said to Jor.

"With what? Walking? Breathing?" she replied with a grin.

He shook his head. "No, not that. With tracking and slaying dragons. This is it. No more."

"The great slayer is retiring? Don't kid yourself. It's in your blood. You can't deny what you are."

"Jor, I'm not sure anymore. I'm just...not."

She shrugged. "If that's your plan, who am I to stop you? I guess I'll have to carry the mantle of Greatest Slayer in Tregaron when you do." She walked ahead of him, her long red ponytail swaying with each step. He knew she was angry; maybe even disappointed in him. It didn't matter. The conviction to end his days as a slayer was powerful. Losing Darlonn was too much.

"I can see the wall!" Jor shouted. The rest of the group caught up to her. Out beyond the forest, a wide open field gave way to the immense wall beyond. From that distance it looked small, though in truth it was the largest structure in all of Tregaron.

A small band of people stood out against the light

green of the field, their dark uniforms clearly marking them.

"The Kull," Driano said. "He's grown impatient. And here with Tower Guards? This does not bode well."

Jor turned to Lailoken. "Now what?"

Lailoken turned to the group. "I fear this may be a mistake. Something isn't right. I've survived against much stronger opponents than a boy with a gem and a touch of power. Why does he need guards out here for us?"

"He is the Kull Naga. A bit strange for my tastes, but he is the Kull," Driano replied. "He never leaves the Tower without guards."

"Then it's time we confront him and find out what he wants with this gem and be rid of this adventure," Lailoken said. He felt the gem thrum in his pocket. "Let's finish this."

Lailoken took the lead. As they neared the edge of the forest, Tozgan and Ori were far behind. "Belthos, do you have training in healing?" Lailoken asked.

"Yes, sir. Not much, but some. The Black Tower isn't known for it."

Lailoken smiled. "Good enough. See if you can help Tozgan. Relieve Ori. I want him with us when we meet the Kull. You and Tozgan stay back. Just in case."

Jor shot him a glance. "In case of what?"

"In case those dragons come back. In case the guards decide to end our lives. I want witnesses. Besides, Tozgan isn't very mobile right now anyway."

"And Myrthyd," Driano interjected, "isn't the most stable Magus I've ever encountered."

"And there's that," Lailoken agreed.

Belthos ran to Tozgan and soon Ori approached the group.

"Thanks for that. I was starting to tire of his stories about Oakenvault. I mean, how many times can one man hear the tale of the most difficult hunt ever?"

Jor laughed and Driano cracked a smile.

"I'd say he's a distant second to my hunt along the western mountains," Jor replied.

"Be ready for anything," Lailoken said. Jor's smile vanished. Driano and Ori nodded. "Let's go, then," Lailoken replied. He felt the thrum of the gem against his chest and moved toward his destiny.

Half an hour later when Myrthyd and his men met Lailoken and his group outside the edge of the forest, the smiling Kull couldn't stop fawning over the slayer.

"Lailoken, what a pleasure to see you again! My instincts tell me you got the gem?"

Lailoken nodded. "Aye, that we did. At a cost."

Myrthyd knitted his brow. "Oh? How so? I see you left a couple of your men back there," he said pointing to the forest. The guards to either side of him puffed out their chests. They approached with unsheathed swords and flanked Myrthyd, a display of his power.

"We lost Darlonn. The enemy was strong, as were the men who ambushed us in the cave. I don't suppose you knew anything about that?"

Driano huffed but remained quiet. Jor had unsheathed her sword and matched the menacing guards' scowls.

"My good man, what are you accusing me of? I'm the Kull Naga, not some terrible southern noble with a grudge."

"Kull Naga, how good it is to see you again," Driano said, breaking the tension and bowing slightly.

"Driano," Myrthyd said, a touch of disgust seeping into his voice. Even Ori raised an eyebrow at the name. "I see you did your part to shepherd this group back from their quest. Where is your novice?"

Driano sighed. "Former novice. He's with Tozgan, attending to his injuries."

"Former novice?" Myrthyd asked.

Driano nodded. "Swore off the Order. Claims to be done with his time."

"Then he is no longer welcome in Tregaron. That filth can stay in the mountains. Better yet," he said, turning to the two guards at his right, "Take care of the boy. Leave nothing. Kill him." The guards nodded and marched quickly toward the forest.

"No!" Lailoken called. "Stop this! Leave the boy. He's done nothing wrong."

"I cannot have loose ends, slayer," Myrthyd said, his voice dripping with hate. "Too many stray threads spoil the garment."

Overhead, the three Garnet dragons returned. Following close behind was another Garnet dragon carrying a snowcat in its claws, and on its back...

"*Alushia?*" Lailoken whispered. He was sure the vision was a trick. It was impossible to believe!

The dragons roared, the larger Garnet breathing a wall of flame that sliced the sky.

"Perfect timing. Give me the gem, slayer, or do I need to remove it by force?" Myrthyd commanded.

The dragons raced downward, flames erupting and spreading toward them.

Lailoken unsheathed his sword, preparing for the dragons. "In time, Kull. Now, we must kill."

"Indeed...we must. Men!" Myrthyd said, and the guards charged Lailoken.

FORTY

Alushia clung to Ryn's neck as the landscape beneath her crawled by. The loping movement in the air jarred her body, but she soon adjusted to the motion. It was a perfect distraction from the revelation she'd heard moments ago.

The Garnet dragon, her mother, Etain—she was sure of it!—let loose a shocking secret. The Kull Naga, the boy Myrthyd who was no older than herself, was her...brother? She wasn't sure she'd heard the words correctly. Maybe she'd misunderstood. Time was not kind to her, and she had to forget the words the moment they were spoken, as the dragons were in a dire need to stop her father from handing the Blood Stone to Myrthyd.

We can make it! she heard Ryn's voice in her mind.

Do not harm Lailoken or Myrthyd. They must be allowed to live! she heard her mother in her mind. The voice startled her. It was powerful and commanding. The other two Garnets said very little. Their wills conformed to her mother.

Wind whipped past Alushia, her hair flowing behind her. Her short sword clanked on Ryn's back. Her knuckles were white and sore as she held on to whatever bit of hide she could cling to, praying to Menos she'd not fall from this height.

Hold tight. I see them in the fields ahead!

Over the rush of wind and the flapping wings, Alushia barely heard Brida's cries of fright, a sound she rarely made.

The dragons descended. Etain was in the lead, followed by the two smaller Garnets and then Ryn. Walls of flame spread across the sky and the dragons flew through it as though it were a cloud. She closed her eyes when Ryn smashed through the fire, which had no effect on them.

The ground rushed up to great them. Waving fields of rough grass grew closer and more daunting. "Ryn, slow down!" she yelled. She heard him laugh in her head.

It's fine, trust me.

A man wearing a black cloak surrounded by four black clad soldiers was talking to a man with three others next to him. Two of the guards left the meeting and headed for the forest. As they dove closer, she recognized them.

"Father! Jor! Myrthyd...no! Don't, Father!"

Lailoken had unsheathed his sword and stared upwards. Myrthyd pointed at him and the remaining guards lunged at her father.

"No!" she yelled, unable to stop the events unfolding below her.

Hurry! her mother said. *We must end this!*

Ryn opened his mouth and sent out a streak of fire that made Alushia cover her eyes and lose her grip, almost falling to her death. Brida roared.

The men on the ground scattered as flames struck between them, burning the ground.

Don't harm them! her mother scolded.

I would never. I only intend to break them apart, Ryn replied.

Alushia clung tight as Ryn circled the men below.

"You have to save my father!"

Ryn exhaled a wall of flame as a black spike shot up through the flames and pierced his wing. He roared in pain and spiraled downward.

"What happened? Ryn!"

Brida growled as the ground grew closer, sending fear through Alushia. "Hold on, Brida!"

Ryn pulled the snowcat closer, tucking her under him, then slammed into the ground. He tumbled and Alushia fell off him, landing far from where the other dragons had landed and were engaged in the fight. She rolled to a stop, her body aching and her world in confusion. For several long moments, she had no idea where she was. It wasn't until she felt the heat from the flames nearby and the dragon roars did clarity return.

"Brida," she said weakly as she pushed herself off the ground. "Ryn? Are you all right?"

Ryn lay on the ground, still in dragon form, with a black bolt lodged into his wing. Blood oozed from it and in a flash, he transformed to his human form. The bolt fell to the ground and he clutched his arm.

Alushia ran to him. "Ryn!"

She sensed Brida to her right, and when she looked over, the snowcat was sitting upright, shaking her large head. She appeared safe from the fall.

"Alushia, we have to go. We can't help now. Etain can take care of it. I have to keep you safe."

"No! My father needs me!"

Brida approached, sending impressions of worry.

"What is it, girl?"

"I'm telling you, Alushia, we can't stay here. I'm no good in this condition." Ryn winced, his lips a tight line as he held back a scream. "Come on," he said, "Our time here is done."

"But I can't! My father!"

"We're not in a position to..." he winced again, "help. Etain will have to do it. Keeping you safe is my priority."

Alushia turned back to the blaze not far away, watching the dragons move and breathe flame, knowing her father was in the middle of it. With her mother directing the rescue, she'd have to trust.

"Fine, we'll go. Your arm is in bad shape. I understand." She gave one last look toward the flames and let Ryn lead her away, hoping to avoid detection.

She had come here to help, not to run. She hoped they were making the right decision.

CHAPTER

FORTY-ONE

Lailoken fell to the ground, the flames narrowly missing his foot. He fell on Driano while Jor and Ori were splayed out on either side of him. For a moment, it was difficult to understand what Myrthyd was doing. The man had jumped up from the ground and waved his hand furiously while barking orders at the guards, the stone at his chest glowing bright.

Ori knocked a bolt and shot it at the dragon, screaming as he did so.

Jor crawled to her feet and held her sword at the ready. "Come on! Fight me, then!" she cried out, and he heard the men shouting at Jor.

"None shall live! Take the slayer but remove the gem! I must have it!" Myrthyd shouted. Lailoken pushed himself to his feet, his head foggy. Before he understood what was happening, two guards were on him, wrestling him back to the ground. He felt a warm sensation cover him, like he was being dipped in a warm pool of water. Was Driano trying to protect him?

"Kill the slayer! Grab the Blood Stone!" Myrthyd shouted. Lailoken noticed his gem glowed brighter and brighter with each word.

Lailoken struggled against them, fighting to free himself. One of them kicked him in the stomach and he lost his breath. Clutching his chest to make sure the

Blood Stone remained in his pocket, he fought for air. His lungs burned and spittle flew from his mouth.

One of the guards punched his face, busting his lip. He felt warm blood run down his cheeks, but still he clutched his pocket, making sure the gem was inside. Strength sapped by each passing moment, Lailoken worried he'd not break free from their grip. He jerked his hand free of the pocket, a difficult decision, and frantically searched for his dagger or something to help him against the men overpowering them.

A guard held his arm across Lailoken's throat and he choked for air, his mouth working in silent gulps with nothing to show for it. The edges of his vision darkened and his thoughts slowed.

Dragons roared above and everyone looked up. The guard's arm moved off his throat and allowed him to inhale deep, burning breaths. A torrent of flame fell from the sky. The Garnets had worked together and encircled the group. The flames walled them in, flaring taller than the height of any of the men.

The lead Garnet landed, sending shockwaves across the ground with its weight. The two smaller Garnets landed to either side of it and the last dragon flew past, heading toward Tozgan and Belthos.

The guards jumped to their feet, entranced by the new threat. Lailoken scrambled away, pushing himself back from his attackers.

The larger Garnet roared loudly, straining its neck, and flexing its wings wide. The smaller Garnets circled around Lailoken and his group, creating a barrier between the Kull and them.

"These beasts won't stand in my way! I will rid this

world of them and their wretched halflings. Give me the gem, slayer!" Myrthyd screamed at Lailoken. Myrthyd's stone glowed and he waved his hand. Lailoken had no idea what he was doing.

The large Garnet roared again, commanding the attention of all within the wall of flame. Lailoken heard a voice in his head that he hadn't heard in nearly eighteen years, though it was slightly deeper than what he remembered.

Myrthyd, leave this madness alone! You must not continue with your course of action. You cannot wield the Blood Stone. The power is too great. It was never meant for man to use.

Lailoken stared at the dragon. Myrthyd must have heard it, too, as he whipped his head toward her.

"Etain?" Lailoken whispered. It couldn't be. It was impossible!

The Garnet lowered her head as if ashamed.

Myrthyd, stop your evil plan. Nothing good is to come.

"Shut up you, evil beast! Get your magic out of my head. Your manipulation won't work on me!"

"Evil plan?" Lailoken asked.

"What plan?" Driano added.

"What are you people talking about?" Ori asked. "Who are you talking to?"

The guards looked as confused as Ori.

"It's her," Lailoken said pointing at the Garnet. "It's Etain, my wife!" He didn't know how or why, but the dragon in front of him had to be her! It was impossible, but it had to be! The dragons forced this on her. There was no other explanation!

Myrthyd growled. A bright blue flame shot from his hands and bore into Driano. A large hole erupted in his chest, evaporating his heart.

Driano's face flushed and his hands clutched at the cauterized hole in his chest. His eyes rolled back in his head and he fell backwards, slamming to the ground.

A fierce madness grew in Myrthyd's eyes.

"No!" Lailoken shouted. "You're the Kull!"

"Yes," he growled, "and I'll do things my way. The Drakku cannot bring harm to Tregaron. Our people are in danger. Give me that gem!" His stone glowed and Lailoken felt the warm sensation again.

The dragons moved in closer, roaring and clawing at the ground.

Give up this madness! Lailoken heard in his head. It was Etain!

"Get off me!" Jor shouted. Lailoken turned and caught a glimpse of Jor fighting off the guards. She lunged at one, piercing his midsection with her sword. He groaned and fought back. Jor kicked him and pushed him off with her sword. The other guard tried to help, but she kicked him away. Then she withdrew her sword and swiftly spun, avoiding the other guard's attack and severed his head from his neck. It flew in the air, screaming, and landed near the foot of one of the smaller Garnet dragons.

Etain roared loudly, beating her wings, and rose up on her hind legs.

Enough! This must end now!

"Give me the gem! Hurry!" Myrthyd said to Lailoken. He felt the gem vibrate and warm in his pocket.

No! Etain howled in their minds. The sound was so loud that Lailoken pressed his hands against his ears to try to silence it.

"Now, slayer! Give me the Blood Stone!" Myrthyd waved a hand and Lailoken felt the warmth press against him again.

Your spells have no effect on him, Lailoken heard Etain say in his head.

Myrthyd peered at the large dragon. "Very well."

He turned to Jor. "Get the gem for me. Kill Lailoken," he said, his stone pulsating. Jor shook then lunged at Lailoken. He fell to the side, rolled, and jumped to his feet where he held his sword in front of him.

"Jor, stop! He's using a spell on you! Resist him!"

"He needs the gem. I'm told to give him the gem," she replied. Jor snarled and attacked.

Myrthyd moved back from the fight, turning his attention to the dragons around him.

Your evil ways are done, Lailoken heard in his head moments before Jor struck at him. He parried the blow and knocked her to the side, but her fury intensified and she righted herself and went after him again.

Stop this! Let go of her mind! Etain screamed in Lailoken's head. Myrthyd must have heard it, too, as he swatted at the air.

The Kull let loose a volley of flames at the dragons, but they were weak strands that dissipated once they struck the thick hides.

Jor growled. She sliced at Lailoken and he parried the attack. Swinging her sword back, she caught his leg and pulled, the blade tearing through his pants above his boots and biting into his flesh. Lailoken fell to the ground clutching his leg.

"Jor, stop! It's me!" he yelled. She gave no response.

"Kill the slayer and bring me that gem!" Myrthyd yelled, motioning with his hands. "The Drakku must pay for what they've done to our people!"

The smaller Garnet dragons leapt into the air and breathed fire down at Myrthyd, the flames circling the young Kull Naga.

Do not kill him! Etain screamed, her voice reverberating inside Lailoken's head. Her voice, welcoming yet distant, forced his attention away from Jor. When he looked up, she stood above him.

"No, Jor! Please!"

"I must give him the gem."

No! Etain screamed.

Jor slammed her sword into Lailoken's chest, pinning him to the ground. He screamed in agony. The blade slid through his body, the metal piercing his flesh and his insides. It was the most horrific pain he'd ever felt.

Sound drifted away. Thoughts of Alushia pummeled his brain. Images of her as a young girl, Brida at her side, frolicking through fields comforted him. Etain, his lovely Etain, dancing during the summer celebration and giggling, always giggling. Darlonn and Jor, the three of them united in purpose and fulfilling their duties. Mugs of ale. Friends. Laughter. Blood. Dark crimson, thick and warm.

He felt a tug at his chest and barely recognized Jor reaching into his cloak. *The gem*, he thought. She pulled it free and turned to Myrthyd. He walked through the flames, unharmed and smiling.

"You've done well, my dear. Now be gone. You are

of no more use to me."

The dragons circled in the air, their loud roars bursting in Lailoken's ears.

Leave him! The gem is too powerful! he heard Etain say in his mind. *Flee now! We will have our time!*

"Etain," he tried to say, but the words wouldn't come. Warmth spread across his body. Menos. Alushia. Etain.

Lailoken closed his eyes and dreamt of death.

FORTY-TWO

Lailoken stumbled in darkness, aware only of his feet striking a solid surface. He was alone. Nothing felt real yet it was all he had.

Where am I? Etain, what happened to you? What did the Drakku do to you?

He walked carefully forward, concerned that he'd strike something. The blackness was oppressive as it bore down on him.

A distant light called to him and he froze. It was the first thing he'd seen in this strange place. He then strode slowly across the unknown.

A dragon's roar broke the silence. He felt warmth and agony.

Suddenly his chest exploded with pain and forced him to bend over, clutching at it. When the pain relented, he straightened and watched as the light grew larger.

He heard a woman's scream. *Alushia? Etain? Jor?*

It was familiar, but his strained mind couldn't piece it together. He was at the edge of understanding, but then it flew away from him.

The light expanded quickly and he found himself standing on a windswept field with heavily wooded mountains in the distance. They were unfamiliar to him and called him closer.

Overhead, a black streak caught his attention. A

dragon with tattered wings flew by, leaving black streaks in its wake. Near the mountains, another black dragon did the same, leaving tiny lines of black behind it.

"Who are you? What is this place?"

The dragon ignored him. Reaching back for his sword, he found it was gone. Remembering the Blood Stone, he grasped his pocket.

"No! The Blood Stone is gone!"

He fell to his knees and sobbed. Alone and defenseless, he knew he'd failed to save Tregaron. By following his duties, he had given Myrthyd the means to unlimited power.

The Drakku had lived and somehow forced his wife to become one of them. The moment the thought crossed his mind, he knew it was a mistake. She had to have been Drakku when he met her. She took her human form to dupe him.

All these years of searching for her, of slaughtering dragons in his quest to return her home and now...she was one of them all along?

The Etain of his memories was a different woman. She was the love of his life, the flame of his heart. There was no way she was truly a dragon, yet...yet he heard her voice. The dragon spoke with her voice!

The searing ache in his chest returned and he fell to the ground. The black dragon in the sky roared again but he didn't care. His life was pointless now. The family he hoped to bring back together was now lost, never to reunite.

He failed his family. He failed Tregaron. He failed Darlonn.

The Drakku were the enemy. Myrthyd was the enemy. He had no one left to trust.

The fields shifted and darkness swallowed him. The dragon roared again and then called out a name, a word he heard Myrthyd speak—*Nightwraith*. He had unleashed a beast with powers over halflings.

Alushia!

All went black and his mind went silent.

Then, in a whisper, he heard a voice.

I've got you, my love. You're safe.

ACKNOWLEDGEMENTS

Thank you, dear reader, for your time spent with me. I hope it was entertaining and you come back for more. If you'd do me the favor of leaving a review, I would be ever so grateful.

I've wanted to explore and create a fantasy world for a long time now. The name Lailoken is one I've used in gaming for over twenty years, and it's in my Twitter name, too!

The original impetus for this story is two-fold. If you've read my short story collection, *Moments of Darkness*, you'll no doubt be familiar with the Nightwraith idea, as it's one of the stories (though called *Dreamwraith*.) I wanted to build on the concept in this series.

The second driving force was a shared world project I was involved in with twenty authors from around the world. We created stories in the same world to write a loose series. Sadly, it fell apart, but it got me started with this series. I'd personally like to thank fellow authors Mirren Hogan, Greg Aldredge, and Stephane Barr for all of their hard work in building this world, which I have now co-opted for my story (with their permission, of course!)

I want to thank my family for their unending support. To my wife, Jenny, thanks for your love and encouragement when I want to throw it all away.

My words are enhanced exponentially by the deft hand and sage advice from my editor, Jodi McDermitt. Thanks for all you do!

My cover artists, MIBL Art rock! Thank you for your amazing work.

A few readers were instrumental in helping me make the story better. Leland Lydecker, Tib Plants, and Simon Bleaken all gave me excellent advice and pointers...and let me know when things didn't work! Your input was super valuable to me.

Thanks again for reading. Look for *Dragon's Blood: Curse of the Drakku Book Two* coming soon!

ABOUT THE AUTHOR

Jason J. Nugent has been a paperboy, pizza maker, dishwasher, restaurant manager, promotional products sales rep, Chamber of Commerce director, and one-time BBQ champion. He has skated with Tony Hawk, had a babysitter with a serial killer brother, and is followed by rapper Chuck D on Twitter. He and his wife share a home in beautiful Southern Illinois with their son, two cats, and two dogs.

He's the author of the thrilling young adult sci-fi series *The Forgotten Chronicles (The Selection, Rise of the Forgotten, The War for Truth)*, and two collections of horror/dark fiction short stories: *(Almost) Average Anthology and Moments of Darkness*. More information can be found at jasonjnugent.com, where you can also sign up to receive monthly newsletters and new release alerts.